A PRICE TO PAY

A PRICE TO PAY

Chris Simms

CRÈME de la CRIME

This first world edition published 2013
in Great Britain and 2014 in the USA by
Crème de la Crime, an imprint of
SEVERN HOUSE PUBLISHERS LTD of
19 Cedar Road, Sutton, Surrey, England, SM2 5DA.

British Library Cataloguing in Publication Data

Simms, Chris, 1969–
  A price to pay. – (An Iona Khan mystery ; 2)
  1. Runaway teenagers–Fiction. 2. Police–England–
  Manchester–Fiction. 3. Detective and mystery stories.
  I. Title II. Series
  823.9'2-dc23

ISBN-13: 978-1-78029-050-8 (cased)

Except where actual historical events and characters are being
described for the storyline of this novel, all situations in this
publication are fictitious and any resemblance to living persons
is purely coincidental.

All Severn House titles are printed on acid-free paper.

Severn House Publishers support the Forest Stewardship Council™ [FSC™],
the leading international forest certification organisation. All our titles that
are printed on FSC certified paper carry the FSC logo.

Typeset by Palimpsest Book Production Ltd.,
Falkirk, Stirlingshire, Scotland.
Printed and bound in Great Britain by
TJ International, Padstow, Cornwall

To the readers who've stuck with me: thanks.

ACKNOWLEDGEMENTS

My gratitude to the following for kindly helping me with my research: Mr E Hesling, for explaining the inner workings of computers; Mr J Alty, for guiding me through the mystery of Skype; and Mr D Lamb, for a few pointers on what a maths degree might involve.

PROLOGUE

They were going to kill her, the girl was now sure of that. She didn't need to understand what they were saying; the decision showed in their eyes, betrayed itself in the tight set of their lips.

The man who'd been raping her since she'd first arrived blanked her on the final day. Men. What a joke. She'd experienced enough of them in her short life to know what he'd been hoping when she'd first arrived. As they'd bundled her out the van, she'd seen him looking across the courtyard at her with glittering eyes.

Later, in the room they kept her in, she could almost hear the clunk of his thoughts as they'd made their brief journey through his brain: just you wait, I'll be so amazing you won't be able to stop yourself from enjoying it. Each time we do it, you'll like me a little more. In time, you'll grow to love me. To need me.

She hadn't.

Not with the men back in Birmingham and not out here, in this flat-roofed house cowering behind high walls, halfway up some wind-whipped mountain in the middle of nowhere. Instead, she'd continued to fight. So he'd lost patience after a few days, got rougher, started with the slaps and stuff. Big deal, she'd had worse. Her dad used to touch the tip of a cigarette against her inner thigh. Now that did hurt. Made her legs spring open, that did.

But the one who was really nasty – the one who she could tell was pulling the strings, the one who listened to the family's whining reports with a mouth that grew more and more tight with outrage – was the grandma. That face like a giant raisin, maggot holes for eyes, lips like a puckered arsehole.

During the days, they tried to get her to teach their younger kids English. That was fun, telling the little brown-eyed dickheads that the word for tree was 'twat', window was 'wank', spoon was 'spunk'. And grandma? She was 'cocksucker'.

When they eventually realized, she was certain it was the

grandma who'd said to just finish it. Like the girl was one of their goats, herded into the courtyard at sundown each day. Something to take a knife to. Chuck the remains away. Burn, maybe.

So when the door to the room they kept her in opened and some new man stepped inside, she'd been caught by surprise. Especially when he didn't swing a leg back and boot her like the family did. This man stepped closer while sadly scratching his beard. He'd undone her ropes and spoken to her in English, not bladda-bladda. Asked if she was all right.

On the drive back down – big car, a Mercedes – he'd said to her what a terrible mistake it had all been. She thought he was full of shit, of course. She'd seen the wedge of dirty notes he'd handed over in return for her and her passport.

So she'd just bided her time, waiting for his hand to slide on to her knee, the finger to start gently tracing circles. But he never tried a thing.

She fell asleep at some point. When she woke, it was dark. He'd driven her to a big town. Posh apartment, fridge full of food – proper food. Pizza, fish fingers, squeezy yoghurts. Cupboards with Pringles, Maltesers, baked beans. Heinz. Even booze. Nothing decent like vodka – some rank shit. Local. But it worked.

Then it was the sunglasses, jeans, T-shirts and a pair of Nikes. Make-up, even bras and knickers. Still she waited for the catch. And, eventually, it came. She could go back to Britain, no problem. Just one little thing she needed to do for him.

Oh, yeah, shall I unzip your flies now?

But it wasn't that. It was just a belt. Beige, canvas, with two rows of thick compartments that had been sewn tightly shut. Full of cash, he'd said. To get his brother out of the prison in the big city nearby. A cousin would be waiting on the other side of the border fence. All she had to do was flash her passport at the soldiers. British girl like her? She'd stroll through. The cousin would take the belt off her and then drive her straight to the British embassy – and she'd be free to go home.

She thought he was a lying twat. But the way she figured it was this: he was giving her back her passport. And he'd said that he – personally – couldn't go too close to the checkpoint. Which meant there was no way he could stop her walking up to the first official she could find, holding her passport out, lifting her shirt up and saying she was being used as a mule. Fuck his brother and fuck his cash.

So now here she is.

The sun's so hot. Stupid hot. And he got me to wear this dumb blue bib over my T-shirt. Unicef – whatever that means. Sunglasses are OK. Gucci, probably fake. He'd said to keep them on to hide my bruises, but I'd have wanted them anyway, the sand is so bastard bright. The belt's digging under my tits, canvas sticking to my stomach and back. Feels like something was in the Coke he gave me to drink. Not speed or E. Something nice and woozy. Skag, maybe. He said not to worry, he'd be watching from somewhere out of sight. He'd shaken my hand, wished me luck and a happy life. Fucking weirdo.

A few of the locals – the women covered from head-to-toe in those big robes – were being waved into a channel by barking soldiers. I try speaking to one but he took a quick look at my British passport and shouted me forward towards a hut. OK, OK, I hear you. No need for that attitude, no need at all. Probably best, anyway. Get inside – somewhere old beardy-weirdy can't see – then come clean about what I'm carrying. Let them know how I'd been kidnapped back in Britain, too. Tell them everything.

Fifteen feet from the building and the sand feels like marshmallows beneath my new trainers. Whatever was in that Coke, it was good. Three soldiers sitting on an anti-ram barrier glance up and start speaking at me. I smile. Got the urge to just sit down next to them and ask for a cigarette.

'Do I look like I speak what you speak? I'm English, see? This is my passport. The care home sorted it, years ago when we all went to France. You know Paris? Eiffel Tower and that? Ooh la la.'

One's grinning uncertainly. He's only a bit older than me. Quite cute. And he's got the ciggies.

'Papers? No, don't have no papers, only this passport. Listen, mate, can you give us one of them you're smoking?'

They're chuckling now. The cute one calls over to the hut. Another steps out, this one in a shirt. No helmet or gun. Fuck it, he'll do.

'Hey, you in charge? I'm carrying something. Could be cash, but it's probably drugs. I've been made to. It's here, under here, look.'

The way they stiffen almost makes me laugh. Eyes bulging like ping-pong balls. Jesus boys, you never seen a push-up bra before? The one without the helmet is turning, diving at the open doorway—

From the top of a building two hundred metres away, a man wearing a pale lavender shirt and designer sunglasses pressed send on a mobile phone. A hot white flash crackled along the bottom seam of the belt wrapped tightly round the girl's abdomen. A millisecond later it was eclipsed by a booming ball of fire that obliterated the girl, the three soldiers, the side of the command post and a visiting major from the Israeli Defence Force.

ONE

Iona lunged for the last seat at the table.

The detective approaching it from the other side gave an outraged gasp. 'Look at bloody that! The Baby-Faced Assassin strikes again.'

'Hey, mate,' Iona grinned up at him, now shuffling the chair forward and placing her pen and pad on the table. 'It's dog-eat-dog in this world.'

'Wouldn't have liked to have played musical chairs at one of your birthday parties,' he retorted.

'Who said you'd have been invited?' she shot back.

A ripple of laughter passed through the people sitting closest. The officer retreated towards the chairs lining the back wall, speeding up before all of those were taken, too.

Iona glanced left and right. They were in the main briefing room of the Counter Terrorism Unit's operations floor in Orion House, just off the M60 on the outskirts of Manchester. The oval table sat fifteen officers, sixteen if you included the superintendent who they were now all waiting for. Several of her colleagues had mugs of coffee or tea in front of them. Low conversations rolled around. The usual stuff, last night's telly, football, acceleration speed of the unmarked Subaru just added to the motor pool. Iona screened most of it out, ears homing in on a murmured conversation taking place at about three o'clock.

Most men, she suspected, had no idea that most women possessed this ability. That and superior peripheral vision. If the guy two places to her left knew about the vision, he wouldn't be glancing quite so obviously at her chest. The conversation between the two middle-aged officers at three o'clock carried on.

'Worrying thing is, I bought my daughter a similar thing.'

'A refurb?'

'Yeah – off the internet. Ebay.'

'Piss cheap?'

'Absolutely. Don't get me wrong, it's quality; she does all her coursework on it. Skypes the wife using its built-in webcam most evenings.'

'Where's she studying?'

'Down in Bristol. Medicine.'

'And you've no idea where it came from originally?'

'Nope. Some big corporation, I'd assumed.'

'You assumed. Did you check the hard drive?'

'Wouldn't know how to. The place selling it said the memory of every computer is wiped clean, checked for viruses and all that—'

The doors opened and Superintendent Graham O'Dowd made straight for the empty seat at the table's mid-point. Conversations began to rapidly die.

'I paid an extra twenty-five quid for a year's warranty,' the officer hurriedly whispered. 'That was it, job done.' He sat back and crossed his arms. Like every other person in the room, his attention was now on O'Dowd.

The superintendent placed a laptop on the table and switched it on. A moment later, the wall-mounted screen behind him came to life. A cursor started moving about, files opened, slides flashed up and were quickly minimised. The room watched in silence, collectively trying to sneak a preview.

O'Dowd finally looked up. 'OK, gents – and ladies.' His flinty eyes settled on Iona for an instant. 'Apologies to be dragging you in at six in the afternoon.'

Iona glanced at the row of windows: black. How she disliked mid-winter. Dark when you got up, dark when you went home. Only the promise of Christmas four weeks away lifted the gloom.

'The reason is that things have started to move very fast on this. I'll start at the beginning; apologies to those of you already up to speed. Three days ago, a final year student at the University of Manchester purchased a refurbished laptop from a seller of such things hawking his wares in the student union. This is the laptop he purchased.'

The image on the wall above him was of a sleek-looking piece of kit. Gun-metal brushed chrome casing, embellished with silver letters: DELL. A tape measure had been placed alongside it to give a sense of scale.

'Our student takes his new purchase home and – while waiting for it to boot up – has a root through the carry case it came with. Also made by Dell, black leather.' He brought up a new slide. Like the laptop, the carry case had been photographed from directly above. As O'Dowd had said, it was made from black leather that shone at one edge where the photographer's flash had caught it. 'In one of the inner pockets, he finds several sheets of A4.'

He clicked on one of the minimized slides. Iona's glance rose above the head of her boss. It looked like a profile you might find on a dating web site, but one where all details of the match-making company had been removed. The face of an attractive blonde girl smiled out at the room.

'Meet Shandy, if that's her real name, which I doubt it is.' O'Dowd was now speaking more quietly, his gaze fixed on his screen. 'As you can see, according to this, Shandy is seventeen. She has blue eyes. You'll also see her physical measurements listed: height, weight, bust, hips, even feet. You'll also see at the bottom a more worrying category: the fact she has her own passport.'

The implications started branching out in Iona's mind. Some kind of escort agency? One that specialized in overseas stuff? Why else would the form mention a passport? Surely an international angle. Trafficking. Did the girl know or had she been duped? She looked happy enough at being photographed. Proud, even.

'OK, most of you – I would hope – are concluding this is sex trade stuff. You might be thinking the sex trade normally works in reverse: namely, that third-world or eastern bloc girls are trafficked into western countries. And you'd be right.'

The cursor moved down once more and a new slide took over the screen. 'This is Rihanna, sixteen. A print-out of her profile was also in the carry case.'

Iona looked briefly at the new face on the wall. Pretty, again. The girl had black hair, tied tightly back like Shandy's. Iona then focused on the final category. No British passport. She went back to the face. Was that a puncture hole in the left nostril? 'Sir, neither girl is wearing any kind of make-up or jewellery.'

O'Dowd's hand paused over his keyboard. 'True.'

Iona felt the attention of her fellow officers shifting to her. Most faces looked at her expectantly, non-judgemental. But a few had that air of anticipation you see on the faces of people watching YouTube clips. The skateboarder going for an overly ambitious jump. The mountain biker losing control on a steep path. For those officers, the demise of their former DCI was all down to Iona. And now they waited eagerly for her to fall. She cleared her throat. 'I don't know if the resolution is there, but that could be a hole in her nostril – a piercing.'

The mass of faces turned back to the image.

Iona shrugged. 'You'd have thought for normal sex-trade stuff, they'd have been made to look . . . I don't know . . . glamorous. Seductive. Those shots seems very plain. More natural.'

O'Dowd tilted his head. 'Good point. Not sure where it's going, but good point.'

'It's the sort of thing modelling agencies do,' Iona replied. 'Test shots for when they're considering whether to take a girl on.'

As Iona began to jot her own observation down, O'Dowd nodded. 'I'll see if our people can confirm if the mark is a piercing. Next up is Aisha.'

Some murmurs broke out before someone spoke from across the table. 'Christ, Iona.'

She looked up from her notepad at the officer. 'What?'

Nodding at the screen, he said uneasily, 'Haven't got a sister, have you?'

For one crazy moment, she feared it would be Fenella's face up on the wall. Her eyes cut to the new slide. Of course it wasn't her, but – oh my God – the officer had been right. The girl was mid-to-late teens, oval-faced, button nose. Even her hair was cut in a similar style to Iona's collar-length bob. Whereas Iona's eyes were a striking emerald, the girl's were a deep and lustrous chestnut. But apart from that . . .

'Hard to judge what this one's ethnicity might be,' O'Dowd stated.

Iona considered her own: a mix of a Scottish mother and Pakistani father. The resulting skin tone meant people took her nationality to be anything from Spanish to Turkish to Mexican. Iona skimmed the girl's sheet: she was even five foot three, almost the exact same height. Her eyes continued down to the base of the form. A passport holder.

'Wasn't she on the news recently?' someone else asked.

O'Dowd rested his chin in the crook of his forefinger and thumb. His middle finger began to brush back and forth across his lips. 'Correct. Can you remember where?'

The officer who'd spoken puffed out his cheeks. '*Manchester Evening Chronicle* website? Did she win something . . .'

'She jumped off the flyover which crosses the M60 at Denton. It was six fifty-one in the evening, three days ago. She landed in the fast lane and was run over by at least seven vehicles.'

The silence in the room seemed suddenly more intense. A chair made a tiny creak as someone moved their legs. Iona felt coldness wash across her scalp. She could sense eyes on her. She glanced about, causing at least four colleagues to break off their stares. It was creepy.

'There's footage from a motorway camera in the central file, but you don't need to watch it. Not right now, at least,' O'Dowd announced. 'Fortunately, about the first thing the student who purchased the laptop did after leafing through the sheets of paper he found was go online. And the first site he clicked on was the *Manchester Evening Chronicle*'s: where he saw Aisha's face looking back at him.' He scribed a series of semicircles in the air. 'Four weeks ago, she went missing from council care and was featuring in the "Have You Seen This Person?" panel the *Chronicle* runs on their site's homepage.'

He lowered his hand to click on another slide. Another sheet, topped by the words Croydon Social Services. 'The girl's real name was Teah Rice, mixed race – mother British, father unknown. The mum's had another three kids since Teah, all taken into care. The last two as soon as they were born, while the mum was still on the maternity ward. Teah was born in Croydon, south London. Entered the care system aged twelve and was moved to a home just outside Stockport in August. It was assumed she had absconded to head back to her haunts round Croydon. Police down there were keeping an eye out for her. Everyone keeping up so far? Because it's about to get much, much murkier.'

'Sir?'

O'Dowd nodded at the officer. It was the one Iona had listened to chatting about his daughter's laptop before. 'Why was she up here? Has she got family in these parts?'

'No. The opposite, in fact. She was moved up here because – thanks to an abundance of cheap, large houses – Stockport is the UK's number-one choice for care home providers setting up shop. Young people are sent from local authorities all over the country.'

Iona felt herself frown. Stockport was five minutes on the train from Manchester. For kids put into care homes there, what about their existing social networks, their old school or familiar adult faces? She wasn't the only one to give a sad shake of the head.

O'Dowd sat forward. 'The purchaser of the laptop – somewhat unsettled, as you would be, by these developments – decides to go back to the person he bought the thing from. He wasn't quite sure what he was going to ask – considerations which all became irrelevant when he got to the shop the laptop seller had occupied.' He reached for his keyboard again.

A photograph taken at street level appeared. The bricks above the shop's main windows were blackened where smoke had billowed out. The flat above it had also been gutted by the fire, judging from the sooty smears trailing away on the wall above window frames that were devoid of glass. The roof had collapsed in at the centre, exposing the charred remains of the rafter at its apex.

'It's suspicious,' O'Dowd stated. 'The fire investigation officer thinks accelerant was splashed around the ground-floor premises. It's also a murder scene, since the laptop seller's body was found on the first-floor landing. This is a bit gruesome.' He clicked to a new slide. 'Eamon Heslin – one-time owner of PCs To Go.'

The man's blackened corpse was arched back, as if he'd died screaming. His hands, bound together at the small of his back, were rigid like claws. The carpet he was lying on was almost completely burned away and the floorboards beneath glistened wetly. Water from the firefighters' hoses, Iona thought.

'Despite appearances,' O'Dowd said, 'he was probably dead before being incinerated. Muscles and tendons contract with heat, giving that appearance of . . . well . . . agony.'

The DCI rested his chin as he'd done before, middle finger flicking up and down. 'So, we have some profiles suggesting a sex-trafficking ring, but possibly one taking girls from the UK overseas. Teah Rice was in council care. The identities of the other two – the names Shandy and Rihanna will have to do for now – need looking into. Urgently. We have a murdered seller of refurbished laptops.'

'What was the type of laptop this student purchased?' asked the officer who'd purchased his own daughter a second-hand model.

O'Dowd consulted his notes. 'A Dell Latitude, if that means anything to you.'

'A Latitude? How much did it cost?'

'Two hundred and seventy-five pounds, with some pirate software, a mouse, keyboard and the leather carry case all thrown in.'

'For a Dell Latitude?' the same officer scoffed. 'I bought my daughter a very basic netbook the other day from one of these internet outfits that sell refurbished gear – and that was three hundred and fifteen pounds with a year's warranty. Latitudes are top of the range; I'd say it was a knock-off.'

'It's now with the Tech department who're trying to access its hard drive and ascertain where it came from, along with how many other profiles for girls might be stored on it. But I think you're right: it would suggest our laptop seller took ownership of an item he shouldn't have. And it would seem the actual owner was very keen to have it back.'

'Did the shop this Eamon character owned – had it been ransacked?' The question came from someone sitting behind Iona.

'The Fire Investigation boys are yet to confirm that. The place was a right shit-heap, apparently. Guts of computers lying every-where. Shelves full of monitors, crates of gubbins. He built them to order, as well as installing and maintaining systems – plus mending ones with cracked screens and viruses. That sort of stuff.'

He clicked on an interior shot from the shop. It looked like Heslin had a hoarding problem. 'What didn't get roasted took a thorough soaking when the firefighters arrived. We've sent a team to comb through it, but we don't expect to recover much evidence from the scene itself.'

Iona half-lifted a hand. 'Sir, I'm probably missing something obvious here: why is the CTU involved in this? I haven't seen any terrorist threat so far.'

'No – you're absolutely right. The reason why we're all over this is about to become very clear. Let me bring up the fourth and final profile.' His hand reached for the keyboard once more.

TWO

E mily Dickinson squinted at the stream of headlights flowing towards her along Oxford Road, hoping for a more substantial pair that would indicate a bus. Wind gusted specks of rain beneath the roof of the shelter and she tried to burrow down more deeply into her duffel coat.

OK, so she knew the weather wasn't going to be like it was in her home town of Brighton. But the rain up here seemed a near-continual annoyance some weeks. She'd started thinking that, even on dry days, the bloody stuff was there, waiting in the wings for a reappearance.

The duffel coat was the business, though. Far too expensive for her student budget, but what she'd saved through the laptop she'd got off the guy in the student union – what a win! Dad had given her £600 for computer stuff. She'd got a Dell Latitude, all the software she needed and a nice carry case for £300. Even with the £125 she'd spent on the duffel coat, she was still up £175.

She peered across at the brightly glowing lights of the student union building opposite. Dark and wet out here, warm and dry in there . . . It was tempting to scoot back across and rejoin Anna and Jess in the Union bar. Why not? She smiled. Friday night and that £175 wasn't going to spend itself.

The few people also beneath the shelter started edging forward. Emily looked to her right. A number 252 was detaching itself from the slow-moving procession, indicator giving a friendly wink. I'm here, the flashes seemed to say. Time to take you home.

It drew up alongside the kerb and they started filing on, passes held up for the driver. To her relief, only a quarter of the seats were taken. She found herself an empty row, slumped into it and hugged her new laptop close. The windows were misted up and she cleared a small port-hole with one elbow, feeling the thrum of the engine quicken as the bus pulled away once more.

It was odd being at uni so far from home. Brighton was a good place: buzzing night-life, the breezy atmosphere you got from seaside towns. Manchester was different. Often, to her, it had a murky, lurky feeling. The people were friendly, on the whole. There were pubs, clubs, bars, cafés, take-away joints, cinemas and cool shops. Much more than in Brighton. But just beyond the glitter and hustle there were sides to the city that made you pause. Or quicken your step. An abandoned house with metal grilles for doors and windows. Narrow alleys choked by wheelie bins. Patches of waste ground enclosed by spiked fences. A bed of flattened cardboard boxes beneath a railway arch. Cobbles showing through crumbling asphalt. She couldn't quite put a finger on it. If the city were a person, you'd never quite feel you knew him. And it was definitely a him. An outwardly friendly guy with an easy, confident smile. But look closer and you'd see a long-healed scar running across the lips. He was fun to be with, but you could tell he was also a bit of a rascal. And, sometimes, you suspected worse. Much worse.

The bus had got to Wilmslow Road, passing Manchester High School for Girls on the right. Then it was on to Palatine Road and Emily tinged the bell. The vehicle's speed dropped, and as she made her way to the front, she saw no one else rising from their seat.

'Cheers!' she called to the driver, stepping down to the black and shining pavement. The bus trundled off into the night and, after putting her earphones in, she pulled her hood up and started making her way along Leardon Street to her shared house at its far end.

From behind a sprawling buddleia bush a man watched her go by. He saw she was fiddling with an iPod Nano, its distinctive white wire trailing up to the neck of her thick coat. He slipped through the open garden gate, double-checking the occupants of the house had been oblivious to his presence in their front garden. All the curtains were drawn.

The trainers he wore had been chosen for their quietness. Didn't matter – she wouldn't be able to hear a thing. He could hear the hiss-thunk of music coming from beneath that great hood. With purposeful steps, he closed the gap. From the jacket of his padded coat he produced a hammer and, the moment he was in striking range, he raised it high then swung it down at her head, both feet momentarily leaving the pavement. It connected with a muffled crunch.

Her legs instantly buckled and she collapsed down and to the side like a tower block being demolished. Her hood had slid half off her head and he could see her eyes were open. He slid the laptop's strap off her arm. Did she need another? The hammer hovered for a moment. No, she was proper fucked. He continued on, laptop now hanging from his shoulder as the first tendrils of her blood made their tentative way across the cold, wet paving.

THREE

O'Dowd remained silent, giving the entire room plenty of time to study the profile on the wall behind him.

Like everyone else, Iona looked at it in silence. Zara, aged seventeen. A face that was a shade too chubby for a teen-ager; the kind of skin made pale and pasty by, Iona guessed, a lifetime of cheap, poor-quality food.

She saw kids just like her every day round Manchester. Kids stuffing maxi size bags of crisps and swigging cans of Coke on their way to school. Kids without coats wandering the rainy streets at teatime. Kids clustered just inside the entrance to the Arndale, shrieking at the screen of their mate's mobile phone. Kids whose parents probably worked long shifts for shit pay and then headed straight for the booze shelves at the nearest supermarket.

The girl's eyes were still bright, though. And her smile revealed teeth that were white and well aligned. Care home kid? Iona wondered. Who could tell?

The same horrible running order ran beneath her photo. British passport. Eventually O'Dowd cleared his throat. 'This girl exploded at a border crossing on the Israeli-Lebanese border five days ago.'

A few seconds of stunned silence. Someone somewhere whispered, 'That's her?'

'It is. A few among you may remember the incident being reported; it briefly made the news that day. Her identity, however, remained unknown until yesterday. Make no mistake, ladies and gents, this represents a huge and deeply worrying development. Girls like this – young, white, British, non-Muslim – do not become suicide bombers. They just don't.

'For those exact reasons, this girl was able to approach, completely unchallenged, the Israeli position. Soldiers even directed her away from the main crossing point. There are no survivors to verify how she seemed; the blast took out a good chunk of the border building along with four members of the Israeli Defence Force, including a major. Needless to say, there was little left of the girl – whose real name, it turns out, was Jade Cummings.'

Around her, Iona could see officers sitting slack-jawed in their seats. Someone said very quietly, 'Holy shit.'

O'Dowd drew breath sharply through his nose and sat up straight. 'OK, that's your dwell time over. Time to re-engage brains. How do we know this girl's identity? Serendipity, as they say. An officer with the Greater Manchester Police was returning from a diving holiday in the Red Sea. He saw a paper at Tel Aviv airport that contained a story about the bombing. Included was a photo of the girl's face.' O'Dowd grimaced. 'When these types of bomb go off, it's not unusual for the upward blast to take the head of the bomber clean off. Often it's propelled a considerable distance. When the officer returned to work yesterday he happened to be on the team handling the investigation into the murder of Eamon Heslin. He was going through the profile of each girl and – bingo – there's the mystery bomber he'd seen in the paper at Tel Aviv.'

Someone at the back gave a humourless laugh. 'Hooray for holidays in the Red Sea Riviera.'

O'Dowd's expression didn't lighten. 'The security services in Israel were contacted immediately; they were able to confirm our photo matched their head. So, our priority is now finding out how Jade Cummings came to be over in Lebanon with a couple of kilos of high explosive strapped to her body. Is there a link to the fact she was in care? Did she have any boyfriends, and if so, what were their ethnicity?' He flicked to another slide: one with the photos of Shandy and Rihanna side-by-side. 'We also need to find out what the hell is going on with these two. That will be made much easier if we can work out where this laptop came from. Obviously, Eamon Heslin can't tell us that and cracking open the hard drive may take time.'

He sat back, interlinked his fingers and surveyed the room. 'Any reports of muggings, break-ins or thefts from cars, public transport, offices or homes need to be pursued. Not just those where a Dell Latitude was taken – remember, due to the nature of this thing, the person probably won't have made a report. But an incident may have been rung in by the security staff of an office building that was burgled, someone in a shared house, the attendant in a multi-story car park, British Transport Police if several passengers were robbed on a particular train, the list goes on.

'If you examine the CCTV footage from when Teah Rice jumped, you can see a female figure trying to coax her back. She leaves the scene when Teah goes over the edge: Good Samaritan or friend? We need her found.'

He brought up another slide, this one with two sets of names. 'Because of the multiple angles we've got to go at, I'm assigning two task forces for this investigation. First will be headed up by DCI Roebuck. It will be his normal team plus Detective Sergeant Everington, who I've pulled away from DCI Palmer. I'm giving you the profiles of Rihanna and Shandy – so you'll be working their identities and trying to establish their current location. Your search will start with Stockport Social Services then go to Manchester's, then the entire north-west and, if needs be, national. I also need you to cover the issue of where this laptop originally came from. Basically, you've got the events leading up to Eamon Heslin's death.'

Iona stole a glance at a fellow member of Roebuck's team. He widened his eyes a fraction in response: the task was going to be huge.

'Second team, under DCI Sullivan, will be covering aspects following on from the death of Eamon Heslin – principally, the recovery of evidence from the murder scene and all necessary actions arising from what's found. You've also got the Teah Rice thing. A few of you may have noted the absence of DS Chadwick and DC Grant this afternoon. They are en route to Croydon to interview Teah Rice's relatives and social worker. OK, that's it. Report to your respective DCIs who will let you know exactly what you'll be doing.'

People started getting to their feet, conversations breaking out across the room.

'Everyone!' O'Dowd's voice rang out above the din. 'MI5 and MI6 are sniffing about – sorry, offering us every assistance. If we need it, we'll take it. But let's try not to. You lot all jumped through hoops to get into this unit. This is our chance to show everyone – including that lot down in London – how bloody good we are.'

Iona started making for the door when O'Dowd spoke again. 'DC Khan? One moment, please.'

He started closing down his laptop as the room drained of people. Once they were alone, he nodded at the empty chair next to him.

She sat down and said nothing. Did I do something wrong? Am I in trouble? Is this because of the comment about the girls' lack of make-up?

'How are you finding things, Iona?'

She tried to conceal her surprise. It was the first time she'd ever spoken one-on-one with the super and now here he was using her Christian name. 'Fine, sir. Good. No, not good. I love it.'

He smiled briefly. 'And being in Roebuck's team?'

Iona thought about her new boss, Peter Roebuck. She knew there were a few in the CTU who found his urbane manner irritating, she suspected because it hinted at a privileged life. In the preliminary meeting she'd had with him, he had been quick to mention that he'd been given a bursary to study at King's School in Macclesfield. She knew the fact she'd won a sports scholarship to Manchester High School for Girls was on her file: it had been a slightly clumsy attempt on his part to find common ground. She looked O'Dowd in the eye. 'No problem whatsoever.'

'Good. Him and I go back a long way. He's as straight-up as they come.'

Iona understood the implications of the comment. Unlike the last person you worked under, was what he'd really said. DCI Paul Wallace had been a racist snake who had left Iona to confront a terror cell without any back-up.

'Obviously, the way things ended with Wallace . . .' O'Dowd looked uncomfortable for the first time. 'He was a popular man in the unit. Charismatic. Even with all the facts laid out about what he did—'

'Sir, I understand. There'll always be people in the CTU who'll wish he was still here and I wasn't. They'll never admit it, but we both know that's what they'd prefer. I can live with that.'

He gave her an approving look. 'You'll go far, Iona, trust me. Now, Peter has OK'd this. In the lounge downstairs, we have Philip Young – the student who brought in the laptop and carry case with the profiles.'

The lounge, Iona thought. The pleasant interview room for members of the public not suspected of any terrorist crime.

'Understandably, he's feeling anxious about what he might have stumbled across. We need to make him feel at ease, but not complacent. It's a tricky one. Me? I'm a fifty-four-year-old with a receding hairline. You are the closest thing this unit has got to someone his age. You're a maths graduate, yes?'

Iona nodded. My file really has been doing the rounds.

'That's also his subject. Where did you study?'

'Newcastle.'

'OK. Not sure what connections the city might have with Manchester. But you've got the maths. Now, he's already been interviewed by uniforms. We need to sit down with him and see if there's anything else in his head that's useful. Are you OK with that?'

'Yes, sir.'

'Excellent. And Iona? Just to be clear, he has no idea about the fate of Jade Cummings. Let's keep it that way – for the time being, at least.'

FOUR

Philip Young looked up from the sofa on the far side of the room. He was holding a copy of that day's *Guardian*. Iona guessed it had been bought specially for him; it wasn't the kind of thing you normally found lying around the building. She spotted a waxed cup from a proper coffee shop on the table before him. Someone had done their best to make him feel at home.

She didn't think it had worked very well. There was a slightly queasy look on his face, like he was about to sit an important exam or be interviewed for a coveted job.

Appearance-wise, he was meticulously plain. Absolutely nothing made him stand out. Loose-fitting jeans and a baggy top. Drab blues and grey. A pair of black Adidas trainers. His hair – brown and straight – was parted at the side. Iona guessed Philip was aiming to get through his time as a student without attracting attention and then land a steady job and have a nice, quiet, respectable life. Shame he hadn't been able to resist an unbelievably cheap laptop.

'Mr Young,' O'Dowd announced as they crossed the room. 'Sorry to keep you. This is my colleague, Detective Constable Iona Khan.'

'Hi.' Iona smiled. As they'd come in, he'd looked surprised at the sight of her. She deliberately didn't hold eye contact so he could continue his appraisal, aware that a petite female in her mid-twenties was far removed from the burly male officers who'd no doubt been dealing with him so far.

'We appreciate you giving us your time, Philip,' O'Dowd said, taking one of the seats opposite him.

The student glanced at Iona again as she settled into the other chair.

O'Dowd pointed at the small camera mounted in the ceiling above them. 'I'll need to record this conversation, I hope that's all right.'

Philip glanced up. 'Um . . . yes. I signed a statement for the officers at the other station already—'

'I know. I have it here.' O'Dowd nodded.

His eyes went to Iona yet again. 'Sorry,' he mumbled. 'But you look really like the photo of that girl . . .'

Of course, Iona realized. That's why he keeps giving me the eye. 'Yes, sorry if that threw you. You're not the first person to notice.'

He was frowning. 'Are you going to be doing one of those reconstruction things? Playing her part in it?'

She wondered if he realized where he was: detectives in the Counter Terrorism Unit would never appear on the telly. 'No, a professional actress would probably be recruited for that.'

'Oh.'

O'Dowd sat forward. 'We'd just like to talk you through a couple of things. I realize it might seem like you're being taken over the same old ground.'

As Philip folded the paper over, Iona could see its corners were trembling. He'd been having a go at the Sudoku puzzle. She reached out and rotated the paper round. The bottom row was partly filled in, as was the right-hand corner. She stared at the numbers, feeling her brain starting to whirr. It had always been this way for her with numbers; they were like a language she had always been able to speak. 'Is that a five you need? Third from the left.'

He cocked his head. 'Five? I don't know, is it?'

'I reckon, because that means the one four across is an eight, so then you can put a three in the corner box.'

He spent a few seconds checking Iona's calculations. While his head was bowed, Iona gave O'Dowd a quick wink.

'Oh, yeah.' Philip looked at her with a mixture of awe and intrigue. 'Are you . . . like a technician or something?'

'No, just a normal detective. Old habits die hard – we always did the puzzles in my student house.'

He leaned back a bit. 'Where did you go?'

'Newcastle. Maths.'

'Maths? Me, too.'

'Yeah, my boss mentioned. And you're a third year?'

'That's right.'

'Which modules have you gone for?'

'I want to be an actuary. Mainly, I'm doing stats. A bit of Option Pricing Theory.'

Iona couldn't imagine applying the beauty of maths to something so boring as finance. 'Fair enough.'

'And you?'

'Me? I just stuck with pure maths – number theory was a favourite.'

'So, how do you end up in the police with a maths degree?'

'Oh, they'll take anyone,' she smiled.

'I can tell you, Iona here is a rising star. A real asset.' O'Dowd's clunky interjection brought the conversation's flow to a stop.

Iona saw Philip blink uneasily. 'So, this laptop.' She waved a hand at the sheets O'Dowd had placed on the coffee table. 'Very nice bit of kit. With an Intel i7 processor, too.'

'Yeah.' Philip sounded wistful. 'Top notch. I suppose it's in bits now?'

O'Dowd crossed his legs. 'I'm not sure. They won't be using a hammer on it, though.'

'You mean, I might get it back?'

'Well, no. Not if it's stolen property.'

He sighed. 'Which – let's face it – it probably is.'

'I've not seen it up close,' Iona said. 'Were there any markings on it?'

'A label at the front had been removed. The casing was all scratched where it had been scraped off with a blade. The guy – the one who was selling – said it had probably come from a bank.'

'And this person, Eamon Heslin, had you any previous dealings with him?' O'Dowd asked.

'No. I'd spotted PCs To Go before. It's along Oxford Road from the student union as you go towards the Aquatics Centre. But I'd never been in. Poky-looking place.'

'On the day in question, he was in the student union itself?'

'That's right.'

'But not as an official seller – as part of any shop or stall in the building?'

'No, he was there . . . you know . . . just asking people as they went past.'

'Asking what?'

'If you wanted a cheap laptop. I know I shouldn't have got one, but when I saw how much he was asking – and for a Latitude.'

'A Latitude with a few extra bits thrown in,' O'Dowd added pointedly. 'Keyboard, mouse and a proper leather carry case.'

Iona shifted in her seat; her boss's tone was more like that of a school teacher. 'He asks,' she cut in breezily, 'if you'd be interested in a cheap laptop. And, for two hundred and seventy-five pounds, who wouldn't?'

He glanced at her with something like gratitude. 'Yeah.'

She smiled briefly. 'Did you buy it there and then?'

'No – I hung to the side and listened to what the deal was.'

'He had a crowd?'

'No – just this girl. She paid three hundred for hers, with just a carry case that wasn't even leather. I bargained a bit and got the other stuff thrown in. And for twenty-five pounds less.'

Iona glanced at her senior officer. Seeing that he was consulting his notes, she said, 'Another laptop was purchased?'

'Yeah – he sold the one he had to her. I asked if he had any more. He said yes and we went back to his shop.'

'How many of these Dells was he selling?' Iona asked, keeping her voice relaxed.

'Not sure.'

'But you think he had others?'

He considered her question. 'Well, he didn't say I was lucky or anything. You know, that it was his last one and I'd been just in time.'

Iona narrowed her eyes, like he was the most fascinating person she'd ever spoken to. 'Try and remember if you can: did he say there were others for sale? As in he'd taken delivery of a batch of them.'

'A batch?' Philip shook his head. 'I don't remember him saying that.'

O'Dowd finally looked up. 'What was that about a batch?'

Iona turned to him. 'I was trying to ascertain if Eamon Heslin had any more of these particular Dells for sale.'

O'Dowd looked at the student. 'And did he?'

'I don't remember him saying.'

'The girl who bought one before you,' Iona said. 'What did she look like?'

'I don't know. Normal.'

Normal, Iona thought. Not the most helpful of descriptions. 'Normal height, you mean?'

'Yeah.'

'So, five foot eight – somewhere round that?'

'I'd say five ten.'

So, Iona thought, she was actually quite tall for a female. 'And what colour hair did she have?'

His eyes closed for a second as he dredged his memory. 'Black. Really black, like it had been dyed. And it was tied back in a ponytail.'

'Good,' Iona encouraged. 'Anything about what she was wearing stand out?'

'She had this purple duffel coat thing. Fur on the hood. It was long, knee length. And she had black leggings on underneath with high top trainers. I think they were probably Converse – they were an unusual colour. Green or maybe orange.'

Iona sent him an appreciative glance. 'I wish everyone who comes in here was as observant as you. Now, going to his shop: what happened there?'

'How do you mean?'

'Did he have the laptop on a shelf, in view? Or did you wait while he fetched it from some other part of the premises?'

'Oh, right. I waited at the counter while he fetched it from a back room. That's when I saw he had other stuff – peripherals – so I decided to try and haggle a better deal.'

O'Dowd tapped his pen against his knee. 'At what point did you find the sheets of paper in the carry case?'

Philip raised his chin a moment. 'When I got home. After I took the laptop out, I went through it to see how many compartments and pockets there were. They were in this zipped inner part. Nearly missed them. It was when I saw the girl's face on the *Manchester Evening Chronicle*'s website . . .' His words faded.

'When you actually paid for the laptop,' Iona said, steering the conversation away from the girl, 'did you use a card?'

Philip's head shook. 'He wanted cash. I stopped at a hole-in-the-wall on the way to his shop.'

'Did he give you any kind of receipt?'

'No – but he said I could bring it back if it started playing up within the first three months.'

'Did he not make any kind of note of the date? What about your contact details for his email list?'

'Yes, he took them.'

'How about the girl in the duffel coat who also bought one?'

'Yeah, he jotted hers down.'

Good, Iona thought. 'When you say jotted, he wrote this stuff down?'

'Not mine. He entered my details into his computer. By the till. The other student's, he jotted them down in a little booklet thing.'

'What details did he take from you? Name, email and phone number?'

He nodded.

'Home address?'

'Yes.'

'Anything else?'

'Erm, no. That was it.'

'OK, you've been a massive help, Philip,' O'Dowd suddenly announced.

'Is that it?'

The super skimmed through the remaining parts of Philip's statement. 'It would seem so, for now. A car will take you back into town.' He got to his feet and extended a hand. 'Thanks for your assistance.'

Philip reached up, and somewhat awkwardly, shook. 'Do you think there's a link between the fire and the profiles from that laptop?'

'We need to find that out,' O'Dowd replied, looking down at the younger man.

Philip spread his hands. 'Am I in any kind of danger?'

'I don't think so,' O'Dowd replied in a reassuring tone. 'But we'll give you a number. If you have any cause to feel unsafe, call it and a patrol car will be with you in no time. OK?'

He nodded uncertainly.

Iona held up a hand. 'Thanks, Philip. See you about.'

Once they were out of the room, O'Dowd started to speak

in a low voice. 'Good work there, Iona. You did well. Our officers at the scene need to prioritise finding the computer Heslin had by his till. If he took details of his customers, he probably took details of his suppliers: I doubt the two laptops came from a legit source.'

'If they were stolen, would he even put the details on his system?' Iona responded, hurrying to keep up with O'Dowd's longer stride.

'Let's hope so.' He shouldered his way through some double doors, a hand holding one open for Iona.

'Sir, if there was incriminating evidence found with one laptop, couldn't there be stuff on the one the girl in the duffel coat bought, too? What if there are other laptops out there? We could end up having to track all of them down.'

'You're assuming the laptop that girl purchased came from the same place as the one Philip Young bought.'

'They were both Dell Latitudes, sir. Heslin wasn't selling any other type that day in the student union.'

As they started up the stairs, O'Dowd grunted in agreement. 'I'll get some resources allocated for tracing the girl in the duffel coat and any other purchasers.'

Iona saw an opportunity. Grab it, girl, a voice in her head urged. Once this investigation kicks in properly, you'll probably never get the chance to speak directly to the super again. 'I could do it, sir.'

He looked back at her. 'Do what?'

'Organize the tracing of the duffel-coat girl – and any other students who may have bought a laptop. Assuming they're students, I'd be well suited, you know, with my age. And I'm female. We know the other laptop was purchased by a female . . .' She wondered whether she'd overdone it, enthusiasm tipping over into grasping ambition.

His step slowed. 'I'm happy with that, if DCI Roebuck is. I'll let you have a word.'

She kept the smile off her face. 'No problem, sir. Do you think Philip could be in danger?'

O'Dowd considered the comment as they reached a landing, turned back on themselves and started climbing again. 'I don't think so. There's a decent chance Eamon Heslin was killed for taking what was probably stolen property. But I think it stops there. What's more important is finding where Philip Young's laptop came from. That and the whereabouts of the other two girls in those profiles.' He stopped at the top step, now almost talking to himself. 'Because if they've already been spirited out of this country, God forbid it's for the same purpose as Jade Cummings.'

FIVE

They felt the muted thud as the front door slammed shut above them. A girl with a long blonde ponytail sent a frown up at the ceiling. 'She said we'd be out there by now. This is doing my head in, being stuck here.'

Her companion continued to twizzle a strand of kinked black hair between her fingers while letting out a yawn. She tossed a celebrity chat magazine aside and draped another across her lap. 'Who cares? I could do this for weeks.'

'What? Be locked up under some house? We don't even know where this is.'

The girl dragged her eyes away from the gallery of images filling the page and glanced about the room they were in. There was a widescreen TV in one corner. Scattered on the carpet before it was an untidy jumble of DVDs. A games console was to one side, cases for it intermingling with the ones containing films. A glass-fronted fridge was next to it, the top shelves laden with cans of soft drinks. Beneath them were several bars of chocolate, a few apples and a punnet of red grapes. A few trashy novels sat on the bookcase in the corner: celebrity autobiographies written by people still in their twenties, romance novels written by ex-models, a few copies of feminine erotica. On the opposite side of the room was an expensive-looking CD player. Plan B was playing on a low volume. 'Yeah,' she replied. 'I could.'

The other girl sighed. 'Well, I can't. Wouldn't mind so much if she'd give us back our mobile phones. Could at least send a few texts.'

'Yeah, but she explained that, didn't she? No bloody signal down here.'

'So? I type them out here and she takes my phone upstairs and sends them there.'

'And then your phone signal gets picked up by the police. She said how it works – they trace it and next thing, they're banging on the front door. We go back to that crappy care home and that's it.'

The other girl stretched her long legs out, sinking deeper into the beanbag as a result. 'You really think they'll be out looking? They never have before.'

'Madison, have you ever been missing this long before?'

'No. Never been missing at all. Not for a few nights.'

'I have. And she said there's been stuff on the local news, didn't she?'

The other girl listlessly ran her fingers across the soft surface of the beanbag. 'She said. How do we know? Got no television, internet, radio, newspapers; just those shit magazines and whatever she decides to tell us.'

The other girl looked irritated. 'So . . . what? Nina's lying to us? Why would she do that?'

Madison said nothing.

The other girl turned back to the magazine, plucking a Malteser from the packet at her side. 'She wouldn't lie.' The Malteser went into her mouth.

'You'll be turning into a right lard-arse,' Madison muttered with a grin.

The other girl held up a middle finger, one cheek now bulging.

'You get better tips if they fancy you,' Madison added. 'Nina said.'

The girl crunched down on the sweet, brown eyes lifting to the doorway. 'I'll do a bit on the running machine later.'

'Yeah, right. Like you didn't do yesterday. Or the day before. Your arse'll split those hot pants when you try and get them on.'

The other girl started laughing. 'Fuck off, it will, Mads. Besides, I've got the tits – you haven't. Only thing I'll be splitting is customers' hearts.'

Madison cackled with laughter before peering down at her own, modest cleavage. 'A handful's fine.'

'Handful?' She made her voice go squeaky. 'Yeah, if you're some kind of midget with little, teeny-weeny handies.'

'Sod off,' Madison giggled as she reached for the computer print-outs lying on the carpet beside her.

The main image was of the interior of what looked like a small casino. But beside the card tables was a dance floor and running down one side of the room, a bar. The photographer had used some kind of lens or filter to add a golden haze to the rows of bottles, gilded decor and massed ceiling lights.

The clientele was exclusively male. Some wore suits, others were in tailored shirts and smart trousers. All had black hair and dark skin. Several had neatly trimmed beards.

Sprinkled among them were a few girls. They all wore the same outfit: gold hot pants, gold high-heels, gold waist jackets over crisp white blouses. Some were carrying trays of drinks, two were up on a low stage dancing, others were just chatting with customers.

The wording at the top of the sheet said, Club Soda. An exclusive club for those with discerning tastes. Chartres Street, Beirut, Lebanon.

'Chloe? Did Nina tell you one of the girls got a five-hundred-quid tip last week? Just for carrying drinks to a table.'

'I know. But it's two fifty just to get in the place. Thirty-five quid for a whisky and Coke. Arabs, isn't it? They're all loaded.'

Chloe gave Madison a mischievous look. 'What do you reckon you'd get for tugging one of them off in the toilets? Twice that?'

Madison's face fell. 'Shut up!' She looked nervously towards the corridor. A heavy door blocked the stairs up to the ground floor. 'Nina would flip if she heard you say that. It's not like that.'

'Oh, I love you, Mads, you're so fucking innocent.' Chloe smiled. 'All places like that are like that.'

'No touching,' Madison said. 'All they're allowed is to talk to us.'

'Not even for a grand? Not to shag, only a hand-job.'

'Shut up, Chloe.' Madison struggled out of the beanbag and looked uncertainly at her friend. 'Would you? For a grand?'

'Any day. Easy money. What about Liam? Would you give him one?'

'Liam? Who brings down the food and stuff?'

'Yeah. When he was showing us how the running machine works, I was checking his arse. Good and tight, it was.'

'Liam? He's like thirty or something. That's gross. Besides, I don't like his eyes. It's like the pupils are too big. Black thoughts, he's got.'

'And? What does that matter? I'm talking about his body. And after a week down here, I'm thinking old Spencer would be worth it.'

'Creepy Spencer? From the care home? I worry about your head, Chloe.'

Chloe laughed raucously. 'OK, maybe not Spencer. But Liam? Get him in the back bedroom. I'd have some of that, oh yes.'

Madison tied her hair back in a ponytail. 'Anyway, he's got the hots for Nina – no question.'

'You reckon?'

'God, yeah. When she's talking, watch him – not her. It's like he's hypnotised, head bobbing away like one of those stupid plastic dogs you see in the backs of cars.'

'Missed that,' Chloe sniffed. 'Still, I could handle sharing him. I'm not selfish.'

'You're wrong, girl. Up here.' Madison tapped her temple. 'I'm having a go on the rowing machine.'

'You work it!' Chloe shot back, reaching for the Maltesers.

Madison paused in the doorway. 'Anyways, two hundred quid for every shift? And a share of the tips as well? They can wank their own selves off, the dirty bastards.'

Chloe burst out laughing again.

SIX

'I remember it being on the news,' Jim said from his position on the kitchen floor. Iona's mum's dishwasher was pulled out from the wall. He continued to examine the tubes and wiring behind it. 'They had to shut the M602 before Salford, didn't they?'

'No – she went off a bridge over the M60 near Denton. That was a different one,' Iona replied, her laptop on the kitchen table before her.

Moira made a clucking sound. 'So many young lives wasted. How terrible this world can be.'

'So why are the CTU interested?' Jim asked as he reached for a pair of pliers.

'Oh,' Iona said, now regretting that she'd brought the girl's suicide up. The fact that so much of her work couldn't be discussed with anyone outside the unit was made more awkward by Jim's lack of success in his own application to get in. 'It might be linked in with some other stuff. The reason why I mentioned it is this other person you can see at the edge of the picture. I can't stop thinking about what she must be going through: trying to talk the young girl back, then watching as she drops off the edge. The way the woman turns round and walks off, shoulders hunched . . .'

'Ow, hen.' Moira's Scottish accent had been softened by her whisper. She stroked her daughter's hand. 'Whoever she was, she tried. At least she did that. She'd be feeling a lot worse if she hadn't.'

'Yeah, but now she's probably traumatised. Now she's got that memory. She'll be able to hear the traffic screeching below. Poor woman.'

It was quiet a moment before Jim gave a cough. 'Your seal's petrified, Moira.'

The older woman's eyes lingered on Iona for another second. 'Didn't even know I had a seal behind there.' Her voice lifted. 'Is it well trained? Would a fish make him happier?'

'Mum,' Iona grimaced.

Jim wriggled out from behind the machine, a rubber ring in his fingers. 'That's where the water's coming from. The rubber's all cracked. Water'll have been draining into the base of the machine. That causes this floating switch to rise up and cut the power.'

Moira's eyes sparkled as she glanced at Iona. 'He's clever. Isn't he clever?'

Iona rolled her eyes. 'Yes, Mum. You don't need to remind me.'

Jim looked mildly embarrassed as he shut the lid of his toolbox and climbed to his feet. 'I can get you another one in the morning. I'm not back on duty until lunch, so I'll pop by and fit it before then. I'll leave my toolbox here.'

Moira glanced at the sink full of dirty plates with a smile. 'No bother to me. It's Wasim's turn to wash up.'

'What's my turn?'

Iona looked to where her father's deeply sonorous voice had come from. He was standing in the doorway, a loose thread hanging from the elbow of his tatty beige cardigan.

'That washing-up,' Moira said, pointing at the sink. 'Jim's solved the mystery. We need a new seal. Arf, arf.'

Wasim turned towards Jim. 'That's all? Well, I thought we were looking at a new machine.'

'No, that one should see you for a while yet,' Jim responded, retrieving a bunch of keys from by the sink. 'Right, I'd better be off – I'm meeting Mark. We're going out to Hayfield.'

'You're not racing around on your mountain bike, are you?' Moira asked. 'You do realize it's dark outside?'

Jim gave her a broad smile. 'Best time for it. No ramblers to get in our way.'

'He's mad.' She looked at Iona. 'Tell him he's mad.'

She held up her hands. 'I'm not getting involved.'

'Thanks for tea, Moira. As tasty as usual.' He plonked a kiss on her cheek. 'Was, see you about, mate.'

As the two men shook hands, Iona busied herself with the computer. This was when things got uncomfortable.

'Iona?'

Glancing up, she saw him leaning down, a trace of uncertainty in his eyes. She turned her cheek and, as he kissed it, she gave his forearm what she hoped was an affectionate squeeze. 'See you soon, Jim.'

'Yes. OK.' He backed away and reached for his jacket. 'Cheers all.'

'Oh.' Moira jumped to her feet. 'We've got some chutney for you. Green tomato. Wasim made it, so it'll knock your bloody block off – the amount of chilli he shoves in.'

'Just how I like it,' Jim grinned.

'It's in the back porch.'

As Moira and Jim left the kitchen Wasim approached the dishwasher. Stopping short of it, he regarded the machine almost affectionately. 'A seal. Who'd have thought?'

Seeing him then send a despondent look at the full sink, Iona reached for the keyboard of her laptop. She muted the sound then clicked on the CCTV footage of the A57 where it passed over the M60 at Denton. The girl was hard to spot, at first; the pole of a streetlamp obscuring part of her thin frame. In fact, it was only when the member of the public began speaking to the girl that you became aware of her presence by the railings.

With her back to the camera, the person – a woman in a long white parka-style coat with a fur-fringed hood – advanced cautiously forward, one hand held out at waist level. She was obviously trying to reason somehow because the girl began to shake. A rejection or a dismissal of what was being suggested. A car passed them, brake lights showing as it slowed down for a second. Then it continued on its way once more. Iona found the callous indifference of the driver depressing.

The woman edged forward once more, hand still out. The girl kept her head bowed, eyes on the racing traffic below. Then her hand let go of the lamppost and she stepped out into the air. Immediately, she dropped from view.

'Iona?'

'Mmm?' She looked up. Wasim had pushed his sleeves above his elbows and was turning off the tap. From in the porch, she heard Moira saying goodbye. The back door closed.

'I said, are you OK? With Jim . . .'

'Of course.' She smiled. 'How could I not be? The guy saved my life. He risked everything for me – his career, everything.'

Her father smiled patiently. 'Yes, but you two were—'

Iona cut in. 'He was my boyfriend, I know. But that's irrelevant.'

'It can't be easy, him coming round each week –'

Moira bustled back into the room. 'When will you give that poor man another chance?'

Iona flicked an angry glance at her. 'What do you mean? I have to take him back through a sense of guilt?'

Moira's step faltered. 'No . . . but . . . he's trying so hard, hen. Don't you think he deserves another chance?'

'Mum, I don't love him. I . . .' She felt tears in her eyes. 'I've tried. Christ, I've tried. I care about him, but . . .' Her voice lost its strength. 'That's all.'

Her mum crossed her arms, 'Maybe your old feelings will return – in time.'

'Moira!' The anger in Wasim's voice startled both women. 'Will you leave the issue be? You cannot manufacture feelings for someone. It's not possible.'

'I'm not saying that,' she replied. 'All I'm saying is, feelings she still has might be rekindled if only she would—'

'He's still drinking, you know?' Iona sat back, watching her mum's face cloud over with confusion. Good, she thought. Time you took those blinkers off.

'He's not. He said he wasn't.' Moira gestured at the empty bottle of red wine on the side. 'He didn't touch a drop.'

'He's not stupid, Mum. Of course he wouldn't. He's lying, though, when he says he's on the wagon.'

Moira's head shook. 'Hen . . . you can't go pointing your finger like that –'

Iona stood. 'Come on, then. He's on his bike, yeah? It's eight o'clock on a Friday night. He's not meeting Mark to do any night riding. He's going home via an off licence to drink himself stupid.'

Moira lifted her eyebrows. 'That's an awful thing to suggest.'

Iona grabbed her car keys. 'I know which way he cycles home; I did it with him often enough. He'll cut across Chorlton-cum-Hardy nature reserve, on to Barlow Moor Road where he'll stop at the cheap booze shop. That's the one he always used to use on a Friday. He rotates between them, you see. A bit from here and a bit from there.'

'How can you be so sure?' There was a defiant, doubting edge in Moira's voice.

'Because I lived with him for almost three years! I sussed him eventually. He'll get the booze and then he'll go home for the night.'

Wasim squirted viscous green liquid into the sink. 'That's a very unfair thing, Iona, to spy on him.'

'I know, Dad. And I feel awful suggesting this. But Mum needs to see. You both need to know. He's not being honest with any of us. If I'm wrong, you can chastise me all you like.' She turned to Moira. 'Are you coming?'

SEVEN

He watched the house from the end of its backyard. The shadows were thick here. Trailing leaves from a creeping plant shrouded him. With the black hood of his coat drawn about his face, he was all but invisible.

Some lad had almost fallen down the rear steps earlier on. He'd stumbled across a patch of paving lit a honey colour by the kitchen window's glow. He'd managed to halt his stagger less than two metres from where the man stood.

Swaying, the youth drained the last of a can and tossed it to the side. He'd then undone the flies of his trousers and begun to piss. The man kept absolutely still, listening to the spatter of liquid as it hit the ground before his feet. The lad had muttered to himself for a bit before starting to wiggle his penis from side to side, amusing himself with the pattern he was making in the grass.

If any of that goes on my trainers, the man thought, I'll be out of this bush breaking your fucking neck.

Totally oblivious to how close he'd come to dying, the young man had walked unsteadily back to the house and rejoined the party inside.

Now, almost four hours later, the music had finally died down. Lights were still on but no one was moving. He checked his watch. Two fifty-seven. It was very cold. He'd lost all sensation in his toes, and as he extracted himself from the cascade of frost-covered leaves, his movements were clumsy.

Remaining where he was, eyes fixed on the house, he shook his legs and pumped his arms, forcing blood back into his fingers and toes. Now he was able to move smoothly and without sound.

He glided across the garden to the back door. Open, as he knew it was. The kitchen table resembled a futuristic cityscape – the slender necks of wine bottles rising up out of a silvery mass of cans.

He peeped into the front room; someone was stretched out on the sofa, breath coming out of his open mouth like sighs of defeat. Another sleeping form was curled up in an armchair, male or female he wasn't sure. The closed door opposite the front room had a hand-drawn plaque on it. Pippa's Pad.

He took the stairs two at a time, careful to put his feet down at the edge of each step to reduce the chances of causing a creak. How many houses had he burgled in his younger years? Creeping about as the owners slept. Once on the landing he stood motionless. The first door had a Liverpool FC banner nailed across it. You'll never walk alone. Probably a bloke's, he reasoned. Opposite was the bathroom, a white toilet roll trailing across the lino floor. Next door was closed, as was the one at the far end of the short corridor. There was no attic to a third floor. A voice murmured.

Stepping lightly, the man made his way to the furthermost door. He listened. From inside, another voice said something. A male voice. Low giggling. Two male voices. Bedsprings squeaked rhythmically for a while.

The man moved back to the other closed door. He sniffed at the crack. A faint smell of perfume. It must be where she was. The handle made no sound as he turned it and waited. No sound of movement from within. He looked through the gap.

Street light shone in through the half-drawn curtains. She was sprawled across the double bed, still in all her clothes. Locks of red hair curled out from her head like streams of party ribbon. He stepped inside and eased the door shut. There was a key in the lock.

His eyes searched the room. A laptop was on the desk in the corner, next to a low pile of books. The carry case was on the floor next to it. He picked his way across the carpet and took a closer look: a Dell. Immediately, he started pulling the leads out of the sockets. Once it was free, he slid it into the carry case before checking the side pocket. No fucking profiles of the girls down in the basement. Damn it! He leafed through the loose sheets of paper by the books. Dense text interspersed with the odd chart or graph. It meant nothing to him. Would Nina want him to take all the cables, too? Probably. She'd said nothing – absolutely nothing – could be left that might link back to them. Cables could carry finger prints.

He'd unplugged the power lead when she began to stir, raising her head and looking away from him towards the door.

''S there?' she slurred.

He kept still, wondering whether her head might collapse back against the pillow. It would make things easier if it did. But she began to rub at the side of her face with one hand. The movement abruptly stopped. He knew that she'd sensed him standing on the other side of her bed.

As her head started to slowly turn in his direction, he jumped across, one knee landing in the small of her back. The beginnings of her scream were cut off as electrical cable looped about her throat.

He crossed his forearms over and pulled outwards with all his might. Coughing dryly, fingers scrabbling at the thin length of plastic, she thrashed from side to side. It was like walking Macy and Mavis, he thought, remembering his two lurchers when they caught the scent of a rabbit on the golf course near Brinnington. She arched her spine backwards at one point and he forced her flat once more by leaning on her shoulders with his chest, face pressed into her hair. More coughs emptied her lungs of the last of their air.

He kept her pinned to the bed, waiting patiently until her twitching had stopped. When he let the cable slacken no sound came from her mouth. He didn't want to take his nose out from her hair. It had a nice smell. After a few more seconds of breathing it in, he got to his knees and looked down at her. She could have been asleep, except for the bulging eyes and protruding tongue.

There was a time, he realized, when he might have peeled the bed covers back. She may have been dead, but she was still warm. Her body would be loose, her legs could be moved. It would be almost like she was alive.

But that was before Nina. Everything had changed since Nina. She was . . . he didn't have the words. She was a goddess. That was the best he could do. Something that didn't belong on earth. Yes, he knew she had been down with the dregs once. Forced to work in houses where the men filed in one after the other, mornings, afternoons, nights. A queue that never died. But she'd risen up, fought her way out. It was proof of how amazing she was. She should be dead, but she wasn't. She was a miracle. And, for reasons he could not fathom, she loved him. Why? How could that be? He didn't know. It was just another part of her mystery. But she said she did. She'd even said that, one day – when enough money had been put aside – they'd leave everything behind. It would be just the two of them. Together.

But first, this shit had to be sorted. He laid tresses of hair over the girl's face and zipped the cable inside the carry case. At her bedroom door, he removed the key, locked the door behind him and padded quickly down the stairs.

EIGHT

Iona leaned back and examined the poster design on her screen. 'What do you reckon?' she asked Euan, the civilian support worker she got on well with.

He leaned his head to the side. 'You won't be getting any awards for design,' he sniffed. 'There's no colour, for a start.'

She smiled. 'Does it get the message across? Quickly and clearly?'

He read the wording out under his breath. 'Important police notice. Have you recently bought a laptop? Was it from PCs To Go on Oxford Road (next to Musharaff Newsagent's). If so, call blah-de-blah-de-blah.' He paused. 'How about some drop shadow for the important police notice bit? Or at least some sparkles.'

'Euan, stop arsing around! Does it make sense?'

He nodded. ''Course it does. It's spot on. Where's it going?'

'All round the University of Manchester's union building. Rest of the campus, too. I'm having three hundred of them printed as A4 notices. Uniforms will hand out another few thousand as flyers. That's why I wanted to make sure it's fine before I put the order in.'

'Well, the phone number's correct.'

'Yeah. I've briefed the switchboard on what to ask before transferring the call through.'

'And what will they ask?'

'Was the laptop bought for cash, what was the make and model, when was it purchased.'

'Then I reckon you've got it covered. What about students who aren't on the Oxford Road campus for their lectures? Ones on placements or studying from home or just skipping lectures because they're . . . they're,' he let his voice go dreamy and distant, 'work-shy layabouts who spend all their time watching telly or going to the pub.'

'Touch jealous there, Euan?'

'Moi? How could you tell?'

'Every student has an email address on the university's system. I'm trying to arrange for a blanket message to go out today and follow-ups tomorrow and Monday. There's also the student news-paper – the notice will be carried on the front page.'

'As part of a story?'

'No, just the notice.'

'They didn't want to know what it was about?'

'Of course they did. But I wasn't saying.'

'Looks like you've thought of everything. Talking of emails, I've got about a million to sort through. Quick drink this evening?'

'Hopefully. I'll see how I go with this.'

'OK.'

As he returned to his corner desk, Iona minimised the poster PDF and clicked on the CCTV clip of the girl's suicide once again. I need to stop watching this, she said to herself. It's getting obsessive. But there was something about the fifty seconds of footage. It started with the girl climbing over the railing. It was that action that had drawn the attention of the control-room camera operator. From that point on everything had been recorded. The passer-by appeared about ten seconds later, her step slowing as she spotted the girl clinging to the post.

What, Iona wondered, had she said? What could anyone say or do to stop such a thing? Look, I don't know you. We've never met. I've no idea of the harrowing sequence of events that have led you to this. Maybe you're homeless. Perhaps everyone in your life that was meant to care for you has done exactly the opposite. School failed you as well? So, you'll be lucky to get even a non-permanent, minimum wage job. Even less chance of a contented, happy life. But don't kill yourself! It's not that bad, surely? Come on, cheer up, climb back over that railing. We could go to a café and have a chat. Well, actually, I'm in kind of a hurry. My husband's at home, you see. Where it's warm. He's cooked me a nice dinner. It's ready now. I've got some spare change, though. I think. Yeah, I have – nearly a quid. That's almost enough to get you a cup of tea. Someone else will walk by soon. Beg twenty pence off them and you're in business. That is, until your drink's finished and you're back out on the cold pavement. All your problems waiting with their arms outstretched . . .

Iona watched the girl vanish from view. Gone. Silent as a raindrop, down she went. The woman in the parka-style coat lowered her outstretched hand. The noise, Iona thought. She'd be hearing what was happening below. The woman jammed her hands into her pockets and turned away, shoulders going up. Her pace increased and she passed out of the frame. The bridge stood deserted. A few seconds later, the footage cut.

Iona continued to stare at the screen. Why did the woman just walk away? OK, she could understand her not wanting to peer over the edge. Who would? The first reaction of many witnesses to serious accidents was to just get away from the scene as fast as they could. Some kind of survival thing. But they normally rang the emergency services once they'd started thinking straight. They did that much, at least. This woman, though. She hadn't.

A tab appeared in the corner. Play again? No thanks, Iona thought.

She was about to make a note of the woman's odd behaviour when her mind bounced back to the previous evening. It had left her feeling cheapened, parking at the top of the side road opposite Bargain Booze and waiting for Jim to arrive. As the minutes ticked by it had got too much for Moira.

'Come on, hen,' she'd said. 'This isn't right. Let's head home before he goes past. What if he sees us here?'

Iona had kept her hands in her lap, eyes on the shop. 'No. He won't go past. He'll stop. You need to see for yourself.'

'But . . . it's not fair. Even if he does stop, how do you know he's buying alcohol in there?'

She'd glanced at her mum for a second. 'It's a Bargain Booze. Come on, Mum, you're hiding your head in the sand.'

'I'm not hiding my –'

Jim appeared. He jumped from his bike and D-locked it to the railings at the pavement's edge. Moira had sunk down in her seat, one hand forming a visor over her eyes. 'Oh, bloody bollocks, he's only to look up.'

But Jim's head only lifted as he turned round and checked for pedestrians before darting through the door, rucksack on his back.

'He might see us when he comes back out. He'll be facing our way.' Moira sounded like a claustrophobic, desperation fraying her voice.

'We can't be seen, Mum. Trust me, I've been on enough surveillance courses to know the windscreen of an unlit car like this only reflects back exterior light. It'll be vodka. A quick fix.'

'All right! I believe you. Please.'

'Do you understand, Mum? Why must it be my job to try and save him? I couldn't, anyway. Even if I had the . . . necessary feelings for him.'

Moira tipped her head. 'The poor man. What did it do to him, those months in Iraq?'

'There are whispers at work – a sergeant who works down the corridor from Jim at Booth Street mentioned it to me.'

'Whispers?'

'His timekeeping. The state of him some mornings.'

Moira spoke from behind clenched teeth. 'Can we just go? Before he . . .'

Iona turned the ignition and had pulled back out on to the main road before her sentence was finished.

Something was happening on the other side of the room. An officer had got to his feet, phone still pressed to his ear. He was making short movements with his free arm and people at surrounding desks were turning in his direction.

The man replaced the phone and clapped his hands together. 'The lab just established the previous owner of that student's laptop!'

Iona was on her feet, mouth opening with the question.

Someone beat her to it. 'They broke the encryption?'

'Not yet. The inner surface of the battery compartment had

been security tagged. Someone shone a UV pen in. The words jumped out.'

'Where did it come from?'

'CityPads. An estate agent's. The office is in the Northern Quarter, opposite the Tiki Bar.'

Iona had a vague idea of the location. The Northern Quarter was full of old textile warehouses and disused mills: testimony to Manchester's once-proud role of cotton producer to the world. With the area's recent renaissance, there'd been a rush of developers converting the empty buildings into trendy offices, galleries, bars and apartments for young professionals.

Someone else raised a piece of paper. 'Did you say CityPads?'

'Yeah,' the officer who'd taken the call from the lab responded. 'Why?'

Roebuck was now at the door of his private office, looking on with interest.

'I was just about to action this. The owner reported a theft of four Dell laptops last Monday.'

The DCI strode out into the main office. 'Details, please.'

The officer studied the print-out in his hand. 'Four laptops and the contents of the petty cash box – seven hundred and forty-three quid.'

'A break-in?' Roebuck demanded.

He shook his head. 'No. Keys were used. It says the assistant office manager hasn't turned up for work since the thefts. Unauthorized leave.'

'The theft was reported when?'

'First thing Monday morning.'

'Day after Jade Cummings exploded at the checkpoint on the Israeli border.'

Roebuck paced closer to the officer. 'This assistant manager: he took them, then?'

'That's the current focus.'

'City centre uniforms dealing with it?'

'So far. Sergeant Ritter, Bootle Street nick.'

Bill, thought Iona. The guy I worked briefly with on the investigation last year. The one who told me about Jim turning up for work vacant and lethargic.

'Got a name for this missing assistant manager?'

'Khaldoon Khan.'

Iona blinked. Same surname as me. Which could well mean he's from Pakistan. A few glances flashed in her direction.

NINE

P hilip Young had just begun to open his front door when a voice spoke behind him.

'Not the ground-floor flat, are you?'

He turned to see a shaven-headed man standing at the bottom of the steps. Thirty or thereabouts. Angular face, slightly beady eyes. Over the top of his navy fleece was an orange tabard with the words Npower emblazoned across the left breast. He looked like he was having a really bad day.

'No, sorry. I live up the stairs. First-floor flat.'

The man rubbed the top of his head with the palm of one hand before glaring at the windows to his right. 'I'm booked in. Saturday morning, eleven fifteen. She knew I were coming.'

'The lady who lives there?' Philip struggled to recall her name even though he often saw letters and catalogues addressed to her in the shared hallway. Debra, was it? Maybe Diane. Something with a D in it. He assumed she was a nurse or something to do with a hospital, coming and going at all sorts of unusual times. 'Have you tried her bell?'

'Yeah,' he sighed, detaching a pen from the clipboard in his hand. 'I'll leave a card. She'll have to book again.' He started up the steps, almost barging Philip aside to enter the building. 'Waste of my fucking time.'

Philip was shocked. Courier drivers, gas meter people: did the companies they work for deliberately pick types who, if you saw them in a pub, would tempt you to find somewhere else to drink? Now he was in a quandary. Did he delay going up to his own flat or did he just ask the guy to shut the front door behind him when he was done? He hesitated. Derek, his flatmate, would be back from playing squash in around an hour. There was no time to lose. Not if he was going to watch the new film he'd bought on the widescreen TV in the front room. Anouska. That was the name of the babe on the download's Jpeg. Her eyes slanted ever so slightly. He guessed she was from somewhere east of Russia. Mongolia or one of those other obscure countries going out towards China. Late teens at most. As he'd purchased the film, he'd vaguely wondered what circumstances led to a girl like that doing the films she did. Not that he was complaining: her body was flawless. He thought of her going at it hammer and tongs with some bloke. The scenarios in the films were always so ridiculous. A TV repairman knocking on her door. Maybe a pizza delivery boy. He looked to his side. Perhaps a boiler technician, or whatever the man next to him writing a note was meant to be. 'Can you pull the front door behind you on the way out?'

'No worries.'

'Cheers.'

He selected the key for his flat door and was just about to go up the stairs when bright lights blossomed in his head. Their appearance coincided with a piercingly loud ringing noise. He wondered if the two things were somehow connected as he felt his shoulder jar against the wall. From the corner of his eye, he saw the man was now beside him, one arm lifting up. He was holding something. Did he . . . ? He did! He just hit me.

Philip raised both arms, wanting to shout.

The man's empty hand lashed out, sweeping Philip's forearms aside. The one holding the hammer swung down once more. Philip shied away and the metal ball of the hammer glanced off his temple and smashed on to the bony part of his shoulder. A horrible stabbing pain surged down his left arm.

His voice returned. 'No!' He sank down and spread the fingers of his good hand over his head, unable to see where the next blow was coming from.

The man took more care this time, swinging the hammer at a slight angle so, when it connected, it was with the part of the skull just above Philip's ear. The young man pitched face-first on to the hallway floor, arms loose at his sides. One leg started jumping about as if he was trying to kick his shoe off.

The man pushed the front door shut and slid the bolt across at the bottom. A swift search of the flat upstairs, find the laptop and its carry case then leave by the back way.

A lock rattled as the door on his right began to open. A woman started to speak, her voice groggy with sleep. 'Will you bloody pack it in? Do you know how much noise you're making?'

The crack in her door was a good eight inches wide. He could see a bare foot, a section of fluffy pink dressing gown. Above it were puffy eyes and tousled hair. Her glance had gone to the student's prostrate form. 'What on earth is . . .'

He ran shoulder-first at the door, causing it to crash against her. She flew back and then fell on her arse, a look of utter bewilderment on her face. A line of blood opened above her eyebrow. He continued forward, hammer-arm arcing down like that of a fast bowler.

She stared up at him, disbelief keeping her mouth open even as the hammer caved in the top of her skull.

TEN

'Oh, I'm not sure, Andrew. I'm really not. You bought me the mobile telephone and I think that's quite enough, I really do.'

'Mum, will you stop fretting? Wait until you see what this can do. Honestly, you'll love it.'

'But what if I break it? Look at all those fiddly keys. The last time I used a typewriter was your father's. That was . . . I don't know when. Really, Andrew, I'm not convinced this is a good idea.'

'You can't break it. These things are sturdier than they look.'

'And expensive, I don't doubt.'

'Not really.'

'Andrew Williams!'

'It wasn't! It's not new, Mum. I bought it from this little place along from the Aquatics Centre. He gets in computer equipment big organisations don't want any more – banks, the university, probably. Those kinds of places. He cleans them up and sells them on.'

'If it's from a bank, won't it be full of bank information?'

'I don't know if this particular one came from a bank. Even if it did, he formats – I mean, wipes them clean. Like a blackboard.'

'He must be very clever. They frighten me, these things. Don't laugh, Andrew, they do.'

'Sorry. Now, where shall I put the carry case? You won't be taking it out of your flat, so this could go in a cupboard. Or to the charity shop, if you want. It's only a cheap one.'

'It looks too good to give away.'

'No, it's just nylon. Binto? I've never even heard of that make. The seams are already coming loose.'

'Leave it on the sofa. I'll find somewhere for it.'

'You're not just saying that so we still have the case if you decide not to keep the computer?'

'No.'

'Sure?'

'Andrew.'

'All right. Now, think of this as a tool waiting for your orders. They do what you tell them to do, nothing more.'

'Tools don't wait for orders, Andrew. Spoons, forks, knitting needles: they don't take in what you want, then act accordingly.'

'OK, good point. I know what you're thinking, though. You're thinking of Hal, aren't you?'

'Hal? Who's Hal?'

'The computer in *2001: A Space Odyssey*. The one who takes over the ship.'

'Yes! The film your father loved watching?'

'Well, it's not like that. You can send emails on this.'

'Email. There you go again. Email, shme-mail. I don't understand.'

'You know how you write to your friend in Cape Town? You can write to her on this.'

'What's wrong with paper and pen?'

'Nothing. But rather than stamps, envelopes and visits to the post office, you just press send. It will appear on her computer a few seconds later.'

'Judith? Did she get you to buy this? Was it her?'

'She might have mentioned it would be good for you to have one.'

'That sneaky so-and-so, I should have guessed.'

'See? You're smiling. You know it makes sense. Come on, I'll show you how it works.'

'What's that bit there?'

'A lens.'

'A lens?'

'It has a built-in camera, Mum. I've already set it up. The concierge has given me the code for the wireless network here. We can chat to each other – just like on the telephone – but see each other, too.'

'It will film me? Why would I want to be filmed, for goodness' sake?'

'It won't film . . . well, it won't record you. There won't be anything stored. The image is live – you'll just see my face on the screen and I'll see your face on my screen. Think of it as a video phone. When we press the button to hang up, the picture cuts, too.'

'And how much will these calls cost?'

'They're free.'

'Free? How can they be free?'

'It's the internet, Mum. A whole new world. You'll be one of those silver surfers before you know it.'

'Silly.'

'You wait. OK – here's something else I set up for you. This icon, here? If I click on that it takes us to this web site.'

'Spotify? Is that an actual name?'

'Of a service, yes. Right, you and Dad liked records. Who was a favourite? Who did you like listening to?'

'What do you mean?'

'When you and Dad were courting, before I was even born, who would you listen to with him?'

'Oh, gosh. That's such a long time ago.'

'Jazz. You listened to that together, didn't you? Name me a jazz singer you liked.'

'Billie Holiday. He listened to her a lot. When we lived near Grasscroft.'

'That cottage with the damson tree in the front garden?'

'That damson tree – the fruit I took off that little thing! How its branches didn't break under the weight of it all.'

'What was a favourite song of hers?'

'Of Billie Holiday's? Your father played one a lot. It had the word fine in the title, I think.'

'There's one listed here called "Fine and Mellow".'

'That could be right. Look at all those songs! Is this a kind of library?'

'Sort of.' Andrew pressed play and the clear tones of Holiday filled his mum's small flat.

She started, as if pricked by a pin. Then her mouth opened slightly. She stared at the machine with the word Dell embossed on its silver case. The singing continued, misting her eyes with a rush of memories. Memories of such sudden and unexpected power they caused tears to roll down her finely wrinkled cheeks.

ELEVEN

'This is it,' Roebuck announced, coming to a stop outside a dark, sombre-looking box of a building. Iona counted the rows of windows. Five. Five floors – each one once packed with piles of cloth, people hurrying to fulfil orders from across the globe.

Another unmarked car from the CTU pool was pulling up behind them, a pair of blue lights taking it in turns to wink from behind its radiator grill.

'Got some more intel,' an officer announced from the back seat, a laptop across his knees. 'Proprieter is Shazan Quereni, business first registered at Companies House three years ago. Mainly deals with residential lettings within the city centre. Five staff – four now with Khaldoon Khan disappearing.'

Roebuck's eyes were on the rear-view mirror. 'Anything more on him?'

'No. Border Agency said they'd have full details within the hour.'

There was a click as Roebuck's seat belt was released. 'Come on, then. Let's see what this Shazan character has to say.'

The lobby was unmanned; a noticeboard named the companies on each floor.

'Spyro-gyra web-site design. Kelly and Lee photography. Spotlight Market Research. Zig-zag, whatever the hell that is,' the officer who'd been sitting in the back of the car muttered. 'How times change.'

They clumped up the stairs to the second floor, six sets of feet. The wide stone steps, with their cast-iron railings, looked like they'd been built for a race of giants.

Shazan Quereni was waiting to meet them at the door of CityPads' office. Thirties, big belly, shock of wavy black hair. Iranian, Iona guessed. He looked taken aback at the number of officers who filed in. 'Coffee? If we have enough cups . . .'

Apart from a side room with a door that was slightly ajar, the office was open plan. Screwed to the wall above each desk was a whiteboard listing various properties and their statuses. Empty. Viewing 11 a.m., Tuesday. Under offer. Awaiting contracts. Sold.

Three women were doing their best not to stare. A call came in and they all reached for their phones to answer first.

'We're fine, thanks,' Roebuck replied. 'Could we speak in your office?'

Shazan nodded. 'Of course. There are two chairs. If we need more—'

'Two is fine,' Roebuck responded. 'Alastair? With me.' He turned to Shazan. 'Is it OK if Damian, Paul and Martin ask a few questions of your colleagues, here?'

'No, that's quite all right.'

'Is someone missing?'

The owner pointed at an empty desk in the far corner. 'Nirpal is out on a viewing. He's due back shortly. The desk next to his is Khaldoon's.'

'Iona? Could you check over there?'

She made her way across, catching a look from one of the women. Tied back blonde hair and pencilled eyebrows gave her a sharp, inquisitive appearance. 'Sorry to barge in like this,' Iona said. 'Not your normal Saturday morning, I bet.'

The woman's smile was uncertain. 'Are you all detectives, then?'

'You mean our uniforms?'

The response had come from Martin Everington, a detective drafted in from DCI Palmer's team. Iona knew that, after her, he was the youngest member of the CTU. He was also the rank above, having joined the unit straight after graduating.

He brushed at his denim jacket. 'Dress-down day. We have them each Saturday.'

'Really?'

Iona rolled her eyes. 'Don't listen to Martin, he's full of it. Yes, we're detectives.'

'In the normal police?'

'I like to think I'm normal. Martin there, he can be a bit odd.' She sent him a jokey look that wasn't returned.

The woman's eyes narrowed. 'I mean you're with Greater Manchester Police?'

'That's right.' Iona didn't want the line of questioning to continue; the fact they were CTU was something the women, at this stage, didn't need to know. 'Which desk is Khaldoon's?'

'The one on the right.'

'Thanks.' She sat down in the man's empty chair, getting an unwelcome impression of a bony behind from the dip in the cushioning. She leaned back to survey the workstation. The other officers started asking the three women usual background stuff: how did Khaldoon seem in the days before he disappeared? What sort of a person is he to work with? Has office equipment ever gone missing in the past?

Quietly slipping on a pair of latex gloves, Iona studied the surfaces before her. Empty leads trailed where the laptop once sat. A telephone. A Manchester United mug full of biros. A mouse mat calendar. A couple of folders, Perspex sheets inside profiling flats. She examined his whiteboard. Four sales already this month. Three properties awaiting contracts. She wondered if that was good. Probably was, if he was assistant manager.

She opened the slim drawer at the top. Paperclips, a lump of Blu Tack and a bottle of correction fluid. The middle drawer was locked, as was the large one at the bottom. She leaned forward to check right to the back of the top drawer. No key. She ran a hand along the underside of the desk, hoping it might have been secreted there. Nope. A glance at Nirpal's desk revealed similar-looking leads. The three females all had a Dell laptop on their desks.

She waited for a pause in the questioning of the blonde-haired girl. 'Excuse me? Sorry to interrupt. Your laptops – they're replacement ones, yes?'

She nodded. 'Shaz got them with his own money. The insurers are dragging their feet, surprise, surprise.'

'And Nirpal's?'

'With him. That's the idea, the mobile office. We can pick up emails and access the server wherever we are.'

Iona looked at the cables once again. 'But when they went missing, was that overnight?'

'Yes.' Her eyebrows lifted. 'Ah – you're wondering why we didn't have them with us?'

Iona nodded.

'Khaldoon was in charge of IT stuff. You know, backing up the system each evening, fixing it if the thing started running slowly. He called all our laptops in last Saturday for some updates or something. Said they'd all be ready for Monday morning. That's the last we saw of them – and him.' Her mouth turned down as she raked the chair Iona was sitting in with a seething look.

'Petty cash, too?'

'Yeah, that was in Rachel's desk.'

The girl nearby looked over. 'He had a spare key to my drawer. Unlocked it and emptied the lot.'

Iona pointed at the drawers of Khaldoon's desk. 'Anyone got a key for here?'

They shook their heads.

Iona wondered what might be in there. It seemed certain the man was behind the thefts. It had obviously been pre-planned. Gather in every laptop, grab the cash and go. But, in doing so, he'd sacrificed his job: maybe the life he had. Surely he knew we'd come after him? But if he was trafficking women – and worse – losing a job at an estate agent's would have been no major loss. Not if –

A figure with short, spiky hair appeared in the doorway. He was wearing a suit and had a laptop carry case in one hand.

Iona started to stand. 'Are you Nirpal Haziq? We're with Greater Manchester—'

He took a step back and bolted to the side. Footsteps drummed down the corridor. 'Bloody hell!'

The other officers' heads were turning as Iona darted across the room. 'Radio the car out front! Asian male, early twenties, charcoal suit!'

She emerged from the office and looked left. His bag was lying abandoned on the floor. The stairway door banged shut and she sprinted forward, kicking it open and checking he wasn't waiting on the other side before jumping through.

Martin shouted out from behind her. 'I'm with you!'

She ran through to the top of the stairs and bounded down the first flight, glancing over the handrail. People were down in the foyer, their loud voices drowning out any sound of footsteps.

She was at the bottom within seconds. 'Where'd he go?'

The group looked at her blankly.

'The bloke in a suit, about twenty!'

They turned to each other before one glanced back at her. 'Who?'

She ran over to the doors and looked out on to the street. One of the drivers was out of his car, radio in hand. He looked at her with raised eyebrows. Turning on her heel, she barged back through the doors. Martin was on the landing. 'First floor!' she shouted. 'He's up there!'

He turned back and reached for the door as she sprinted up the steps. 'You sure?' he called over his shoulder.

'Yes. Go on!'

They burst through together and started scanning the corridor. Empty.

'I'll go this way.' Iona set off to the left. The corridor took a right-angled turn and, up ahead, she saw an open emergency exit door. A metal fire escape led down to street level. No sign of him. She met Martin back at the stairwell. 'Gone. Out the fire escape.'

'We'll get uniformed support – he's still close. Has to be.'

Iona pictured the warren of narrow streets that made up the Northern Quarter. 'Damn it!'

They were halfway up the flight of stairs when her mobile started to ring. Office number. 'Iona here.'

'It's Stuart. Is Roebuck with you?'

'Yeah – well, no. He's on the floor above. What's up?'

'Let him know we've had word from the Border Agency, will you?'

Iona kept climbing. 'In relation to . . .?'

'Khaldoon Khan.'

'What did they say?'

'He left the country on Monday the nineteenth. Early morning flight.'

The very day the laptops were reported as missing, Iona thought. 'Going to?'

'Islamabad. Left Manchester at seven fifty. Paid in cash.'

Now at the top of the steps, Iona glanced at Martin. 'Don't suppose it was a return, was it?'

'No. And it wasn't just him, either.'

'He wasn't travelling alone?'

'No. He paid for two tickets. Him and a female.'

'Really?' Iona could now see Shandy and Rihanna in her head. Had he gone abroad with one of them? Was another bombing imminent? She dropped her voice to a whisper. 'Have you a name?'

'I do. It was a Sravanti Khan. His fifteen-year-old sister.'

TWELVE

Nina's arms were folded as she surveyed the table. On it were two Dell laptops. Beside each of them was a carry case and an assortment of cables.

Liam watched the cigarette that burned in her hand, following the smoke as it flowed up over the smooth, shiny folds of her silk blouse. He wanted to do the same with his finger, but her rigid posture made him worry that he'd done badly. To touch her now would be a mistake. He'd so wanted to do well. To put a smile on that troubled face.

She uncrossed an arm to drag deeply on her cigarette. Then she jabbed it at the laptop on the right. 'It was in her bedroom?'

He gave a single nod.

'Damn.'

'What's the problem? I mean, apart from it not being your computer . . .'

'Look at the makes.'

Liam didn't understand. She was angry. Was she angry with him? He'd done what she'd asked him. He thought back to the balls-up that had caused all of this. When Eamon Heslin had called round to sort out something with the network in her office, she'd also asked him to take away a load of old equipment. Printers, monitors, other bits and bobs. She didn't need it any more, but she still used the stuff to negotiate a reduction in Eamon's fee. Always watching the pennies, that was Nina. But he wasn't meant to take her Dell laptop. It had been on the desk next to the other stuff, but not with it. And when she'd realized the mistake, it had been too late. Eamon didn't have it any more. The wheeling-dealing little twat had already sold it on.

'So . . .' Liam hesitated, afraid of sounding stupid. 'It's a Dell laptop. But it's not your one. Yours doesn't have that mark in the corner where a label's been scraped off.'

She took another drag on her cigarette. He wished she wouldn't smoke so much. It wasn't good for her skin, all that smoking.

'I'm not talking about the laptop, I'm talking about the carry case.' She sent him a suspicious glance. 'And you are sure there wasn't another case in her room?'

'No. I mean, yes. There wasn't another computer or case in there.'

'You're sure? You said her bedroom was dark.'

'Dark, but not so I couldn't see.'

'Shit. And the one from this morning, nothing was in his flat?'

He thought about the student. Philip Young, Flat 1a, 109 Shawcross Grove, Rusholme. Two-bedroom flat, no computer in either. The woman he'd had to kill downstairs. The way she'd looked at him and not the hammer. She'd seemed sad, like he'd disappointed her. He shoved the memory back. 'No, I went through everything. There was a printer in the front room. Computer games. But that was it.'

'This,' the tip of her cigarette waggled above the table. 'It is not good.'

It wasn't often that traces of her accent crept back. Only when emotional. Or when she was wound up, like now. Her English was so good: miles better than his. Normally, you couldn't tell she hadn't been born in Britain. More than once, he'd wondered if she'd sound like that in bed. Maybe she'd even speak the language of where she was originally from.

He wrenched his mind back to what was before him. Still, he was confused. 'I . . . I don't know what is not good.'

She placed the edge of a thumbnail on her lower lip, nibbled at it like it was something incredibly expensive. 'OK. This laptop you just got from the girl's room – it's in a case made by PC World, yes?'

He nodded.

'And the one from the street,' she poked the end of her cigarette at the other case. 'This is made by Binto.'

Folding his arms, Liam nodded again.

'This is what I think,' she continued. 'Heslin was mixing up carry cases and laptops. He told us – when we went to his shop to get my laptop back – that an Asian man had called in and sold him four Dells, remember? Same model as mine. This is how one Dell laptop is inside a Binto case and another is inside a PC World case – he buys in stuff, puts the laptops in one place, the bags in another, the keyboards in another, printers in another. So on. When he sells one on, he isn't being careful to put the same items back together again.'

He wasn't going to argue: she was usually right. 'So, you're saying your laptop might not even still be with its carry case?'

'Yes. That is what I'm afraid of.'

'And you have to have the case and the computer back?'

'Yes.'

Liam was silent again. 'Why? Because of fingerprints?'

'No. I am not known to the police. There were some sheets of paper in the carry case. About the girls downstairs.'

'And your carry case is made by Dell?'

'Yes, it's made from black leather. Good quality leather. It cost quite a lot. We need the carry case and we also need the laptop.'

The way she said it, he knew what she really meant. I need the carry case and the laptop – you must find them for me. He glanced at the second carry case on the table. The girl in the street with the black hair. That had been a waste of time, then.

The student called Philip as well. Fucking students. Shouldn't have been buying dodgy gear in the first place. It was their own fault.

When they'd called in on Eamon in his shitty little shop, he said straightaway the laptop he'd taken wasn't there. That he'd sold it. He stuck to the story, eventually mumbling it through missing teeth and mashed-up lips, hands tied behind him. She'd stared down at him for a long time waiting for his sobbing to stop. Once it had, she asked for details of every person he'd sold a laptop to in the past few days.

It was all in the computer by the till, he'd said. She went downstairs. While she was gone, he'd asked Eamon if he had any food in the place. There'd been biscuits in the tiny kitchen. He'd run his hand under the cold tap for a while to make the throb in his knuckles die down. Then he checked the cupboards. Ginger snaps. Eamon hadn't wanted one. That was fair enough: wouldn't be easy crunching up those things with a mouth the state of his. He leaned against the wall and ate quite a few while they waited for Nina. Eamon had started sobbing again. At one point, air caught in the blood and snot up his nose. A shiny balloon had emerged from his nostril. Liam had almost choked on his biscuit – it looked so funny! A red nose balloon!

When Nina came back up the stairs, she had printed off a list. She was clever; found it, no messing. Asked Eamon if the names were the ones. Emily Dickinson. Philip Young. Teresa Donaghue. Andrew Williams. The four people who had bought a laptop since he'd walked off with Nina's. Eamon's head had bobbed up and down. One of them has it, they must have, he'd said. If it wasn't downstairs. Nina had said it wasn't. 'Liam?'

They'd gone to the top of the stairs. She brought her face close to his. Close enough so he felt the heat coming off her smooth skin. She'd placed a hand on his arm. 'Finish him then burn this place and everything in it. There is a load of equipment down-stairs, including a Dell laptop. For a minute, I thought it was mine, but it's not. Destroy it and everything else down there. I'll see you back at mine.'

Nina stubbed her cigarette out, looking disdainfully down at the two laptops as she did so. Then she unfolded the list she'd printed in Eamon's shop. It made a cracking sound as she opened it out. There was just one more name on the list. Andrew Williams, 41 Victoria Drive, Brinnington. 'You know where this place is?'

'Brinny? Yeah, I grew up near there. It's close to Stockport. Not the sort of place you get many students, though.'

'I hope this person has my laptop and its carry case. If not . . . it is bad.'

'You want me to deal with him, too? Not just break into his house and take the computer and case?'

'He might have seen the profiles. He might have seen what's on the computer.'

'Eamon said he'd wiped the memory, though.'

'He would have, wouldn't he? It's safer this way.'

Liam said nothing for a second or two. 'The police don't know about you. But they do me. I've got a record, Nina.' He watched her as she took another cigarette from her pack and lit it. The ones she smoked were black. They had a funny name. Soberoni or something. 'All I'm saying is, we're getting out of here after this, aren't we?'

Her pale blue eyes glittered. 'Mmm?'

'This guy in Brinny. That'll be the fifth I've done over this – six if you include the woman living in the ground-floor flat. I can't be in the country if the police start piecing it together. Neither of us can.'

Her shoulders dropped and her features softened. She cupped the side of his face with one hand. 'Yes, we'll be together soon. The money I'll get for the two we have downstairs, that will be enough. You will love it so much where I'll take you. There is a beach and, right behind it, the mountains. The slopes are a carpet of vineyards – you just fill up jugs at the farm. It costs almost nothing.'

Her palm and fingers on his face; they seemed to suck away his ability to speak. 'And the beer?' he mumbled. 'You said that's good.'

'The beer?' Her eyes almost closed. 'So good.'

She dropped her hand and lifted her eyelids. The spell was broken. 'But first we must finish this thing. Then we can be free.'

He nodded his agreement, so wanting to feel her touch once more.

THIRTEEN

They were crowded round the table in a side briefing room. Too many men, not enough space, Iona thought, as a slightly stale smell began to permeate the air. People with coffee on their breath and shirts that had been worn for a few hours too long. She glanced at the condensation-covered window. If it wasn't mid-winter, I'd open that as wide as it would go.

'OK, everyone,' Roebuck said. 'I'm due in the super's office in under thirty minutes. Marko, what have you got?'

A man with medium-length blond hair and a thin nose sat back. Like most fieldwork officers in the unit, there was nothing to make him stand out in a crowd. 'All four laptops that went missing from CityPads were Dell Latitudes that had been stickered. The laptop Philip Young brought in had obviously had that sticker removed, with resulting damage to the case in its bottom-right-hand corner. We can assume, therefore, the other three laptops will be similarly disfigured.'

'And marked with a UV pen on the inner surface of the battery compartment lid,' Roebuck added. 'I asked that of Shazan Quereni and he confirmed that he had personally written his company's name on each.'

'How did he strike you?' Iona asked.

'Quereni? Pissed off. A lot of important company data was on those laptops. He said several accounts had been jeopardized.'

'Including people looking to purchase Western girls?' Martin Everington questioned.

Roebuck hunched a shoulder. 'Obviously, I made no mention of the profiles. But he seemed entirely unconcerned about us having one of his laptops in our possession – other than wanting to know if and when it would be returned.'

Someone gave a mocking laugh.

'And the employee who ran?' Iona asked.

'Nirpal Haziq?' Roebuck responded.

'Yeah, how did Quereni react to that?'

'He seemed just as surprised as the rest of us. Embarrassed, too.' He looked down at his notes. 'Because he gave up the bloke's file there and then, we were able to get a car to his address within minutes of Haziq doing one. No sign of him, as yet.'

'Do we reckon him and the other one – Khaldoon what's-his-face – are working together?' Marko asked.

'Can't say at this stage,' Roebuck replied. 'We've already put a block on his bank cards. No significant sums withdrawn today. So, unless he had an exit plan in place, he won't be going far. The entire City Centre division have him as a top priority.' He moved that sheet of paper aside. 'Any more on the two missing girls, Dean?'

A detective in his late thirties placed his elbows on the table. 'Not so far. We're still working with social services to compile a list of kids who've gone missing from care homes in the area.'

'And?'

'And because so many of them are now privately owned, it's proving a nightmare, frankly.'

'There's no record kept centrally by social services?'

'Officially, there is. But some homes are better at submitting figures than others. There's been a lot of phoning places is all I can say at this stage.'

'Welcome to the wonderful world of privatisation,' Roebuck muttered. 'I'll need some kind of numbers for the super. What can you give me?'

Dean pulled his notes closer. 'In the last two months, forty-six have run away from homes in the central Manchester area. Twenty-nine are back in care, seven are in custody and ten are still unaccounted for.'

'You're not waiting for a final list, are you?' Roebuck stated. 'Start looking into the ten we know are still missing now. Deal with other missing reports as they filter in, OK?'

'Sir.'

'Right, next on the list is the laptop handed in by Philip Young.'

'Any luck getting past the password?' Martin jumped in.

Iona flashed him a glance: I'd been about to ask that, she thought.

Roebuck looked across at an overweight man with a wedge

of brown hair hanging low over one eye. 'Sorry, I don't know your name.'

He nodded, clearing his throat as he did so. 'Alan Goss.'

'Go ahead, Alan.'

'It's not as easy as I'd hoped. Initially, I thought I could use OPH Crack to get in. But whoever the owner is, they've built in a couple of extra layers. I've just finished trying all the passwords provided by the employees at CityPads who were able to give them: no joy.'

'So it must be Khaldoon's or Nirpal's,' Iona stated.

'If they're working together, why would Khaldoon flog Nirpal's laptop – dropping him in the shit as a result?' Martin asked. 'I mean, there's something important on it, or he wouldn't have run. To me, that suggests they're not a team.'

Good point, Iona begrudgingly thought to herself.

'How long before you do anticipate getting access?' Roebuck asked Alan.

'I'd say hours. There are a couple of things I've yet to try.'

'OK, you get going.' As the IT guy shuffled out of the room, Roebuck consulted his checklist. 'Simon, latest from the Border Agency, please.'

'Khaldoon and his sister, Sravanti, boarded PIA flight three-o-two to Islamabad on Monday the nineteenth. Their seats were paid for with cash and the booking requested they sit together. Sravanti is Khaldoon's fifteen-year-old sister.'

Someone gave a low whistle.

'We've made contact with the embassy in Islamabad and they're going to try and establish where they might have gone.'

'They're British nationals, then?' someone asked from over near the doors.

Simon nodded. 'The family are from Droylesden, west of the city centre. It's an area with quite a large ethnic community.'

'Craig and Nigel have gone to speak with the parents,' Roebuck stated. 'We'll soon know if their son and daughter left the country with their blessing. We know Khaldoon's absence from his office is unauthorised. Has the daughter permission to be away? This trip of hers is, remember, during term-time. Anything for Khaldoon on the PNC?'

A bald man wearing a muted green tie with thin red stripes spoke. 'Nope. Never been so much as cautioned.'

'So, at the moment, we have an otherwise hardworking, law-abiding individual suddenly ripping off his employer and taking a morning flight to Islamabad – along with his younger sister. Something ugly is going on. Iona, you're looking into the identity of the female student who purchased that other laptop. Progress?'

She straightened up in her seat. 'I've had the posters printed and – as soon as this meeting's over – I'll start distributing them round the university campus. Four laptops were taken from CityPads; two of those were, we know, flogged to students. I think there's a good chance the other two could have been, as well.'

Roebuck nodded. 'If you need more uniforms to expedite that, I'll try my best – we need all these things in our possession.' He lifted his final piece of paper, a slightly sour look now on his face. 'O'Dowd asked that I inform you about this. It's from the CC himself.'

Chief constable, Iona thought. The very top.

'As I mentioned earlier, establishing whether the girl called Zara was the one who blew up at the Israeli checkpoint meant contacting that country's security services. They quickly confirmed it was and now we have their ambassador demanding that a team of agents from his country are granted full access to the investigation.'

A voice came from the back. 'Mossad? We'll be working with Mossad on this?'

As soon as Roebuck nodded, murmurs of excitement rippled across the room.

'These guys,' he added, raising his voice, 'as I'm sure you're all aware, do not mess around. The Israelis have years – decades – of experience in counter terrorism. All that knowledge is funnelled into Mossad. They've demonstrated time and again that rules don't come into it when they want someone.'

Iona pictured her father, a lecturer in Persian Studies. She knew from reading his pieces how much he abhorred Israel's long tradition of sending agents into other countries to execute opposition figures. Car bombs, letter bombs, shootings, poisonings. She recalled how a honey trap sprung in Britain led to the abduction of the person who'd blown the whistle on the country's illegal nuclear programme. He'd then been shipped back to Israel, charged with treason and locked away.

'Now,' Roebuck continued. 'The powers-that-be have agreed to keep the Israelis abreast of developments as they happen. But let's not fool ourselves, Mossad will not happily sit back and wait for us to provide them with answers on this.'

A heavy-set man hunched forward, the material of his shirt taut across his shoulders. His eyes were on Roebuck. 'They'll be conducting a parallel investigation to ours?'

'Put it this way: they'll have their own leads and their own sources, I'm certain. And I'm not convinced they'll be keeping us as closely informed as we are them.'

The man grunted dismissively. 'So why are we showing them our cards? Bollocks to that.'

Roebuck sat back. 'We'll show them what we want them to see. It's called diplomacy, Lewis. I know you rugby league players don't have much time for it.' He grinned.

Lewis lifted the corners of his mouth in return. 'You don't win matches by being nice to the opposition.'

A few people started to chuckle as the door opened. Stuart Edwards, the office manager, poked his head through the door. 'Boss, got an urgent one. Relating to the stolen laptops.'

Roebuck's chin came up. 'Fire away.'

Edwards stepped fully into the room and read from the paper in his hand. 'Report just received from a patrol car over in Rusholme. The student who brought the laptop in – Philip Young.'

Roebuck's eyebrows lifted. 'What about him?'

'They think it's his body in the flat below the one he was renting.'

'Sorry?'

'Officers forced the front door of the flats. Two bodies in a ground-floor flat bedroom. The female who occupied it and what appears to be Philip Young. They've both been bludgeoned to death.'

Iona turned to Roebuck. We shouldn't have let him go, she wanted to say. We need to find that girl in the duffel coat. Fast.

Roebuck's face was white. 'Anyone arrested at the scene?'

Edwards shook his head. 'The female – a nurse called Wendy Morgan – was engaged. Patrols are out looking for the fiancé now.'

FOURTEEN

Nina walked down the aisle of her office. Eight women worked part time for her, the shifts of each one arranged by Nina so there were always at least three people in. A phone rang. Keyboards clicked. Business was good; what had started as a front for what she really dealt in had steadily grown. Thanks to her, it was now a viable commercial enterprise in its own right. True, not enough to sustain her large home and very comfortable lifestyle. How far she'd come! Her early years: they may as well be another person's. She didn't want the memories. She wished she could bleach them from her mind. She had no idea if her parents were still alive, her younger brothers and sister. She didn't care. Her mum and dad had sold her at the age of fourteen. She didn't know of any other girl who'd worked her way out of the brothels in the mining town of Vorkuta. Those she'd started with, she was sure, were dead by now. But she had guile as well as good looks. The owner of the brothel was soon won over. Better jobs came her way. Evenings that involved being taken to hotels in the town centre to visit men there. Men who could afford suites.

Clients started requesting her by name. Sometimes for an entire night. A few would even take her down to the hotel restaurant for a meal. It was on one such evening, while escorting an obese finance officer from a mining company, that she had been introduced to him. The one who saw that she was truly special. Sensing he could save her, she'd worked extra hard to enchant him, harder than with anyone before. And it had worked. He paid the necessary fee and took her out of the old gulag town, out of the Pechora coal basin completely.

Europe followed. England. He trusted her. No more clients: she was his. He didn't want anyone else to touch her. Now she helped him run his business. She looked at the long thin white boxes piled neatly on the shelves. A spot of colour was stuck to each one – yellows, golds, beiges, tans, browns and blacks.

So many shifting shades, the differences so subtle. But this wasn't his business. His was the secret one. The one that involved the two young girls in the basement of the main house.

She entered her private office at the far end and closed the door. Four in the afternoon on Saturday. He was due to call. She turned on the computer, eyes moving briefly to the table where she'd so carelessly placed the laptop.

Heslin had known there were hidden aspects to her business. After all, she knew a few things about his set-up, too. The fact she paid him in cash each month to keep their entire arrangement off the books suited them both.

She logged into her video link and waited.

Clearing her throat, she took a small mirror from the top drawer and checked her appearance. Her platinum hair was cut by a hairdresser who visited her at home once every fortnight. The woman had worked for Toni and Guy's but left when she knew enough of her clients would leave with her. Nina adjusted a strand of the jagged fringe and then bared her teeth: a perfect set of veneers.

Her natural teeth were as good as could be expected, but the poor diet and lack of dental care from her early years had weakened them irrevocably. If it wasn't for several thousand pounds of private work, she'd now look like so many of her country-women: a mouth full of brown stumps every time she smiled.

Glancing down, she checked how the silk of her blouse contoured her breasts. They were, she thought proudly, perfectly natural. And something he was especially fond of.

The inner window on the screen clicked, went dull for a moment and clicked again. Suddenly, his face was there. She immediately smiled, eyes wanting to search his face for a clue to his mood. But his gaze was directed down at something off screen. He looked preoccupied, impatient. He usually did. She waited for him to speak.

'There – that one, OK?' He handed something to someone at his side and glanced up. 'Can you hear me?'

She broadened her smile, a tight feeling in her throat. 'Yes. Hello.'

His fine black hair shifted ever so slightly. She wondered where he was. Bright sunlight was bathing the side of his face.

'Is it cold there?' he asked.

'Cold, but not uncomfortably so.' She knew not to show weakness of any kind. He abhorred weak people. They were, to him, victims-in-waiting.

His mouth moved, rubbery lips twitching with amusement. There was something strangely sensual about them. 'It is hot where I am. Too hot.'

'I love the heat.'

'I know you do.'

He was looking directly at her. Examining her. She felt her chin lift slightly, eyes on his. They were so dark. Inscrutable. His fingers came into view, a pistachio held in them. The knuckles of his thumbs jutted out for a second before the shell gave way with a sharp crack. She tried not to shudder at the noise. The bones of her middle fingers had made a very similar sound when he'd snapped them all those years ago.

Still looking at her, he popped the nut in his mouth and crunched on it. Don't look down, she told herself. Even though if feels like you must.

'My beautiful one. You are so beautiful. I wish you were here with me.'

She let herself blink.

'Do you not want to be here with me?'

She inclined her head. 'Of course I do.'

There was a twinkle in his eyes. 'But you don't know where I am.'

'It doesn't matter. Anyway, you said it's hot there.'

He looked to the side and dropped the shells into something, smiling as he did so. 'Soon, my pale jewel, soon. Then we will share such things together.'

She smiled, but not for too long.

'First, though,' he sighed, looking back at her. 'We must work.' He lifted a sheet of paper and continued to chew. It was the profile of one of the girls in the basement. The blonde, slender one. Shandy. 'What is her real name?'

'Madison.'

'Madison.' He considered it for a moment. 'Madison. OK, this one we want. She is a virgin?'

Nina nodded.

'She must be a virgin. The buyer I have, it is a condition. No sale otherwise.'

'She is a virgin.'

He sipped from a shallow cup, swilled the liquid around his mouth and swallowed. His lips peeled back in a proper smile. 'Aaah, this is why you amaze me so. Information like this – only someone with your particular skills. Good. I have her travel arrangements in place.'

'OK.'

'She must be ready for collection on Wednesday.'

'In four days?

'Correct.'

'OK.'

The sheet of paper disappeared from view. He held up another. 'This one, without a passport, Rihanna. Her real name?'

'Chloe.'

He frowned. 'We will stick with the name Rihanna. Have her ready to travel on Friday.'

'You're getting a passport for her?'

'She will not need one; it will be a private flight.'

The jet, Nina thought. He only used the private jet when a girl was exceptional. Chloe Shilling certainly was not that. For a start, she wasn't a virgin. Why go to the trouble of taking her abroad on a private flight? There was only one explanation she could think of. They were going to use Chloe like they did Jade: to carry a bomb. Nina swallowed. 'Where . . .' She stopped. It was not a question she should ask. 'They were expecting to travel together.'

He looked irritated. 'So you explain to them how that is not possible.'

'Very well.'

'And the girl you lost.' He held her eyes once more.

Nina's thoughts turned to when Teah Rice managed to get out. The chase across the golf course, Gorton reservoir on one side, the M60 on the other. If she'd headed to the right at the bottom of the golf course she'd have found help, all the houses there. But she went left. And found herself on the motorway bridge, the lanes of the M60 below her.

It could have been so much worse. The girl had died, yes. But what she'd seen . . . If she'd escaped to report that, everything

would have been over. Nina was actually quite relieved when the
girl had stepped out into the air. 'What about her?'

'My client? He still wants this type of girl.'

'I'm looking. I will find another.'

'It must be soon. You have caused me to lose face.'

'I am sorry.' She thought about the basement. 'I've put precautions in the place.'

'Precautions?'

'I have taken away their mobile phones. There is no access to
the internet. And we lock the upper and lower doors behind us.
There won't be another escape.'

'There must not be.' He leaned closer to the screen. 'Is there
anything else?'

It took a monumental effort not to flinch from his gaze. How
did he sense these things? It was uncanny. The urge to glance at
the table where she'd left the laptop almost got the better of her.
She looked calmly back at him. 'Anything else?'

'You are not telling me something.'

'No.' The shake of her head felt too rapid. Like she was trying
to remove water from her hair. 'There's nothing else.'

He broke eye contact to crack open another nut. He popped
it in his mouth. 'OK.'

She knew that he knew something was amiss. It had been
noted. And, eventually, he would raise it again. He never let
anyone else's secrets survive. Like cockroaches, he sought them
out and stamped them open. She heard a voice off camera and
his attention switched. He listened to the person speaking then
looked back at her. 'Tomorrow.'

The screen went blank and she breathed out slowly, fighting the
shiver that was trying to take hold of her shoulders. The video-link
connection might be off, but she didn't trust the computer. He had
access to it remotely. He might be there, watching her. Listening
to her. The same went for the tiny camera hidden on the shelf unit
behind her. When Nina found a suitable girl, she'd bring them to
this office for an initial assessment. While the girl thought she was
being interviewed for a role answering the phone in the next room,
he was observing them from thousands of miles away. If they were
judged to be suitable, Nina would mention the possibility of earning
much better money – out in a very expensive club abroad.

Nina got up and left by a side door. Once safely outside, she took a cigarette from her packet and lit it with trembling fingers. Chloe. Why had he started using girls for that kind of thing? Carrying bombs. The only explanation was money; someone was obviously paying him huge amounts.

FIFTEEN

Iona shifted the phone to her other ear. The person she was speaking to at the university was humming to himself. 'OK,' he finally said. 'That's been logged as a high priority with the central IT department.'

'Great, thanks. What will happen next?'

'They'll forward the message on to the IT department within each faculty.'

'Each faculty has their own IT department?'

'Yes. Faculty IT departments will then send your email to each student on their list.'

Iona didn't like the multiple stages to the process; it increased the chance of error occurring somewhere down the line. 'Can the central IT department not just email every student directly?'

'It doesn't work like that, unfortunately.'

'Why?'

'Why? Well, historically, when the two universities merged back in 2004, certain schools within what was the Institute of Science and –'

'OK.' She didn't have time for a lesson in the evolution of the University of Manchester. 'How long before each student receives the email?'

'I'd say within two hours. Whether they actually read the email, that's another matter. Don't bet on it, not with it being a Saturday.'

Iona looked at the message that would soon appear in around thirty-nine thousand students' inboxes.

*Can you help? It is vital that a female student at the
University of Manchester contact Greater Manchester Police
immediately.*

*This person was seen purchasing a Dell laptop from an
unauthorized vendor in the student union building on Oxford
Road last Tuesday at about five p.m. She is approximately
5'10" tall, has black hair and was wearing a distinctive
purple duffel coat and green or orange Converse trainers.*

Could this be you? Do you know her?

*Please phone the number below with any information.
All calls will be treated in the strictest confidence.*

'Can I ring you in another hour to check on progress?' she
asked, with more cheer than she felt.

'Yes. You have my direct line, don't you?'

'I do. Thanks again, Lucas.' She hung up and looked at the
table by the photocopier. Euan was placing the posters she'd had
printed into a plastic crate for transporting over to the campus.
Six uniformed officers would be waiting for them. They were
going to need a lot of drawing pins.

Iona jiggled one knee up and down. She didn't believe Philip
Young had been killed by the fiancé of the woman in the ground-
floor flat. She wanted to see the crime scene for herself, but there
was no chance of that. Forensics had sealed the place off so they
could go about their business. It was a painstaking process and
Iona had a horrible feeling the investigation was lagging far
behind what was really going on.

The laptops. It was all about the laptops, she felt certain.
Someone wanted them back. Khaldoon Khan was in Pakistan,
so it wasn't him. Most people in the CTU were sure it had to
be Nirpal Haziq. Could it be someone else in CityPads? The
owner, Shazan Quereni, was being looked at closely. His parents
were from Iran and had fled to Britain in 1979 when the Shah
was toppled from power.

Shazan had been three years old. He'd gone to school in
Longworthy then done a business studies course at Bolton
College. He'd worked in mobile phone sales before becoming
an estate agent. Three years ago he'd set up CityPads. There was
no record of him ever leaving Britain to visit any red-list country.

He had no known association with any domestic extremist groups. He'd been a member of the Conservative Party since 2006. It didn't appear that he was religious.

Iona looked at the papers on her desk. Four Dell laptops had gone missing from CityPads. Philip Young had bought one. The girl in the duffel coat another. Two were still unaccounted for. The thought made her nervous.

At a table alongside Euan's desk, four support workers were going over the log for the previous day. It detailed every incident that had been reported to the Greater Manchester Police. In light of Philip Young's death, the workers had been instructed to comb it for any type of violent crime. One of them was looking over, her hand half-raised.

Iona got up. 'Find something?'

'Yeah, this: a young female, found on Leardon Street in Fallowfield at eleven minutes past six in the afternoon.'

Fallowfield, Iona thought. A residential area popular with students. The worker clicked on the incident number to bring up the details. The attending officer had responded to a call from a member of the public who'd been returning home from work. She'd spotted the girl lying on the pavement and immediately called for an ambulance. The girl had sustained a serious head injury. There was no sign of her being robbed; her purse was still in her coat, as was a mobile phone. She was wearing earphones connected to an iPod.

Iona looked for an identity. Emily Dickinson. There had been a student union card in her purse: University of Manchester. The girl had been taken to the Manchester Royal Infirmary. She was still unconscious.

Iona's stomach tightened as she picked up a phone, called the police station on Bootle Street and asked for the officer handling the case.

'That'll be Sergeant Stephens,' the control room operator had replied.

'Jim? Sorry, James Stephens?'

'That's correct. Putting you through now.' The phone rang twice.

'Sergeant Stephens speaking.'

'Jim, it's Iona.'

'Iona? Why are you phoning me on this—'

'It's a work call. I didn't know I'd be put through to you.'

'Oh. How's things?'

'Yeah, fine. And you?'

'I'm good. Legs a bit stiff from the ride last night.'

She grimaced. Liar. 'Right. Hayfield, was it?'

'Yeah, near there. I fixed your mum's dishwasher before coming in this morning.'

'They'll be grateful for that. Thanks, Jim.'

'Hey, no problem.'

She stayed quiet, not wanting to discuss her family. Too often, it felt he was a part of it. She knew he wanted to be.

'So, what's up?'

She leaned a little closer to the support worker's screen. 'You know the serious assault yesterday afternoon on Leardon Street?'

'Young adult female? They don't think she'll recover. Complete waste of a life.'

'What was she wearing?'

'Wearing?'

'Specifically, her coat. Did she have one on?'

'Hang on – I'll bring up the attending officer's notes. He just submitted them.'

Iona leaned her hand more heavily on the table. The ominous feeling was now making her chest feel tight.

'Here you go . . . purple duffel coat, leggings – black. And green trainers, Converse.'

Iona lifted her eyes to the ceiling. 'Black hair?'

'That's what it says.'

'Was there a laptop with her?'

'Nothing mentioned.'

'Is there an address for her?'

'There is.'

'Jim? I think the CTU are about to be all over this.'

SIXTEEN

Nina stepped out from the converted stables that now housed her office. The path angled to the left, past a clump of rhododendron bushes. There was no sign of Liam's Golf on the drive, which meant he was still over in Brinnington scoping out the address where the purchaser of the last laptop lived.

As she neared the main house, she felt nervous. It had been unwise of her to print the profiles of the last few girls she'd recruited. Stupid and careless to leave them in the carry case of her laptop. Nothing on the profiles linked directly to her – she had purposefully designed them to ensure that. True, if they fell into the hands of the police, questions would be asked. If they worked out that one of the girls had jumped to her death from a motorway flyover, those questions might be followed up by some kind of investigation. But, if they worked out one of the girls had obliterated a checkpost on the Israeli border . . . Nina hardly dared contemplate it.

The bloody internet, she cursed to herself. While Teah Rice had been searching about on it for details of Club Soda, the place in Beirut where she thought she was going to work as a waitress, she'd found a Lebanese news story on Jade.

An unknown Caucasian female who'd been blown apart when the bomb she was carrying had detonated. Teah had realized Jade wasn't working in any exclusive club where the tips alone amounted to hundreds of dollars every night. She realized everything was a lie. And so she'd run.

Nina had done her best to try and coax her back off that bridge. She'd tried to persuade her that she'd been mistaken – it couldn't be Jade's face in that newspaper report. But the girl was inconsolable. All her hopes for finally having got lucky were false. There was no better life waiting for her. There were no nice people in the world. People she could trust. She was stupid to have even thought there was. All everyone did was try to deceive her. The only fate she had was one like Jade's. And rather than that, she chose the motorway lanes below.

Once Teah had dropped from sight, Nina had got away as fast as she could. Once home, she went straight to the computer to see exactly what had caused Teah to panic. Nina herself had been genuinely shocked: she didn't know what happened to most of the girls she lured in with her story about Club Soda. She didn't really care. But getting a girl to carry a bomb? That . . . that took things into a whole new realm of risk.

She looked at the empty space where Liam normally parked. Just come back with that computer and carry case, will you? After she unlocked the back door, she paused before the mirror in the utility room. The strain was showing on her face. Her lips were thin and tight. She took a deep breath and smiled. She tried it again. Better.

A stubby key opened the upper door of the basement. She trotted down the narrow steps and selected a new key for the door at the bottom, checking through the spy-hole for any sign of either girl before opening it.

'Hi you two, it's only me, Nina!' She pulled the door shut behind her. 'Everyone OK?'

Madison Fisher appeared from the side room. She had her usual, slightly suspicious expression. Nina didn't like her. 'Hi, Madison, you been on the step machine again? Cheryl Cole has that exact same one, you know?'

Madison was wearing grey tracksuit bottoms and a black vest top. She ducked her head to the side, causing her ponytail to slide over her shoulder. Grasping it in her left hand, she bent the tip of it up and started looking for split ends. 'Yeah, I read that in *Closer*. Just like I've read all those magazines.'

Nina's attention was also on the lush length of hair. She gazed at it with a hungry expression.

Sighing, Madison flung it back out of sight. 'Nina, when are we going? It's so boring—'

'Nina!' Chloe Shilling was in the doorway of the TV room. She was still in her pyjamas, a Wii remote in one hand. 'Hi!'

'Hi there, Chloe.' Nina's eyes travelled quickly up and down her. She was putting on weight, and the skin on her forehead was starting to bobble with pimples. 'You two not exercising together?'

Chloe grinned. 'I'm playing tennis in there, burning some calories that way.'

The gap between her front teeth seemed too prominent to Nina. Still, some men liked the look – as they did large-breasted, full-hipped physiques.

Madison spoke again. 'Nina?'

The petulant expression was still on her face. You'd better forget looking like that, thought Nina. The sort of place you're going, that will earn you a beating like you wouldn't believe. 'Yes, honey?'

'If we're going to be stuck down here much longer, can you give us our phones back? Just to see my texts; I wouldn't reply to any. And can we get on the internet? I haven't checked Facebook for—'

'Maddy?' Chloe cut in. 'Drop it, will you?'

'But we've been stuck in this—'

'Girls,' Nina raised both hands. 'It's happening, all right?'

Madison turned back to Nina. 'What's happening?'

'The job. It's all sorted. You're going. It's been arranged.'

Chloe let out a squeal of delight, ran down the corridor and threw her arms round her friend. The two of them started shrieking with excitement.

Nina watched them. Madison had probably been purchased for somewhere in the Middle East. Saudi Arabia, she guessed. There was no telling where she'd be sold on to after her initial stint there. It might be somewhere else in the region; it could be back into Europe. Portugal, Spain, Italy, Ireland, Croatia. Nina knew of many places – often located near golf courses – where men from all over the world flew in, often on business trips. During the day they would be out enjoying themselves on the courses, then in the evenings they would have a few drinks and take taxis to where the girls were kept.

Someone with Madison's looks wouldn't end up in a bad place. Not like Vorkuta, where Nina had started. She would be fed, kept in relative comfort. But she would be made to work hard. A girl like Madison? By her early twenties, it would all be over. Then she might be sold on to somewhere less respectable. Across into Eastern Europe, for instance. Once there, it could only get worse. Much worse.

Her eyes cut to Chloe, who was bouncing up and down on the balls of her feet. 'Club Soda! Club Soda! Club Soda!'

Nina drew in her breath and smiled. 'Let's go and sit down. I'll talk you through what's next.'

'I can't believe we're going,' Chloe said breathlessly, breaking from Madison to give Nina a hug. 'Thank you, thank you.'

Laughing lightly, Nina squeezed back for a moment. Looking over Chloe's shoulder, she caught Madison's eye. The other girl's face still hadn't totally relaxed. You're sharp, Nina thought. Too sharp. I should never have approached you. 'Right, come on; let's talk business.'

Chloe let her go and they proceeded through into the room they used as a lounge. Nina noticed the fridge stocks were down. Various sweet wrappers were on the sofa. If Chloe had been playing tennis, she'd been doing it while sitting down. 'OK, so first – it's all on.'

'Oh my God,' Chloe gasped, using one hand to fan the air beneath her chin. 'I can't, like, even believe this. When?'

Nina sat back. 'You won't be travelling out together. I'm sorry.'

Madison's eyes narrowed. 'How come?'

Nina looked at Chloe. 'You know we're arranging for your passport? There's been a slight delay on that. Don't worry – only a small one. Madison, you're good to go.'

'How big a delay?' Madison asked, glancing at Chloe. The other girl had slouched back on the sofa.

'Only a few days,' Nina responded brightly. 'Madison, you could get your apartment ready so it's all nice for when Chloe catches you up. I'll make sure you get some pay upfront. It'll be fine.'

Chloe reached out and found Madison's hand. 'It's all right. It's not like either of us will be on our own for long.' She glanced at Nina. 'Is it?'

'No, of course not. Two, three days. That's all.'

Madison placed her other hand over Chloe's. 'I don't want us to be split up. You said we'd fly out there together.'

Nina kept her smile in place. 'I know. But it's just one of those things. The owners of the club – the ones who've paid for your airfare – have already booked the tickets. I can't do anything about it, sorry.'

'It's OK,' Chloe whispered. 'If one of our rooms has a balcony, can I have it? I've always wanted a balcony.'

Nina let out a little laugh. 'You'll both have a balcony. The staff apartments are brilliant. Amazing views over the Avénue de Paris. There's a gym in the basement – just for residents.'

Madison kept her fingers entwined with Chloe's. 'How soon will I be going?'

Nina swept her hair back with one hand. 'This Wednesday.'

SEVENTEEN

Superintendent O'Dowd waited for the last few people to shuffle into the meeting room. Flanking him were DCI Sullivan and Roebuck. From her position two chairs to Roebuck's left, Iona looked around. The room was, if anything, even more crammed than for the super's initial briefing. For the last few in it was standing room only.

There were at least five people whose faces weren't familiar, including two women. They were seated directly opposite Iona, several files ready on the table before them.

'Is that everyone?' O'Dowd asked, checking the screen of his Blackberry.

'No more room if it isn't,' someone shot back.

A few weary chuckles.

O'Dowd laid the device before him on the table. 'Right, with the exception of DCIs Roebuck and Sullivan, along with our two guests,' he inclined his head in the direction of the two women, 'can everyone ensure their phones are put to silent?'

Around the room, people reached into their pockets. Iona didn't need to check hers; she'd switched the ringer off on the way in.

O'Dowd made a clicking noise at the back of his mouth as he sat back. 'This investigation seems to be mutating before our eyes, ladies and gents. I don't use the analogy lightly: people are dying and they're dying fast. This morning, two murders. And yesterday a serious assault at about six in the evening.

'Killed earlier today was Philip Young, the student who brought in a laptop and carry case, the side pocket of which held the profiles you'll all now be familiar with. Killed alongside Philip Young was a forty-two-year-old nurse called Wendy Morgan. She was tenant of the ground-floor flat below the one Philip Young had rented. Wendy Morgan's fiancé was initially being sought in connection to the murders, but crime scene analysis is now starting to cast doubt on that. Then DCI Roebuck's team ran a check on the overnight log. Peter?'

Iona glanced at her senior officer, careful to keep her expression neutral. That was me, a voice in her head complained. I helped make that discovery. And O'Dowd doesn't even know it. She silenced the voice with a blink as Roebuck brought the print-out she'd given him closer. 'At eleven minutes past six yesterday evening, a call was received. A member of the public had found a body on the pavement outside his house in Fallowfield. The description fits that of the female student Philip Young saw in the student union who bought a Dell laptop directly before he did. She is Emily Dickinson, aged nineteen, here in Manchester studying microbiology. There is no sign of the laptop she was observed buying at the scene or at her house.'

O'Dowd grunted. 'In case any of you think this could be a very ugly coincidence, all three victims had sustained blunt trauma wounds to the head. Probably caused by a hammer. Emily Dickinson survived her attack, but the prognosis from the hospital is that it's doubtful she will be able to communicate in any meaningful way. She remains in an induced coma. Questions?'

'How many laptops went missing from CityPads?' someone asked.

'Four,' O'Dowd replied. 'So two of the buyers – assuming all four laptops were sold on – remain unaccounted for. The focus of this investigation, therefore, has altered and expanded. We need to locate those two other laptops and their new owners as a matter of extreme urgency. We also need to know what's on the one we do have in our possession.' He nodded to the man from the IT department. 'Mr Goss?'

He pushed his fringe back. 'We've now got into the main hard drive. Unfortunately, it's been formatted. Wiped clean. So I can't say whose it was, other than an employee at CityPads.'

O'Dowd sat forward. 'You're saying there's nothing on the thing? No profiles, nothing?'

'I can do a registry search, but – at this stage – it's not looking good.'

O'Dowd pursed his lips. 'Next up, the two girls from profiles – Rihanna and Shandy. I'd like to introduce Linda Bakowitz who is currently assisting us in an advisory capacity. Ms Bakowitz will provide us with some very useful background information in relation to the sexual exploitation of children here in the northwest.' His Blackberry buzzed and he quickly checked the screen before replacing it.

Iona gazed at the woman as she removed the top sheet of paper from her folder. She was somewhere in her forties. Draped over her shoulders was a length of green and gold chiffon that looked like it might have come from India. Her short hair had been chopped into and dyed a deep purple. One nostril was pierced.

'Thank you,' she said quietly, eyes still on her notes. 'As Superintendent O'Dowd mentioned, I currently work with the GMP on the issue of child sexual exploitation. For the past few years, I've been involved with the Child Sexual Exploitation Gangs and Groups Enquiry – or CSEGG. We've been working with government, police, local authorities, the youth justice sector and health professionals to try and ascertain the scope and severity of the problem.'

Iona sat back. The woman spoke with an assurance that suggested she knew her stuff.

'Many of you will be aware of the recent high-profile cases related to organized gangs grooming vulnerable young girls in order to then sexually exploit them. Despite what many of you may believe from media coverage, it is not only practised by certain ethnic groups.'

She looked carefully around the room and Iona realized she was searching for anyone readying themselves to question her assertion. No one did.

'The issue reaches across all races and classes,' she continued, 'and affects – we believe – thousands of children. Certain individuals are more vulnerable. Children who've been placed in the care system, for instance. We estimate they are over four times more likely to face exploitation. My colleague here, Margaret

Hammersley, can give you some anecdotal evidence.' She looked at the lady at her side.

'Thanks, Linda.' She hooked light brown hair back over both ears, fringe splaying out across her forehead like a fan. 'I've been carrying out research in several care homes across the region, conducting surveys where possible or just chatting to the children about their experiences – when they're willing to talk. While I've been in houses – often during the afternoon, in broad daylight – I've seen cars pull up on the road outside and simply toot their horns, like a taxi picking up a fare. A girl – usually a girl, sometimes two or three – will rush to the window, see which car it is, then start heading for the front door. The vehicle might be a BMW or a Lexus or something more ordinary. The men driving can be late teens through to forty, sometimes older. Staff may try to ask the children where they're going: they get a similar response to any parent asking their teenage offspring unwelcome questions, I imagine. "Out," is the general response.'

'Hang on.' Iona looked to where the comment had come from. Someone from Sullivan's team, heavy features emphasised by his look of outrage. 'Why don't the staff stop the girls from leaving, if it's that obvious? What's going on?'

Margaret Hammersley made a small chopping motion with one hand. A gesture, Iona thought, that hinted at the frustration she felt. 'They don't have that power – to restrain a child or young adult against their will. Or confine them. Not in those circumstances. Not at that time of day. They can advise. Ask things like, "Do you think it is a good idea to go off in that man's car?" You can probably guess the answer.'

The officer thought for a second. 'Then take the car's registration. Report that.'

'Staff often do. One home near Stockport collected nineteen registrations during a one-month period. But the local police can't do much more than make a note of them – perhaps run a check on the database. Unless an allegation comes from the actual girls, their hands are pretty much tied, too.'

O'Dowd gestured at Roebuck. 'That's another one for your team; gather in registrations of all cars that have been picking up girls from care homes. We'll need those details on HOLMES, see if any cross-matches come up.'

Roebuck turned to Euan. 'Got that?'

Iona saw he was already typing it down. 'On it.'

'So, you now sense the nature of the problem for children in care,' Bakowitz stated. Several heads were shaking in weary disbelief. 'Another vulnerable group we've identified is children being transported overseas for forced marriages. Legislation in 2008 prevents someone being taken abroad against their will – figures giving us an insight into the problem are still far too sparse for my liking. However, summer is the peak for it. A charity based in Derby that helps those in danger of forced marriage received seven hundred and sixty-nine calls this June alone. A home affairs select committee report dating back to 2008 found, during that year, over two thousand students went missing from school registers. These are children who, come September, simply do not reappear in their class. The desk is empty. It transpired some had moved to new areas and joined a new school: many had not. Thirty-three in Bradford alone are still unaccounted for.'

O'Dowd sat forward. 'Ms Bakowitz, if you could elaborate on which countries are known to be involved in . . .'

'Bridenapping? Of course.' She pushed her notes to one side and began to speak from memory.

Libby Williams lowered herself stiffly on to a chair. Once comfortable, she raised her phone back to her ear. The laptop was in front of her, positioned on a lace-work placemat to stop it from scratching the table. 'Yes, the screens have stopped flitting about.'

Her son spoke. 'Well done. Tell me what you can see.'

'It's that one with all the thingumyjigs.'

'The icons?'

'Yes. There's that little waste-paper basket in the corner. And in the middle is that green dot for the music.'

'Spotify?'

'Yes.'

'Good. You're on the desktop, that's what it's called. Now, Mum, see if you can find an icon that is a blue square with an S in the middle. I think I put it by the Spotify dot. It will have the word Skype below it.'

'Yes, that's right beside it. Do I move the cursor over and click on it?'

'Get you! Clicking now, are we? Yes, click away.'

'The desktop has now gone. It's been replaced by a grey screen. Oh, now it's making a noise. I can see a little photo of you. It says you're calling.'

'So now you just click on the green telephone at the bottom.'

'Oh my Lord, I can see you. You're waving!' She couldn't help laughing. 'You're waving!'

'Mum, I'm waving at you. Close your mouth unless you want a fly to get in.'

'And I'm there, too, in a little square in the corner. I can hear your voice so clearly!'

'That's the idea. You can hang up the phone now and we can talk like this.'

'You want me to put the phone down? Will it not cut the connection?'

'No – we're on the internet, Mum. The phone line is completely different. Go on, put that big old lump of plastic in your hand down. Good. Still hear me loud and clear?'

'Yes. How remarkable. I wish your father was still alive to see this. Amazing. Your picture isn't straight, on the wall behind you.'

'Mum! We won't continue with this if you start using it as a way of tidying up, OK?'

'Well, it isn't straight. So, can you see me just as clearly?'

'Yes. Well, no. Not if you lean to the side like that. Mum, you need to be in front of the little camera. And now my screen has gone pink. Mum, is your finger over the lens? It is, isn't it?'

She laughed and lowered her hand.

'Oh, you're back again. But wait, did you feel that over in Poynton?' He frowned theatrically. 'I think it's an earthquake. Oh! Oh! Everything's shaking!'

She watched with an amused expression as the view of her son started to bounce up and down and from side to side. 'That's you, silly. You're wobbling your computer about.'

The movement stopped and he grinned at her. 'You sussed me.'

Across the street, Liam watched the man. His head and shoulders were visible through the living room window. He was chatting away to someone, having a right laugh by the look of it. Then he'd put his mobile to one side and continued to speak. The guy's face shone faintly with reflected light. Liam guessed he was looking at a laptop's screen. Nina's laptop. He checked his watch: just after three. Another couple of hours and it would be completely dark. He continued along the road to check what was behind the house. A backyard or small garden, hopefully.

'We know bridenapping goes on in at least seventeen countries, worldwide,' Linda Bakowitz said, eyes trained on the meeting room wall where it joined the ceiling. 'China to Mexico, Russia to South Africa. In some regions of Kyrgyzstan, a Central Asian country bordered by Kazakhstan, Uzbekistan and China, it is thought that up to eighty per cent of marriages are forced. Many regions view the practice as a tradition, not a crime. It goes on in Chechnya. Dealers operate in Vietnam, taking young girls over the border into China. The same for Somalia and Kenya. Within Europe, it's estimated seventeen per cent of marriages in Georgia are forced, fourteen per cent in Turkey.'

She directed a finger at Euan's laptop. 'The entire process has been greatly facilitated by the internet – that's kidnapping in general, not just that of girls for marriage. You'll know better than I that things like Twitter and social networking sites make it easy for criminals to communicate. Large amounts of money can change hands online, too – going from one currency to another in the process. Foreign travel, across the EU and beyond, is easier now than ever. We know the international links are there. I recently attended a seminar with the Serious Organized Crime Unit's team. We went over the case of a British boy kidnapped last year. The family paid a ransom to an account traced to Paris. The investigation that followed led, eventually, to arrests in Pakistan, Romania and Spain.'

O'Dowd coughed. 'For the purposes of this investigation, we have a young girl who disappeared from a care home near Stockport—'

'An area with one of the country's highest concentrations of care homes,' Margaret interjected, emotion straining her voice. 'All those big houses at cheap prices. Local authorities in London and the south east short on space and budgets ship the children up here.'

'So we've gathered,' O'Dowd replied. 'And one of these girls has then reappeared at a checkpoint on the Lebanese-Israeli border – with horrific consequences.'

Bakowitz interlinked her fingers. 'Given that the girl in question was Caucasian and taken to the Middle East, I'm of the opinion she'd been trafficked originally for sex, not marriage.'

Iona took a quick glance about. Everyone's eyes were glued to Bakowitz.

'It is deeply disturbing,' she added quietly. 'And it goes beyond anything I've experienced before. These girls are, as I've said, vulnerable. Suddenly, all this attention is being lavished on them. They're bought gifts. Nice stuff, at first. Little treats. A meal in McDonald's, trinkets from Accessorize, often a pay-as-you-go phone. That mobile opens up a direct channel of communication. Then it's invitations to house parties – where there are cigarettes, alcohol, drugs. They're lured in very carefully.' She tapped her fingers against her file. 'But, there's a huge difference between being exploited sexually and detonating a bomb that's strapped to your body—'

'If she detonated it.' Iona realized she'd spoken her thought aloud. She looked up. O'Dowd was scrutinising her. Next to him, DCI Roebuck's eyebrows were raised. Christ, Iona said to herself, knowing she now had to back her comment up. 'Sorry to butt in,' she started nervously. 'But we don't know she was aware of what she was carrying, do we? She may have been told it was something entirely different. In which case, someone else may have actually detonated it.'

The room remained silent.

Damn it, Iona thought. Why did I open my—

'Good point,' O'Dowd said, consulting his file. 'Jade Cummings was reported missing from her care home in mid-October. She died on November eighteenth. That's a six-week period. Long enough to indoctrinate someone to the degree they'll commit suicide for the cause?' He glanced at Iona. 'I doubt it.'

She felt a surge of relief. I didn't drop a clanger, after all.

'Research on this tells us,' O'Dowd carried on, 'that, unless the bomber has lost loved ones in what they perceive as unjust circumstances – an airstrike or drone attack, for example – the process of indoctrination is long and slow. The religious argument must be accepted first; then the case for sacrificing yourself. Six weeks . . . I can't see that as being sufficient.'

'If the indoctrination only started at the point of her disappearance.'

Iona looked across the table. Martin Everington had thrown the comment in. She saw that he was slouched low in his seat while cartwheeling a green biro through the fingers of one hand. She suddenly wished he'd drop it. He was so bloody confident.

He looked up at the senior officers. 'What if the grooming – religious or whatever – had been going on for a while before she went missing? We're talking like her disappearance wasn't her choice. But – maybe – she went willingly.'

Iona saw heads nodding round the room and was acutely aware that few had reacted that way when she'd spoken. Martin's eyes touched hers and she immediately looked away. He had a point.

O'Dowd traced his finger over his sheet. 'Jade Cummings had been in care since the age of seven. She had one period with a foster family when she was nine, but that fell through within eight months. She'd been in a home near Reddish ever since.' He looked at DCI Sullivan and was about to speak when his Blackberry buzzed again. Rather than pick it up, he glanced down at the screen and gave a dismissive flick of his fingers. 'Where was I? Jade Cummings. Let's review things from the angle of her being groomed not for sex but suicide. Re-interview staff and children from the care home, if necessary.'

DCI Sullivan immediately looked at Martin. 'Happy to do that?'

'With pleasure, sir.'

Iona kept her eyes on the table, smarting at the turn of events. One minute her contribution looked like it was taking priority, the next it had been swept aside by Martin's. She could feel gloating glances settling on her from every direction.

O'Dowd was about to say something else when his Blackberry buzzed again. 'Christ sake.' He glanced at the screen, frowned, picked the device up and read the message more carefully. The room watched as he pressed a few keys. 'Charles? I just got your text. What's going on?'

As he listened to what was being said, a ping came from

Sullivan's jacket. He retrieved his phone and scanned the screen, straightening up as he did so. He turned to the superintendent, a forefinger raised.

'Great, let me know as soon as,' O'Dowd said, cutting his call. 'Andy?'

DCI Sullivan spoke. 'Word from Eamon Heslin's apartment. Some paperwork has been recovered that lists what could be several clients. Might be whoever bought those laptops. It's being biked over as we speak.'

O'Dowd clenched one fist in response before jabbing a finger at his mobile. 'That was the liaison officer at the embassy in Islamabad. Khaldoon Khan and his sister have relatives in the mountains of north Pakistan. They think that's where they headed from the airport.'

Iona stared at the super. Were they talking about the tribal areas that bordered Afghanistan? Because if they were, it was a region so hostile to America and its allies, any Westerner risked death by going there.

EIGHTEEEN

Iona pulled on to the drive, coming to a halt behind a white Range Rover with personalised number plates. Turning the engine off, she reflected glumly on the latest shuffle of cards.

Gone was her leading role tracing the remaining laptop owners through the university. That had been handed to a uniformed team who'd been hastily seconded from Trafford Division.

Now she'd been tasked with interviewing some of the clients whose details had been found in Eamon Heslin's apartment. The details had been hand-written in a small ledger and the sums of money detailed had all been cash. Probably jobs he was keeping from the taxman's attention – a fact to be overlooked because of the slim possibility that someone at one of the companies could have purchased the two missing Dell laptops. It was a very slim possibility, in Iona's opinion. The names were of corporate clients, mainly small businesses whose IT systems Heslin probably repaired or maintained. They wouldn't be interested in knock-off laptops.

Worse, she thought, is who I've been paired with to make enquiries.

'Impressive-looking property,' Martin Everington said from the passenger seat beside her.

From what she could see of the house between a cluster of rhododendron bushes and squat fir trees, it stank of poor taste. New build, but with a mass of faux-classical touches. Twin pillars either side of a huge front door. A frieze of semi-nude statues set into the brickwork below the gutter. Five bedrooms, at least. 'Depends on your taste.'

She glanced at the Range Rover's personalised number plates. The things really got on her nerves. It didn't bother her if vehicle owners went against DVLA regulations by manipulating the spacing between numbers and letters; for her, memorising a plate that actually spelled a word was far easier than a random sequence of letters and numbers. It was more the sheer vanity and self-importance of it all. It was a car, for crying out loud. A metal compartment with seats and a wheel at each corner. To Iona, the need to try and stand out from the crowd indicated pompousness on the owner's part. That, or some strange form of insecurity. She wondered which one would apply to the person who drove the Range Rover.

'Well,' Martin announced, opening his door. 'The sooner we get these crossed off, the sooner we can join the lot looking into Jade Cummings.'

They took the path's left-hand fork and followed it away from the house and towards a long, thin, single-storey building. Converted stables, from the look of it, Iona thought. Through the row of windows that had been put in place of the stable doors, she could see a few women sitting at desks and talking on phones. The far wall was lined with box-laden shelves. They reached the door at the far end. Office, read the brass plaque. Before she could reach up, Martin rang the buzzer.

A second later, it opened.

'Miss Dubianko? Detective Sergeant Everington. I called before?' His warrant card was raised; the standard Greater

Manchester Police one giving no indication of the unit he was
part of. 'This is my colleague, Detective Constable Iona Khan.'

The woman was, Iona guessed as she held up her own card,
in her early thirties. Tall, pale blonde hair, gym slender and, Iona
couldn't help noticing, very large breasts. Fake? She certainly
had that well-groomed sheen shared by people with the time and
money for such things as personal trainers and regular beauty
appointments. Iona would have written her off as typical Cheshire
set if it wasn't for the woman's angular cheekbones, wide mouth
and glacial eyes. Iona had never seen eyes such a pale shade of
blue.

She glanced over their identities, eyes settling back on Martin.
'Come in, please.'

Her warm smile revealed a perfect row of teeth. They were
so white that, if they'd been in the mouth of someone thirty years
older, Iona would have suspected they weren't real.

'Thank you,' Iona said, stepping in before Martin. 'We appreciate you seeing us at such short notice.'

'That is not a problem, honestly. Can I get you both a tea or
coffee?'

'No thanks,' Martin said from behind Iona. 'This really won't
take long.'

Her eyes went to Iona. 'And you?'

I think he already decided that, Iona thought. 'Not for me,
thanks anyway.'

'Very well.' The woman had an elegant way of moving as she
walked round the desk and took the leather chair on the other
side. She gestured to the chairs opposite and looked expectantly
across at them.

'The name of your company has come up as part of a wider
investigation,' Martin explained, sitting down.

'Would you mind if I smoke?

The request took Iona by surprise. You couldn't wait until
we're gone?

'No, not at all,' Martin replied.

Iona watched as she extracted a cigarette from a packet by
her phone. Was this, Iona thought, some kind of displacement
activity? The tactic of a nervous person? But the well-manicured
fingers that lifted the lighter showed no sign of any tremors. The

cigarette itself was brown and thin and with a gold filter. Foreign. A cultural thing, Iona concluded. The woman had probably come from a part of the world where smoking was as unremarkable as blinking your eyes.

'So, this investigation?' she said, eyes firmly on Martin.

'Yes,' Martin replied in a languid voice, crossing one leg. 'We're looking into a small IT business. Recently, it was destroyed in a fire. Some records were recovered that mentioned here.'

'What?' she said. 'My business?'

Martin wiped the air with a hand. 'Miss Dubianko, we're really not concerned if you had the odd dealing with this company on a cash-in-hand basis.'

Iona watched as the woman gazed at Martin. Her eyes were so pale they seemed to almost act as mirrors. Iona could get nothing from them.

'Do you know the company I'm talking about?' Martin asked.

As she pulled on her cigarette, the bones beneath her cheeks became even more pronounced. For a second, it was easy to picture her skull beneath that flawless skin. Iona waited for the woman to reply, but she remained silent. There was a flintiness about her that spoke to Iona of a life not always shrouded in luxury.

'Miss Dubianko,' Martin said, 'the owner of the IT company, unfortunately, is dead.'

Now she blinked. 'You're not talking about Eamon Heslin, are you?' Smoke trickled from her mouth and nostrils as she spoke.

Martin nodded.

'Oh my God.' She leaned forward and ground her cigarette out. 'In the fire?'

'Sorry, I cannot give you any more detail than that,' Martin replied.

'That's terrible.' Her eyes moved slowly to the side. 'He was only here the other day . . .'

'He was?' Iona asked.

'Yes,' she replied in a small voice. 'When I set up the busi-ness, he did the networking for me in the main office. Whenever there's a glitch, he fixes it. Usually remotely. But a cable needed to be replaced, so he popped over in person. I can't believe he's dead.'

Iona jotted the information down. 'There was some kind of monthly contract?'

'Not really. I sometimes bought items from him, when he had them for sale. Printers, a couple of computers.'

Iona studied the set-up on the lady's desk. The monitor sat on a desktop PC from which a mass of wires and cables hung. 'Did he recently sell you a laptop?'

'A laptop? No – I just use this computer. And I can pick up email on my Blackberry. That works fine for me.'

Martin looked about. 'What do you do here, Miss Dubianko?'

'I sell hair.'

'Sorry?'

'For extensions. I supply most of the best salons round Manchester.'

'Synthetic hair?'

'No, human.'

Iona thought of the thin boxes piled up in the main room.

'Really?' Martin asked, sounding intrigued. 'There's a big . . . obviously, there is a big demand.'

'There certainly is. Thank you Cheryl Cole, Lady Gaga and the rest.'

For the first time, the woman's eyes sparked with feeling. When she'd said the names, the faintest trace of an accent had shown through.

Martin smiled. 'Sorry to be nosey – this has nothing to do with why we're here – but where do you get your hair?'

'That would depend on the colour.' She reached into a drawer and placed three of the boxes Iona had seen in the main office on the desk. They looked like the type a florist might use for packaging a single red rose. 'This is black – most of my black hair is sourced from India or the Philippines. Of course, you can buy it dyed, but I think it lacks a truly natural appearance when it is dyed.' She opened the lid and there inside, like a severed horse's tail, was a lustrous length of ebony hair. 'Brown is trickier, there are so many shades. I get some from Venezuela, Colombia, Nicaragua. Countries where the Spanish blood has mingled with the local. Blonde – that's much, much easier. Latvia, Lithuania, Estonia – those are my main countries for blonde.' She removed another cigarette from her packet, lit it and gestured at Iona with the glowing tip. 'Your hair, that is wonderful. It would command a good price if you grew it long.'

Suddenly self-conscious, Iona couldn't help reaching behind one ear and making a little raking movement with her fingertips. 'I think you'd have a long wait! It must take years for the women to—'

'Yes. But so many people in these countries are poor. The money can be a great blessing.'

Martin was peering into the box. 'Do you pay a lot, then?'

'Not nearly as much as I sell it for.' She laughed for the first time.

It was a hard, ugly sound. Iona's smile faltered as she registered the woman's mercenary smile. The purpose of the visit came back to her; along with the certainty it was futile. 'So Eamon Heslin didn't offer to sell you a laptop when he was last in?'

The woman tapped ash from her cigarette. 'No. He had some new monitors he'd picked up somewhere, with bigger screens. But the ones I have are fine.'

'When was this?'

'Five, six days ago? Shall I check?'

'If you don't mind. We're trying to piece together all of Mr Heslin's movements in the run-up to his death.'

She opened a red diary with her cigarette hand, wisps of smoke snaking about as she tracked across the columns. 'Yes. On Tuesday the twenty-first. A morning visit: eleven o'clock.'

She rotated the large book round. Iona sat forward and could see the entry written there. Eamon, eleven o'clock, just as she'd said. Eamon Heslin only started attempting to sell the stolen laptops from CityPads the day after that, she thought, glancing at Martin. From his face, she could tell he'd come to the same conclusion. Heslin had targeted the student union for getting rid of the stolen Dells, not clients. Iona closed her notebook.

'OK, that's us done,' announced Martin.

'Why is the laptop so important?' Dubianko asked, flicking the cover of her diary shut and pushing it to one side.

Martin was readying himself to stand. 'Eamon Heslin had several for sale. We're trying to locate anyone who may have purchased one.'

'There is something important about these laptops, then? There must be if you are . . .' She lapsed into silence, a worried look on her face. 'He wasn't killed because of it, was he?'

Martin's hands were still clutching his knees. 'There's really no reason for alarm, Miss Dubianko. It's just some material was recovered from the carry case of one handed in to us. Material that has given us cause for concern. Listen, if you remember anything else – or are just feeling worried – you can get me on this number.' He checked his pocket and looked at Iona. 'You don't have a card, do you?'

Iona produced one and Martin took it a little too eagerly from her fingers. 'Here,' he said, writing on it. 'Ask for me by name, OK?'

Nina's smile was tentative. 'Thank you. But I still do not follow.'

'As I said, I really wouldn't worry. But we'd like to locate the other laptops Heslin had sold. They may provide us with vital information.'

Uneasy about how much Martin was divulging in his desire to reassure the woman, Iona stood. 'Did Eamon Heslin mention any other clients to you? Someone else who may have been interested in buying a laptop?'

'No.'

'How did you come to use him for your computer needs?'

'A Google search. His website came near the top and he was fairly close by.' She also rose to her feet, swiftly followed by Martin. 'So odd to think that he's dead. I had better find a new company to maintain my system.'

That coldness again, Iona thought, starting for the door. Or is she just being pragmatic, like a business person should be? 'I love your name, by the way,' she said over her shoulder. 'Where is it from?'

'Kyrgyzstan. It is a—'

'Small country in Central Asia, bordering China to one side,' Iona replied, thinking of the bridenapping statistics. Around eighty per cent in some parts of the country.

The woman seemed genuinely taken aback. 'You know it?'

'It was mentioned in relation to something, that's all,' Iona replied. 'You were born there?'

'No, I'm British. My parents were from there. They never really spoke English at home when I was growing up.'

'Well,' Martin piped up. 'You speak it beautifully.'

'Thank you.' She stepped closer to Iona. 'And your name? Iona Khan?'

Iona had to look up to maintain eye contact. The woman was comfortably over six foot tall. 'Scottish mother and Pakistani father.'

'Pakistani father?' Her eyes touched briefly on Iona's hair. 'Are you not permitted to cover your head while at work?'

Iona needed a second to process the question. 'I'm not Muslim.' She smiled quickly.

'I'm sorry. I should not have presumed about your religion.'

'It's fine. I get asked all sorts of questions. Thanks again for your time.'

'Yes. Thank you,' Martin said.

'My pleasure,' the woman smiled, holding one hand out.

Martin took it, and for a second, Iona thought he was going to stoop forward and kiss it. But after a quick shake, he let it go. 'We'll find our own way back.'

Iona had a perplexed smile on her face as they headed towards her car. The woman's forthright manner was strange. The comment about buying Iona's hair, for instance! Iona couldn't imagine growing it long and then chopping it all off for some cash. Something so personal, so integral to how you saw yourself. She realized it was the way the woman so calmly said it had a value. To her, it was a commodity – nothing more. 'She had a heart of flint.'

'You what?' Martin sounded surprised. 'She was very pleasant.'

Iona gave him a quick glance. 'Oh, right. By the way, you can roll your tongue back in now.'

'Roll my tongue back in?'

'Come on. You were like a puppy back there. Practically drooling.'

Martin snorted. 'OK, she might have been mildly attractive.'

Iona felt a little pang in her chest. The woman was tall, blonde and stunning: everything she was not. Chiding herself for being so insecure, she said, 'Nice touch with the business card.'

'What's that meant to mean?'

His voice had been defensive so Iona smiled innocently, glad to have landed one on him. 'Nothing. We're meant to be offering our reassurances to the public, lowering their perceptions that crime is on the increase. I've read the departmental memos, too.' She paused before shooting him a cheeky grin. 'It had nothing to do with you fancying her.'

He tried to adopt an affronted expression, then gave up. 'I feel she rather liked me, too. Unmarried as well. Not even an engagement ring, I couldn't help notice.'

Iona wanted to laugh. 'Is that all it takes? A flash of those ice-blue eyes and a smile or two?'

'We had a certain chemistry. Admit it – you felt it crackling in there, the electricity.'

Iona raised a hand and clicked her fingers. 'And back in the real world . . . talking of rings, did you notice the fingers on her left hand?'

'The kinks in the middle two?'

'Kinks? She'd had them badly snapped, at some stage. No rings are ever going to fit over the lumps in those joints. What about her business? Selling human hair – how creepy.'

'Just business,' Martin replied. 'Buy cheap, sell expensive. The woman wasn't breaking any laws. And from the look of her office, she employs a few other people, too. Small businesses like hers are the backbone of this fine country.'

'I suppose so.' Iona wanted to, if not like the woman, at least feel respect for her. Aside from being stunning, she had much of what Iona aspired to. Confidence, independence, drive and ambition. But all Iona actually felt was mildly unsettled.

They reached the fork in the path and, as they continued towards her car, Iona studied the main house. 'Something like that. I know we're only on the edge of Denton, but what do you reckon? Three quarters of a million quid?'

'Probably. It practically borders the golf course. Nice and private.'

A burst of drum beats carried across the lawn. Vocals kicked in, but the noise quickly died. Iona kept looking. Did she have kids? She didn't have any photos in her office. The noise didn't resume. Odd, Iona thought, unlocking her car and getting in. 'What's next on the list?'

'An accountancy firm, over in Salford. The A57 will be best. You can get on to the Mancunian Way at Ardwick.'

'No problem.' As she reversed, Iona looked at the Range Rover's number plate once more. N1NA. How naff.

NINETEEN

N ina Dubianko unlocked the door at the bottom of the stairs and strode towards the music coming from the TV room. 'Who was it?'

Madison and Chloe glanced up from the beanbags. Seeing her expression, their smiles vanished.

'Who turned the music up so loud?' Her face was white.

Madison looked at the floor. Chloe half-raised a hand. 'Me.'

Nina continued across to the docking station, lifted it up and hurled it against the wall. The casing came open and the iPod Nano spun to the side, hitting the side of the TV and dropping among the untidy pile of DVD cases. She whirled on the pair, voice shrill with fury. 'I said no loud sounds. I said! And then I have the police visiting here – police! – and I hear music from here.' Her fluent English was gone, the words distorted by a thick, awkward accent. 'This police detective – what if he also heard?' She bent forward to bring her face closer to the cowering girls. 'You stupid fucking bitches. You wish trouble for me? Do you? Do you?'

Chloe had lowered her chin to her chest while Madison remained absolutely still, eyes unfocused and distant, as if in a trance.

Nina straightened up. 'I throw you back on the street. No money for you, no job, no lovely place to live. You don't deserve it.'

Chloe wiped at the corner of one eye. 'I'm sorry, Nina. I didn't mean to, I didn't.'

Nina flicked a hand at her. 'You are sorry now. Now is too late.'

'Please don't . . . don't cancel it. I won't be so stupid again, I promise.'

Nina crossed her arms and looked towards the door.

'Were the police looking for us?' Madison asked in a subdued voice.

'No,' Nina replied, face still averted. 'I am so angry with you.' She was regaining control of her voice, English tones reasserting themselves.

'Nina,' Chloe tried again. 'Please give us another chance.'

'I will speak to you both later.' She dropped her arms and marched from the room.

Up in the kitchen, she lit a cigarette and tried to think. She would have to tell him everything now. Things were too risky; they were too exposed to carry on. The police were bound to work it out sooner or later. They had to.

She took three deep drags on her cigarette, blew smoke upward then looked out of the window as she lifted her mobile phone. Dusk was beginning to fall. Would it be day or night where he was? She had no way of knowing. The call was answered almost immediately.

'Hello.'

She perched on a bar stool, glad she wasn't in the office with its unseen camera. 'Can I talk?'

'You may.'

'There is a problem here. Police.' It was a scenario they had prepared for. Arrangements were there for her to disappear quickly, if needed.

'What problem?'

She sucked briefly on the cigarette. 'I . . . I had a laptop and a carry case taken. By an engineer who thought they were not wanted.'

'You mean stolen?'

'No – I don't think so. It was just a mistake by him.'

'Information was on this laptop?'

She closed her eyes. 'Yes.'

'How much information?'

'Enough.'

'The main files?'

He meant details of his bank accounts. Places where money passed to and fro. 'I'm trying to get it back. But the engineer, he sold it to someone else.'

'Do you know who?'

'I think so. Liam is out now, at the address. I should have it back soon.'

'Liam.'

'Yes.'

'You trust him?'

'Yes. He would never say anything.'

'Everyone will say anything. It's just a question of cost – financial or physical.'

'He . . . he couldn't afford to. He has dealt with people for me.'

He stayed quiet.

'You are angry,' Nina stated softly, disappointed to hear the wobble in her voice.

'I do not know, yet. What else do you need to tell me?'

'The laptop was sold to one person, but I think the carry case was sold to someone different. You were somewhere recently without any internet connection, remember? You asked me to fax those profiles to you. So I printed them off. They were inside the carry case and I think the police now have them.'

'Profiles for the last four? You were meant to shred them, immediately.'

'I know. I didn't. I don't know why.' She stared down into her ashtray. He would be processing the fact that the profiles included the one of the girl who'd shown up on the Israeli border. She wished she could ask what he had got them into. 'The profiles cannot be traced to me. To us.'

'Why did the police visit you?'

Nina thought about Eamon. The idiot wasn't meant to have recorded her details. That's why she paid him in cash. 'The address of my business was among some material the police found. The policeman was asking if the engineer had sold a laptop to me. So they can't have mine. If they had mine, why send two low-rank officers? And one of them a woman.'

'We do not know that. Who were these officers?'

'Youngsters. They were not experts.'

'You saw them where?'

'In the office. Not in the house.'

'At your desk?'

'Yes.'

'Let me watch the conversation. I will ring you back.' The call was cut.

Iona was passing the run-down Multiplex cinema on the A57, when her mobile's screen lit up. Stuart Edwards, back at Orion House. She put the call on loudspeaker and spoke at the windscreen. 'Hi, there. What's up?'

'You driving?'

'I am. Heading to Salford, why?'

'Your student angle just paid out.'

She veered into the slow lane. 'How do you mean?'

'The body of another female student has just been found.'

She glanced quickly at Martin, eyes wide. 'Where?'

'Her bedroom. A house in Moss Side.'

'Any sign of a laptop?'

'Not sure as yet. Word of this reached us, literally, minutes ago.'

Iona accelerated back into the outside lane. The road she was on led directly into the city centre. To her side, the sun was just a red smear above the horizon, its rays glinting on the fuselage of a plane as it made its final descent to Manchester airport. 'How did she die?'

'Suspiciously. That's all we've got at the moment.'

'What's the address? We're on our way.'

Nina felt her shoulders flinch. She pushed the end of her cigarette into the ashtray, took a quick breath and picked up the phone as it rang again. 'It's me.'

'I think you are right. They had no idea. Their superiors might, but I think not.'

Relief caused Nina's head to fall forward. 'I agree. It is nearly dark here. Liam will get the laptop back.'

'The profiles. These are a problem.'

'Yes.'

'Why didn't you destroy them?'

She wished he'd shout when he was angry. This whisper. It terrified her. 'I'm sorry.'

'We must go ahead with the two you have. I have buyers waiting. But not before one other thing.'

His voice had that hitch in it. She knew something bad was coming. 'Yes?'

'The female detective who visited you.'

'Yes?'

'She is perfect.'

'Perfect?' Please, she thought, don't say it.

'The girl you lost at that motorway bridge. This female officer is the same. Black hair, petite, skin like coffee. Are her eyes green?'

'I . . . yes, they were.'

'Do you think she weighs any more than the other one?'

'No. Maybe a little more.'

'The other one was a little thin for what my buyer wanted. What was the policewoman's name?'

'Khan. Something Khan. Iona, that was it.'

'Iona Khan. Was she with Greater Manchester Police?'

'Yes, but I don't know which part.'

'Don't worry about that. I can find that out, along with her address.'

'Her address?'

'The plane that is coming for the one called Chloe. You come on it, too. I also want Iona Khan on the flight. You will get her for me.'

'But she's with the police.'

'It doesn't matter. We're finished in that country. Do what you need to make sure no one can trace you.'

Nina cleared her throat. It was all over. Her business, her lovely home. Finished. 'But how will I get someone like her?'

'Use Liam, if you have to. Kill him after.'

'But she's police.'

His voice dropped even lower. 'Do you think I am pleased with you? You have let me down, Nina. This policewoman – she is the way you can make things better. A little bit, at least.'

TWENTY

Ten minutes later, Iona and Martin came to a stop. Teresa Donaghue had lived in what struck Iona as a typical student house – large, slightly dishevelled, a neglected front garden and the curtains in most windows either closed or half-drawn. There was even a wheelie bin with the lid being forced up by the volume of cans and bottles crammed inside.

The sight of it momentarily took Iona back to her own student days in Newcastle. The long trudge from lectures up the Westgate Road to Fenham. Local kids vacillating between mild curiosity and open contempt at the rainbow-coloured book bag her sister had bought her as a going-away present. Iona couldn't stand the attention it attracted, but still doggedly used it out of loyalty. Years later, Fenella admitted she thought it was utterly gross but had got it because she thought that was the type of thing students used. They still laughed about it.

'Beer and baked beans,' Martin muttered, unclipping his seat belt.

Iona looked at him.

'Student life,' he stated. 'Beer and baked beans.'

'Where did you study?' she asked.

'York. You?'

'Newcastle.'

'Add another word beginning with b, then. Burglaries.' He laughed.

She didn't like his tone and she didn't like his superior attitude. 'No criminals in York, then?'

'Not as many as Newcastle.'

She reflected on how many times her own house had been broken into. Three. Deciding not to rise to it, she got out of the car and approached a uniformed officer at the end of the drive. 'DC Khan and DS Everington. Who can we speak to about this?'

He looked over their identifications and jotted their names on a clipboard. 'Crime Scene Manager's just shown up. Jim Reed.'

'Thanks.'

There were more uniforms hanging around in the hall and two sitting with what must have been one of the housemates in the front room. More voices came from upstairs. Iona climbed them, spotting a white-suited forensics guy outside a doorway further along. 'Jim Reed about?'

He turned round and removed his face mask. 'That's me. Are you with the Major Incident Team?'

'Counter Terrorism,' she replied as quietly as possible, stepping on to the landing.

'Oh.'

'What do you reckon has happened?'

He glanced into the bedroom. 'I'd guess she was killed about ten hours ago. In the early hours. Cause of death would have been asphyxiation, I'm pretty certain. She had something looped round her throat. Smooth surface, about five millimetres in width.'

'An electrical cord?'

'Possibly.'

Iona looked back at Martin, who lifted an eyebrow. 'Not part of some sex game?'

'She was fully clothed,' Reed replied.

Iona was desperate to sneak a peek in the girl's room. 'Any sign of a laptop?'

The CSM shook his head.

'A carry case? Any type of computer equipment?'

He beckoned her over. 'See the desk by the bed? There's a printer there. I'd say that was her workstation. No computer, though.'

Iona's eyes strayed to the female form on the bed. Red hair was spread out across the pillow. 'She wasn't dressed by whoever did this?'

'I doubt it very much.'

'And you found her lying on the bedcovers?'

'That's correct.'

Another figure in a white suit was scraping at the fingernails of her left hand. Among the posters on her wall was one of Daniel Craig as James Bond. Another of Emeli Sandé on stage. Next to that, a tour poster for Adele. The sort of things I'd have chosen, Iona thought sadly.

'OK, thanks for your help,' Martin said from behind her.

Halfway down the stairs, she muttered under her breath, 'I reckon that's number three.'

'Different MO to the others,' Martin shot back. 'No hammer, for a start.'

'True.'

They looked into the front room. A lad of about nineteen was on the sofa, face like a ghost's. There was a girl on the chair in the corner also looking shell-shocked and vacant. The officer talking to the male student paused from taking notes and glanced up as Iona produced her ID.

'Sorry to interrupt, here,' she announced in a gentle but firm voice. 'May I jump in with a question or two?'

The officer looked seriously pissed off. 'Be my guest.'

Iona nodded her thanks and crouched before the bloke. 'I'm Detective Constable Khan. And you are?'

'James Balfour.'

'You live here, too, James?'

He nodded meekly.

'Which room is yours?'

'Far end of the corridor, upstairs.'

'And the room with the Liverpool sticker at the top of the stairs?'

'Craig. He's at the Learning Commons. Phone's turned off.'

Iona pointed to the ground-floor room she'd spotted on the way down the stairs. 'And that one?'

He nodded at the girl in the corner. 'Pippa.'

Next, she pointed at the empty cardboard boxes of beer bottles. Surely not a normal week's worth. 'Party?'

'Yes. Last night.'

'A houseful, was it?'

He hunched a shoulder. 'Fifteen, twenty. A few more swung by after closing time. It wasn't full on, or anything.'

'Did you know everyone who turned up?'

'More or less. I told him.' He glanced at the uniformed officer who now stood with folded arms and a look of impatience. 'A few friends of friends, but no strangers.'

'Was Teresa with anyone, up in her room?'

'No. We were all doing shots. She doesn't normally join in

and they took her legs away. She bailed out around half one, I reckon.'

'She went to bed at about half one on her own?'

'Yes.'

'You saw her go up the stairs to bed on her own?'

'Well, I didn't stand at the bottom and watch. But she certainly set off alone.'

Martin edged closer. 'What was Teresa like? Shy, extrovert?'

For a second, James looked on the verge of tears. 'She was a real laugh. Everyone liked her.'

'Bit of a party girl, then?'

Sensing where he was going, Iona tried to throw him a cautionary glance.

'Yeah,' James said quietly. 'She was.'

Martin nodded. 'Did she like the lads? Was that part of it when she partied?'

James looked shocked. 'No! Back in Dublin, she's got a boyfr— Oh, Jesus, who's going to tell him? He was here last weekend, oh, Jesus.'

Iona crouched before him. 'James? That will be taken care of, don't worry. It will be done sensitively. You know the best way you can help with Teresa?'

He looked at her with moist eyes.

'Think through who was at the party—'

The uniform gave his notebook a little shake. 'I was in the process of compiling a list of guests.'

Iona stood up and stepped back. 'Great, I'll let you get on. Sorry to interrupt. Just one more thing. James, did Teresa make any purchases recently?'

'What kind?'

'Did she mention picking up a bargain? That kind of thing.'

'A second-hand laptop. She mentioned that.'

Iona gave what she hoped was a measured nod. 'Where did she get it?'

'Some guy was flogging them in the student union. She was really chuffed to get in there quick enough.'

'And when did she buy this?'

'Er, two, three days ago. She came back with it from lectures. Tuesday, it would have been.'

'Did she say anything about the seller?'

'Not a lot. He has a little shop further along Oxford Road. Computer stuff, I think. Not new, pre-owned.'

Pre-owned, Iona thought, horrified how a crafty marketing term had made it into this young man's everyday language. 'So, you say this guy had more than one for sale?'

'Yeah, there was a second. I almost jumped on my bike to get down there, but decided there was no way it wouldn't have been taken.'

'James.' She put a hand on his to ensure he was listening properly. 'What time do you think she bought the computer?'

'After her lectures finished. She went into the union to get some more printer paper from the shop. Came out with a Dell laptop.'

'So this would have been . . . ?'

'Three-ish. She finishes at three on a Tuesday.'

'OK, thanks, James. I'll leave you with the officer here.' She gave the uniform a quick glance. 'Thanks for that.'

Dusk had fallen when they emerged from the end of the sloping driveway. A bike was rapidly approaching, the headlight wobbling as the person's legs pumped the peddles. It swerved to a stop and a guy jumped off, cheeks red, hair all over the place. 'What's going on?'

Iona caught the Scouse accent. 'Are you Craig?'

'Yeah.' His eyes cut to the house. 'What's happening?'

Iona raised her hands. 'Get your breath, there's no need to panic. Martin?' She glanced at Martin who was staring at the younger man. 'Maybe get a uniformed officer over, Martin?'

'Sure.'

Iona kept her eyes on the student's face. He was staring anxiously after Martin as he walked back up the drive. 'Have we been burgled?'

'Craig, there's been a serious incident here. You'll have to give us some of your time—'

'Is it to do with that laptop?'

'Which laptop?'

'Teresa's.' Gulping air, he reached into his jacket and produced a piece of paper. 'A copper was handing out these by the Learning Commons. It's asking about anyone who bought a laptop recently.'

Iona saw he was holding a copy of her flyer. A day earlier, she thought, and we might have stopped this.

Once an officer had come for Craig, Iona and Martin returned to her car. Closing the door on the bustle outside, she turned to Martin. 'Four laptops taken from CityPads. If that's the third person who bought one, we need to find the fourth, if they're still alive.'

Martin face was grim. 'What the fuck is going on here?'

'I don't know. But, whatever it is, we're way off the pace.'

TWENTY-ONE

L iam eased the kitchen door open. The sound of the television playing became clearer. He'd been watching the man through a rear window of the house for the last twenty minutes as he'd shuffled around the ground-floor room, turning a laptop on and then plonking it half-open on the sofa before flicking the telly on, too. He scrolled through that evening's listings, highlighting a film for recording later that evening.

Did that mean he was planning to go out? Liam decided he couldn't afford to wait and see: Nina wanted the laptop back straightaway.

The news came on and the man sank lower on the sofa, just the top of his head now visible. There were no mirrors near the television, nothing to give the man a view of the doorway behind him.

Liam stepped carefully across the tiled floor of the kitchen, stopping in the corridor to remove the hammer from his jacket. He peeped round the TV room's door. The room was in semi-darkness; most of the light came from the TV's screen. It kept brightening and dimming as the camera angles switched.

The man was still on the sofa, head now tilted forward. Had he nodded off? Liam moved silently across the carpet, thinking of all the houses he'd robbed while their owners watched television in the front room, totally oblivious to his presence.

He peered down at the top of the man's head. He'd nodded

off, judging by the deep breathing. He wondered whether to just lift the laptop from the sofa and slip back out of the kitchen door. But Nina had said: no one left alive.

It had occurred to him, once or twice, where the girls they shipped out of the country ended up. Probably the same type of place they did in Britain; terraced houses on quiet city streets, flats above shops, back rooms of certain clubs.

The only buyer Nina had ever talked about was one who owned a giant yacht. A man who'd got into gas or oil when the Russian government decided to sell the industries off. But rather than spend his money on things like Premiership football clubs, this man liked to blow his cash on young girls. He had them flown out by helicopter to his floating palace. The man, Nina had once said, was willing to pay any price if the girl matched what he was looking for at that particular time. All that money and – according to Nina – the girls were never on board when he eventually returned to port.

He lifted the hammer up high. Nighty night, mate.

The man made a little snorting sound before the head of the hammer sank into the crown of his skull. He went stiff and, as Liam yanked it back up, he started to topple sideways. Liam just had time to reach over the back of the sofa and whip the laptop away.

As the man settled across the cushions, Liam looked at the words on the laptop's case. Sony. Nina's wasn't a Sony, it was a Dell. Shit! He looked at the man. His deformed head was against the armrest and air was seeping from his open mouth. Liam stepped round the sofa, leaned down and saw that the man's eyes were open. 'Where's the Dell? Where is it?'

The man blinked and Liam thought for a moment that he'd understood. 'Where is it?'

No answer.

His eyelids were beginning to close and Liam slapped him hard across the face. 'Where's the fucking Dell?'

His head rolled forward and blood began to well up in his ear. More suddenly appeared from his nostrils and he stopped breathing.

'Fuck.' Liam dumped the Sony on the coffee table and searched the room, flinging open cupboard doors, pulling out drawers. A carry case was in the kitchen, next to the bin. Binto, like the other one. No Dell laptop, no leather carry case. This was a fucking disaster.

He went back into the front room to retrieve the Sony. Better to come back with something, even if it wasn't right. As he lifted it up, the thing gave a little series of bings. Some sort of a message? Liam looked at the blank screen. The sound came again; a noise designed to attract attention. Someone was trying to get in touch. He extended a forefinger and pressed the pad. The screen came to life. In its centre was a little window.

There was a photo of an old woman in the middle of the screen. The words below read, Mum calling.

Liam wasn't sure exactly how these Skype things worked, but he did known it was a way of talking to someone on screen. Which meant Mum was also on a computer. Did she have the Dell? The bloke had definitely bought one from Eamon Heslin. Did he give it to her?

He moved the cursor over the green phone button and clicked.

The window changed and he found himself looking at the old lady. She was staring right at him with a frown. Her voice came out of the speakers. 'Andrew? Is that you?'

He shrank away from the screen, suddenly realizing he must be in view. There was a smaller window in the corner. The person in that one was barely visible. He realized it was him, in the semi-dark.

'Andrew? Turn on the main light – you're in shadow. I can hardly make you out.'

Liam's eyes were wide. The old woman was in a flat or bedsit of some kind. He could see a couple of potted plants behind her; a photo of the dead man was on the wall.

'Can you hear me, Andrew? I can hear your television playing in the background. Is this working?'

Unsure what he should do, Liam kept silent and didn't move.

'Andrew?' She was squinting straight at him. 'Oh, bother this thing, what's wrong with it?' Her hand reached out as she looked down. 'Stupid contraption,' she mumbled. 'Is my sound turned off? Something is definitely not right.'

A doorbell rang. Liam's head whipped round as the old lady looked up sharply.

'Was that your front door? Andrew, can you hear me? Oh, this silly thing, why won't you work?'

There was a knock. 'Andy? Come on, mate, shift starts in fifteen. Andy!'

'It's no good,' the old lady said, sounding cross. 'I'm going to ring you.'

Liam picked the Sony off the table and made for the back door. As he stepped into the rear garden, a phone started ringing in the kitchen. He glanced through the window. Shit – he hadn't spotted the mobile on the sill during his earlier search. He started back.

'Andy!' The voice again, now at the side of the house. Footsteps crunched on gravel. 'Always bloody late. Every time.'

Liam hesitated for a moment then turned on his heel and made for the back gate, the phone continuing to ring behind him.

TWENTY-TWO

Superintendent Graham O'Dowd lowered his eyes from the ceiling and sighed. 'Three. Three! For all we know, the fourth is dead, too. Lying in a house, at the bottom of a canal, Christ knows where. This is a nightmare!'

DCI Roebuck coughed into his curled fingers. 'Is there a chance the fourth laptop is among the burned-out remains of Heslin's shop?'

O'Dowd glared at him. 'Let's assume it's not, Peter. We assumed Philip Young was not at risk and now we look like a bunch of prats.'

Iona dropped her eyes to the meeting room table. When members of the senior team started falling out in front of everyone, things were going really badly.

'Time's ticking with Mossad, too. They're pushing for a meeting first thing Monday morning. I'll be there via a video link, so what have we got? Andy?'

DCI Sullivan looked up. 'Crime site analysis indicates there's nothing more to recover from the premises of PCs To Go. As it happens, among the debris are several parts that appear to be from a Dell laptop. Whether we'll ever be able to ascertain if it's the fourth one from CityPads I cannot say at this stage.'

'What about Nirpal Haziq?' O'Dowd demanded moodily.

'We're outside his home address,' Sullivan answered. 'Officers are calling on his friends and family, but nothing so far.'

'Has he links to anything dodgy? Has he come to our attention before?'

'No – on both counts. We found his passport during the search of his flat. Unless he has another, he won't go far.'

O'Dowd pursed his lips, obviously sceptical. 'We need him. Increase pressure on the family – search their homes and make a mess of them – see if that encourages them to cooperate. OK, the computer Philip Young brought in. Alan, tell me you found something?'

The IT guy pulled at the collar of his T-shirt. 'Kind of. When I did an audit of the hard drive's memory, something interesting appeared.' He glanced quickly about. 'Without bogging you down in detail, the memory of a hard drive is made up of partitions – back-up partitions, recovery partitions and so on. The standard for personal computers is a type of partition called NTFS – that's what Windows is designed to read. When I compared the memory available on Philip's hard drive with what the manufacturer specified should be there, I found a discrepancy of two gigabytes. Not a huge anomaly, but worth looking at more closely. So I checked disc management and there I discovered a two-gigabyte partition of RAW memory. This can't be opened with Windows.'

'You mean one that survived the formatting?' Martin asked, forearms casually draped across the armrests of his chair.

'I believe so. But it's under a very good lock; one I can't open for the moment at least.'

Martin frowned. 'Can't you just look at what type of file it is and get the appropriate programme?'

The IT guy gave a regretful shake of his head. 'Double clicking on it only gives you the option of reformatting it – and that would wipe it clean.'

O'Dowd started tapping his fingers. 'What are your next steps, then?'

'I've removed the hard drive and plugged it into a dock. Next is to figure out what to plug the dock into.' He shrugged. 'It's designed to work with something, just not a personal computer.'

'You mean an Apple or something like that?' Martin asked.

'Something with a USB port; we've tried a range of phones and tablets but it's not having it. We've yet to try any digital cameras . . .'

'But that could take days,' someone muttered.

O'Dowd placed his palms on the table. 'Keep going at it. There's been no joy from Pakistan yet, either. The embassy rang half an hour ago to say that Khaldoon and his sister haven't shown up on any internal flights or trains heading into the north of the country. Of course, they may have been collected by car or taken by bus. Who knows.'

O'Dowd turned his attention to Roebuck. 'The two missing girls?'

Roebuck looked along the table. 'Dean?'

A tired-looking sergeant puffed his cheeks out. 'OK, every care home in the Greater Manchester Area who's had girls abscond in the past eight weeks was contacted by phone. We asked them to send us documentation that would allow the girl to be identified. However, many of the photos were of extremely poor quality – or were several years old.

'Of those photos, five are reasonable fits for Rihanna, three reasonable fits for Shandy. What we're doing now is arranging visits to those care homes with a copy of the profiles recovered from the laptops. That way, we should get a definite yes or no from a staff member.'

'Why has this not been done already?' O'Dowd growled.

'Reports have only just started coming in – and are still coming in, actually. Only just now, a photo came in that could be Shandy.'

'Who's working with him on this?' O'Dowd cut in, his face turned to Roebuck. 'It needs more resources.'

Roebuck looked at Iona and Martin. 'Where are you two at with the names recovered from Eamon Heslin's premises?'

Martin replied, 'We saw one company earlier on. But the owner hadn't been offered a laptop. Heslin called in on her before he showed up at the student union trying to flog them. That leaves an accountancy firm, which we were going to visit immediately after this.'

'OK, get that crossed off. Then you're helping out Dean with tracing these girls. Both clear with that?'

'Yes sir.' Iona's reply had been in perfect unison with that of Martin. It appeared she now had a partner for the investigation.

O'Dowd had started to consult his file when a series of beeps came from his phone. He tilted the screen then grabbed it properly. 'O'Dowd here. Yes. Yes, OK.' A spark of excitement was now in his voice. There followed a lengthy silence during which he gave the occasional eager nod. 'OK, I understand.'

He hung up, a gleam in his eye. Iona sat up, sensing every officer in the room doing the same.

'Has anyone heard of the Forced Marriage Unit?' he asked. 'It's a government organization, something to do with the Foreign and Commonwealth office. If a British national is being forced into a marriage against their will, these guys can intervene.'

He started gathering his file together. 'They just received a phone call from a friend of Sravanti Khan. Sravanti texted her to say she's being held by her brother in a hotel in Islamabad. He has her passport and he's told her she is going to Waziristan for an arranged marriage. The friend is begging the unit to go and get her.'

The four men stepped out from a rear door of the Israeli embassy in Kensington. All were under thirty years old. They were dressed in casual clothes, one with a baseball cap with the word Redskins across the front. They moved fluidly and with purpose – like athletes on the way to a training session. All had been chosen because they looked European. Three had travelled into the country using Italian passports; the one with the baseball cap had used a French passport.

At the security gate set into the high fence that enclosed the gardens behind the large residence, they were allowed through without a word being spoken or anything being written down.

A Ford Galaxy was waiting for them on Queen's Gate Terrace, several streets away. Three got in the rear of the vehicle. The one with the baseball cap slid into the front passenger seat. 'OK.'

The driver started the car and pulled out. He made his way

to the A315 which would lead them through Notting Hill and eventually the A40 and then M40.

'Where are they?' the man with the baseball cap eventually asked.

'Parked at a service station on the M40. Keys are in the compartment in front of you.'

The man removed two sets, swiftly selecting the bunch that had a small key. 'Weapons box in the boot?'

'No – beneath the floor of the passenger seat's footwell. The carpet lifts off. Everything you need is in there.'

'Comms?'

'The works. All mobile phones have been pre-programmed with the numbers you need. There's also a TETRA scanner.'

'That works on the encryption used by the police up in Manchester?'

'Yes. The entire British police use the same system; it's fine.' He glanced at his passenger. 'So, a real rush, then.'

The man in the baseball cap nodded. 'If whoever's behind this is taken into British custody, it'll be months before we get an answer. If at all.' By tilting his head, he could see his three colleagues in the rear-view mirror. One was already asleep; the other two were staring silently out the window, eyes scanning the lit London streets. Early evening on a Saturday. The pavements were busy with people out to enjoy everything the city had to offer. Twenty-one hours earlier, his team had been at a military base on Israeli-occupied land near the disputed border with Syria. The El Al flight from Tel Aviv to Amsterdam had been busy; a kid a few rows down had screamed for most of it. From there, the ferry and drive had taken another ten or so hours. He yawned. 'How long until these services?'

The driver glanced at the dashboard clock. 'Less than an hour.'

'And from there, how long will it take us to get to Manchester?'

'If the traffic is good, under four hours. But the M6 is normally slow.'

The man pushed the baseball cap over his eyes and settled back in his seat.

TWENTY-THREE

Liam let himself into the kitchen of Nina's house. She was perched on a bar stool, cigarette in hand. As he'd opened the door her head had jerked stiffly round. He remembered a lurching ferry trip to the Isle of Man, the look on passengers' faces when they knew they would soon be throwing up.

'Have you got it?'

'No.' He placed the partly open laptop on the table. 'But we're a step closer.'

'What the hell's that?' Her voice was shrill. Desperate. 'How can we be a step closer?'

'Just listen, right? Let me explain. I went into his house. He was on the sofa with the telly on. It was dark. So I dealt with him and grabbed the laptop next to him. It's not a Dell, but this window opens up on its screen – a video link thing to an old woman talking.'

'Skype?'

'I don't know. Probably. This old woman was there, thinking I'm her son.'

'What do you mean?'

'She was there, on the screen. I thought she could see me at first.'

'His mum? He gave the Dell to his mum?'

'Looks like it.'

Nina took a long drag of her cigarette. She lifted her chin, and as she blew smoke up at the halogen light above her, Liam gazed at the smooth skin of her throat. A tracery of faint veins showed just beneath the porcelain surface. He wanted to kiss her there, pinch the skin gently with his teeth. Maybe trap blood there, leave his mark.

'What did this woman say?'

'Asked me to put the light on because she can't make anything out. Then someone the son works with turns up at the front door. He's calling for him, banging on the door, so I grabbed the laptop and got out the back. Only just made it.'

Nina studied him. 'Were you seen?'

'No. I don't think so – he was coming round the side of the house, but I was on the street by then. I made sure the laptop didn't shut. It logs you out if it does, yeah?'

Nina nodded.

'So, she carried on for a bit – the mum – moaning about it not working properly. Eventually she gave up. I pressed a button now and again to stop it from shutting down.'

'You did well.' She ran a hand along his arm and the breath caught in his throat. 'I wonder . . .' She crushed her cigarette out. 'Put the lights on low.'

Liam crossed to the doorway and turned several rows of lights off. Nina opened the laptop and clicked on the Skype icon. All his contacts were in the panel on the left of the screen. Near the bottom was Mum.

'I reckon she lives nearby. If someone wasn't trying to get in, I could have found you an address.'

Nina wasn't sure if clicking on the woman's icon would immediately open a connection. 'Maybe. Let's check the email.' Nina opened up Thunderbird and clicked on the contacts tab. She then scrolled down to the letter M. 'Here – a phone number for Mum. No address.'

Liam looked over her shoulder. Her ear was inches from his lips. It was hard to speak. 'That's the area code for Poynton. I was sha— I was seeing a girl from there, once. It's not far from here.'

Nina moved away from him. He looked wrathfully at the expanse of floor now separating them. It felt so good when they were close.

She lit another cigarette and turned round. 'OK, he gives her the computer. They Skype each other; she's unable to work out what's going wrong with the picture. She's new to it; he sets it all up for her. He must have. Now she's confused.' Drawing on her cigarette, she regarded the laptop through narrowed eyes. Then she reached for her mobile and keyed in the number on the laptop's screen. 'Is that Mrs Williams?'

Nina's voice was friendly, but businesslike. Liam also noticed she was speaking with a slight accent.

'Mrs Williams, I work for Dell computers. Their technical

support department? How are you today? That's right, Dell. Ah, did he? That was very kind of him. He also registered that laptop with us. This is a courtesy call to let you know there are some connectivity issues at the moment.' She listened for a moment. 'Oh, I'm sorry to hear that. OK, it might be a problem with the service in your area. Where do you live, Mrs Williams? Poynton, in Cheshire. I'm just checking now. And what's your actual address there? OK, thank you. Mrs Williams, the good news is a technician is now en route.'

She looked at Liam and raised her eyebrows. 'Are you planning on leaving your flat, Mrs Williams? Because I might need to call you back. You're not. That's good. Don't worry. He'll be able to reset your computer settings, if needs be. How long? He should be with you in under thirty minutes.'

As Liam's car turned out of the drive, her mobile went off. Him. She felt the usual flutter in her lower stomach. 'Hello.'

'It's all over.'

She looked at her startled reflection in the glass. 'What is?'

'There are new factors to account for.'

'New factors?' She climbed backwards on to a bar stool and pressed her knees tightly together. 'What are they?'

'It's not just police any more. I have heard security forces are involved.'

The girl who blew up, Nina thought. That's what he's talking about. 'Which ones?'

'The flights are now tomorrow. Madison Fisher: she is on a flight to Istanbul at seven fifteen in the morning. TK1994.'

'Tomorrow morning? That's in less than twelve hours.'

'Yes. The flight goes on to Beirut, but she'll be met in Istanbul. That is taken care of.'

Nina looked round for her cigarettes as he spoke again.

'The jet will be at Woodford Aerodrome at four o'clock tomorrow afternoon. You, Chloe and the policewoman. Normal arrangements, you drive airside and people will meet you from the plane. Leave nothing behind – no tracks, nothing.'

TWENTY-FOUR

Iona stepped out of the meeting room trying to focus on the latest task thrown her way. But her mind kept returning to the Forced Marriage Unit, sparking long-harboured questions about her own father, Wasim. He'd been brought up in a well-off, well-respected family in Islamabad. He'd excelled academically. Outside his studies, he was a gifted sportsman and had played for the Pakistan hockey team for nine years, winning gold with them at the 1982 hockey World Cup and at the 1984 Olympics.

Life at the very top of the country awaited. Then, in his late twenties, he'd abandoned everything and come to Britain.

It was only as she got older that Iona began to appreciate what a dramatic event such a move had been: yet the reasons for it had never been explained. She'd just assumed he had no contact with his family back home because of the geographical distance involved. As an explanation, it worked OK while she was young. Only by cornering her mother on a few occasions had Iona been able to form a hazy picture of what had happened. No wonder all contact with his family had been severed.

'Sound fair to you?'

She turned to Martin, vaguely aware he'd been talking into her ear for the entire length of the corridor. 'Say all that again, can you?'

His eyebrows lifted in exasperation. 'The care home Dean wants us to check out? In Heaton Chapel?'

There was a condescending note in his voice that immediately rankled her. 'Yes, what about it?'

'Give me two minutes. Just need to check in with my boss. Tell him what's what.' Martin headed for DCI Palmer's private office.

Iona made her way across the main incident room and sat down at her desk. The civilian support workers from the day shift were gone. No one seemed to be keeping an eye on the log to see what was happening round the city.

She plonked herself down at her desk and logged on. What, she asked herself, am I even looking for? Aside from suspicious deaths, a flag had been put on any type of incident involving violence, muggings or thefts. Anything involving a student also automatically triggered a heads-up for the entire CTU.

She scrolled past the usual medley of lost mobile phones, road traffic accidents and domestic disputes. A report was just coming in from outside a house in Brinnington, south of the city centre. The owner of the property – due on duty at the Aquatics Centre on Oxford Road – hadn't responded to the front door being rung. The colleague had glanced into the kitchen and spotted signs of the place having been burgled. At that point he'd become uneasy and called the police.

Iona went back to the workplace of the house owner. The Aquatics Centre. A two-minute walk from the student union and practically next door to Eamon Heslin's shop. It was worth a try. She lifted the phone and, within seconds, had been patched through to the two uniformed constables who were just arriving at the scene. 'DC Iona Khan, who is this, please?'

The voice of the constable came back down the line. 'Constable Gray. Michael.'

He sounds younger than me, Iona thought. And very nervous. 'Michael, what do you see? Describe it to me.'

'Well, I've gone round the back, by the open door into the kitchen. The television is on – I can hear it – as are the kitchen lights. I can see car keys on the side and a mobile phone on the windowsill. There's a jacket draped over a chair. You'd have thought he's in.'

'You've tried shouting his name?'

'Yeah. He's not answering.'

Trying to focus on the scene, Iona closed her eyes. There could be an entirely innocent explanation – or it could be far more sinister. She made a decision. 'Michael, I need you to check the property – but be very careful. Assume there's a burglar inside.'

'You want us to go inside now? We were waiting for a patrol car.'

'No – I need you to take a look now. Is that OK?'

'Yes.'

'Good. Keep the line open. Talk me through what's happening.'

'Sarah, stay with me. Sir? Remain out here, please.' His voice dropped. 'We're in the kitchen. The cupboards are all open. Stuff's all over the floor. Now in the corridor. The door to the TV room is on my right.'

Iona could hear it playing. Applause rang out.

The constable tried calling again. 'Mr Williams? Mr Williams? We're police, can you hear us?'

The TV played on. Iona pressed the phone more tightly against her ear.

'Doesn't seem to be anyone here. TV room is empty. There's . . . oh . . . Mr Williams? Sir?'

Another voice. Female. 'Jesus, is that blood? Sir, can you hear—'

Iona sat up, eyes opening. 'What's going on? What is it?'

'Check for a pulse. Can you feel . . . No? Nothing? OK, Sarah, get back. We need to be out of here. Detective Khan? He's here – there's damage to his head. My colleague was unable—'

Iona was on her feet, shouting at Roebuck in his side office.

Within ten minutes, Gowerdale Road was clogged with emergency vehicles. Iona and Martin arrived a few seconds behind Roebuck. They pulled in behind his car and approached the taped-off area at the front of number eleven. Roebuck swept through and vanished inside the property.

'Detectives Everington and Khan,' Martin announced as they reached the outer cordon. Since she'd raised the alert back at the CTU, Martin had been subdued. Now, at the crime scene itself, he turned to her. 'Go on, you can take the lead.'

'You sure?'

'Yeah, it was your shout.'

She could see a pair of constables talking to a sergeant beside the front door. The male was tall and appeared to be in his early twenties. The female looked ill and was about ten years older. Iona approached them. 'Is it Michael and Sarah? I'm Detective Khan. It was me you were patched through to just earlier.'

Michael turned and looked down at her, lips parting in surprise. Sarah blinked. Used to people being surprised by her appearance, Iona looked briefly to the house. 'You did well.' She smiled at them.

Michael regained his composure first. 'Er, thanks. Yeah, my first body.'

Iona could see the house was already bustling with people. It was unlikely she'd be permitted beyond the front door. 'Not nice, is it?'

They nodded together. 'He was on his side – head on the armrest of the sofa. Skull looked like it had been caved in.'

A hammer blow, Iona thought. There'd been no word, so far, about any laptop. 'Did you get a look round the front room before coming back out?'

'No, we withdrew as soon as we were sure he was dead.'

She tapped her toe in frustration: they were too late. Unless, by chance, the killer had been disturbed before he'd found it. 'Where's the person who works at the Aquatics Centre; the one who called the police in the first place?'

He nodded at the patrol car on the opposite side of the street. 'In there, giving a statement, I think.'

'Cheers.' She turned to Martin. 'I'm going to pop across. Coming?'

'Iona, we're meant to be over at the care home in Heaton Chapel, remember?'

She looked back at him. 'Seriously? You want to head there right now?'

'OK, OK.' He made a fending motion with his hands. 'Do what you want to do. I'll wait in the car.'

She headed swiftly across the road, smarting at his petulant tone. If this had been your call, she thought, there's no way you'd be so keen to clear off. She leaned in at the driver's window of the squad car. The man on the back seat gazed straight back at her with dull eyes. Probably still taking in what's just happened, she thought. 'Hello there.' She turned to the officer in the front seat and briefly showed her ID. 'Detective Khan. Anything?'

He laid a hand on the steering wheel. 'Not apart from what he reported to the crime scene officers, if that's what you mean. Picking up the victim was a regular arrangement; he'd swing by and they'd car share.'

She peered into the rear of the vehicle once more. The man was now staring off to the side. 'Sir? Could I ask how long was it before you gave up at the front door and went round to the back?'

His eyes shifted to her but his head didn't move. 'A minute at most.'

'And you could hear the TV was on?'

He nodded.

'So you made your way round to the rear of the property. Did you notice any cars pass by on the road?'

He began to shake his head, but stopped. 'Just a man walking off. I could see him through the hedge. Then I saw the gate for the back yard was—'

Iona cut in. 'This man. Which direction was he walking?'

'Away from me. Off up the side road.'

'Did you see his face?'

'No.'

'What was he wearing?'

'I don't know. A darkish jacket.' His eyes lifted. 'He was carrying something.'

Iona felt a stab of adrenalin. 'Did you see what it was?'

'No, it was in his hands. Cradling it, kind of.'

'You mean like you'd cradle a baby?'

'No, not a baby. It was square-ish. Flat. I thought it was maybe a pizza.'

'Was he in a hurry? Was he strolling casually?'

'Hurrying – yes.'

'Where did he go?'

'Not sure. I was looking at the back door by then.'

Iona addressed the policeman in the front. 'We need to conduct a formal interview, right now.' She stood up straight and was in the process of calling DCI Roebuck when he came rushing down the garden path, pursued by another detective.

She started jogging over. 'Sir?'

He caught sight of her. 'Follow us, Iona!'

Roebuck ran towards his vehicle, calling over his shoulder. 'The murder victim had a message on his mobile. His mum, saying the laptop he'd given her wasn't working!'

TWENTY-FIVE

L iam stood in the darkness, eyes on the building where Libby Williams lived. It wasn't going to be easy getting in. The reception area was unmanned, but you had to be buzzed in by a resident or whoever looked after the place. A janitor or caretaker. CCTV cameras were above the entrance and in the ceiling of the lobby.

He almost laughed. It didn't matter any more. He and Nina would be out of the country in a few more hours. So what if the pigs eventually recognized him from the footage? Add it to the forensics they'd eventually pinpoint at the various murder scenes. If they caught him now, he was fucked. One old woman on the list would hardly make a difference.

He pulled on the tabard with reflective panels, placed a baseball cap on his head and strolled across the lawned area. The toolbox in his hand was small; a few screwdrivers in the top tray, just the hammer beneath.

What was the flat number? Six, that was it. Ground floor. That made things easier. 'Mrs Williams? It's the engineer. I'm calling about your broadband connection. You spoke to someone at our office earlier on?'

Her voice was quite posh, like old people liked to sound whenever they spoke into anything. 'Oh, yes. She said you'd be on your way. Come in and turn left through the double doors that are directly in front.'

The door clicked and he stepped inside, aware that the CCTV cameras were trained directly at him. Keeping his head down, he held up a finger as he crossed the lobby. The thought of a crowd of detectives looking at that later on made him grin. If it wasn't for the panel of mailboxes on the opposite wall, the place could have been a service station motel: blue nylon carpets and green fire escape signs. Metal plates at the base of each door, black smears where they'd been bumped by wheelchair tyres. He hated old people.

Beyond the double doors was a corridor. Flats one to seven, said a sign. He followed the arrow. A radio was playing somewhere. Wurlitzer music. Memories of Blackpool flashed up. Shivering in a pub's concrete courtyard, Coke and crisps long-finished, waiting for his mum to come back out and take him home. Then explosions of laughter from inside and behind her cackles the sound of one of those bloody piano things. Its noise would carry on the breeze from a big hall down the road, notes rising and falling, building and building until she emerged, staggering, lipstick smeared, looking like the organ sounded: crazy. Back to the bedsit. Sometimes chips on the way. Slurring her words, she'd tuck him up before vanishing back off into the night.

He focused on the door at the corridor's end. The music was coming from beyond it. The next seaside he saw would be different to Blackpool. It would be sunny and clean and there'd be no fucking Wurlitzer music. And he'd be with Nina, not the pissed slag he'd had for a mum.

He knocked on the door, nice and gentle. The old dear who, earlier on, had been peering at him from the computer opened up.

'Do come in. I hope you're not still working just because of me.'

It took him a moment to cotton on. 'Oh, no – I'm on lates this week. I won't be home until morning.'

'My husband used to work nightshifts.' She led him towards a small sitting room. The Wurlitzer music got louder. 'He was a printer – newspapers. In the days when all the letters were little blocks.' She smiled over her shoulder. 'Before computers took over. Here it is. The Spotify thing is working, as you can hear. I don't know, sometimes I think they're more trouble than they're worth.'

Stepping aside, she gestured at the laptop on the circular table in the corner.

'Nothing worse than a misbehaving computer, is there?' Liam replied, stepping closer. It was a Dell. On and on went the bastard music.

'What with that and mobile phones. I'm forever being bothered by sales people.' She pointed at a clunky-looking Nokia on the side. 'I ignore the thing, mostly.' As if on cue, it started to ring.

She briefly scrutinized the screen. 'Absolutely no idea who that is.' She put it back down. 'I won't even ask what you need to do. The fact those things don't even have wires is confusing enough for me. A cup of coffee?'

Liam was checking the laptop's casing. No label had been scratched off the front corner. Nina's. It had to be. 'You what?'

Her face stiffened slightly. 'I asked if you'd like a drink.'

'Oh, no. Don't bother.' He crouched down and flicked the toolbox clasps up. 'This won't take two minutes.'

TWENTY-SIX

They raced south, away from the city centre and towards Poynton. En route, Martin called Roebuck and got a hurried explanation of what was happening.

Someone had heard the mobile phone beeping on the window-sill, saw the missed call had come from Mum and then listened to her answerphone message. An address for her had then been found in a book on Andrew Williams' bedside table; she lived in a sheltered housing unit called Hope Green on the far side of Poynton. A call had been made to the nearest police station. A few years ago, that would have been in Poynton itself. Cutbacks now meant it was only manned at certain times during the day. Instead, a patrol car was being sent from Hazel Grove.

'Hazel Grove?' Iona replied, jaw set tight as she pursued Roebuck's tail-lights, the sound of his car's siren clearly audible. 'We're going through that now.'

Martin looked at the line of shops zipping past. 'Shit. We'll only be just behind it, then.'

'Just ring the bloody care home, surely?' Iona demanded, keeping in Roebuck's slipstream as traffic parted ahead of them.

'Sergeant Fairfield's doing that now,' Martin responded, one hand reaching for the dashboard as Iona had to brake sharply. 'He's got hold of the concierge.'

The bus moved out of their way and Iona hit the accelerator once more. Barely five minutes later they'd gone through the main part of Poynton at high speed. Countryside was opening up around them when Roebuck started indicating right. As they slowed to take the turning, Iona could see a police car parked before the doors leading into a building trying to look like a normal residential house, only it was about three times too big.

A uniformed officer was visible in the lobby area. He was talking to a middle-aged man in a beige gilet who kept flapping one arm about. The gesture filled Iona with dread. Gravel caused them to skid slightly as the car came to a halt behind Roebuck's. He was already out and asking questions. Sergeant Fairfield was at the rear of the vehicle, unlocking the weapons box in the boot.

'She didn't answer,' the concierge said. 'I knocked three times. Then I heard the police siren,' he nodded at the uniformed officer, 'and came back here.'

'So you didn't open her door?' Roebuck asked.

The concierge shook his head.

'Can you? You've got an access key?'

'Yes.' He removed a bunch from the pocket of his gilet. 'But I only like to go into a resident's room without their permission in exceptional circumstances.'

'And you think she's there?'

'She rarely goes out. Just when her son takes her.'

'OK. We need to go in.' He looked to his side. 'Sergeant Fairfield?'

He gave a nod, one hand hidden in the pocket of his overcoat. 'Do you know the layout of her flat?'

The concierge turned to him. 'I do. They're all the same: bathroom opposite the bedroom in the corridor on the other side of the front door, sitting area and kitchen straight ahead.'

'OK, cheers.'

The concierge led them all down the corridor to room six. Iona could hear someone coughing in number three. Really coughing, like a bit of lung had come away and got stuck. It ended in a loud spit. They were gathered outside number six when the door opposite half opened. A silver-haired man with a sharp nose looked out.

'Back in your room!' Martin whispered, badge raised. The door slowly closed as the concierge unlocked Libby Williams' door and stepped away.

Roebuck pushed it open and Fairfield slipped inside, the barrel of a Glock directed at the floor.

'Mrs Williams! Police! Are you here?'

No reply.

'Mrs Williams?' Fairfield nodded at the closed doors on the left and right before moving swiftly and silently past them and into the room at the far end of the short passage.

Iona felt cold air on her face. It was streaming out of the flat. A window must be wide open. Fairfield looked rapidly about him, gun swinging with each turn of his head. Something off to the side caught his attention for a moment. He vanished from view. When he reappeared, he moved back to the closed doors, checking one room then the other. There was no sign of the Glock when he came out of the bathroom. 'Clear. Front room, boss.'

His voice was flat and Iona knew they were too late. Their man had gone, taking the laptop and leaving another body in his wake.

She whirled round and slapped the corridor wall with her palm.

Nina opened the lower door and knocked. 'Hi, you two, it's me! Watching telly, are you?'

The tinny noise of laughter cut out and Chloe's voice called back. 'Hi, Nina, we're in here!'

She locked the door behind her and walked up the short corridor, bag swinging from one hand. They were slumped on the beanbags, faces turned inquisitively in her direction. 'Anyone for ice cream?'

'You are joking!' Chloe rolled to the side and scrabbled to her knees. 'Really?'

'I got Winter Berry Brownie, Peanut Butter Cup or Mint Chocolate Chunk.'

Both girls let out squeals of delight as Nina jumped on to the sofa and held up the bag. 'Who wants what?'

'Winter Berry Brownie, please, please, please,' Chloe said, both hands outstretched.

Nina tossed her the tub. 'Madison?'

'Mint Chocolate Chunk!'

Nina lobbed it over. 'Hey, I've got some other exciting news. You know your flights? I managed to bring them forward.'

Madison paused, the lid of her ice cream half-peeled back. 'When?'

'How does tomorrow morning sound?' She dug out a lump of ice cream and regarded it with relish. 'Different flights, still. I tried to get you going together.' She cocked her head and looked at Madison. 'I've been meaning to say, have you ever thought of a shorter hairstyle?'

'How do you mean?' Madison tentatively replied.

'It's just that, in Club Soda, the waitresses with short hair seem to get the best tips. Arab men are so used to their women having long hair. They just love a blonde bob. Don't you think she'd look good with one, Chloe? I do.'

TWENTY-SEVEN

They sat in silence, waiting for word from Roger Wilson, the Forced Marriage Unit manager stationed at the High Commission in Islamabad. Everyone's eyes kept touching on the pyramid-shaped speaker at the centre of the table. Conference calls. Iona couldn't stand them.

News had come that Sravanti had been successfully lifted from the hotel where she was being held. Someone – probably a member of staff – had phoned up to the room as the FMU staff and local police had appeared through the hotel doors. The brother, Khaldoon, had fled, but the girl was safe. She'd been answering questions for the last hour-and-a-quarter.

'My apologies about this.' The voice sounded tinny and artificial. A hiss of static smothered the 's' sounds. 'Mr Wilson is just attending to something with the local police, he won't be long.'

O'Dowd needlessly craned his neck forward. 'OK, we understand.' His voice had been reasonable, but the look he sent round the room spoke of annoyance. It was now almost two in the morning. Everyone needed some sleep; things weren't going to go any slower the next day.

'So,' O'Dowd said, turning to DCI Sullivan. 'You think it was Nirpal Haziq sighted over in Levenshulme?'

There was a slightly wooden quality to O'Dowd's voice that caused Iona to look up.

'Yes, that's right.' Sullivan sounded exactly the same.

Of course, Iona realized, glancing at the speaker phone. The knowledge of their voices being relayed to another location was making both men sound like bad actors.

'We know Haziq's parents live on Hopkins Avenue. A patrol car coming away from an incident at a betting shop on that road thinks they sighted him by the train station. He was gone by the time they'd turned the car round.'

'How certain were they?' O'Dowd asked.

'Eighty per cent. Significantly, he was wearing a suit. If it's the same one he was wearing when he ran from CityPads' offices, he hasn't even got access to a clean set of clothes.'

O'Dowd was looking pleased. 'We'll have him soon.'

'How could he have made the journey out to Poynton?' Iona asked quietly, not comfortable with the fact that Nirpal was their main suspect for all the murders. 'Little cash, no car . . . It wouldn't have been easy to—'

'He could have nicked a car,' Martin cut in.

Iona turned to him, irked by the cheerful note in his voice.

'I suppose so. If he's the type to know how you go about stealing one. He's got no priors for that sort of stuff, though.'

'That just means he's never been caught before,' someone else interjected.

Iona could sense the weight of opinion was against her. She could understand why: Nirpal bolting like he did was the act of a guilty person, no doubt. But was he really carrying out the killings? Believing it was him was certainly very tempting.

Whispers came from the speaker phone and O'Dowd slashed his hand for silence.

'Hello, Superintendent O'Dowd? It's Roger Wilson.'

'Mr Wilson,' O'Dowd's head was bobbing eagerly at the lump of angular plastic. 'Thanks for this. I realize you'll—'

'Don't be thankful. I'm not sure how much help this will be.'

O'Dowd's hopeful smile faded. 'Well, we'll be grateful for anything you might have. By the way, I'm here with DCIs Sullivan and Roebuck and a few of the officers on their teams.'

'Very well. Shall I run you through the pick-up, first?'

'Please.'

'After receiving the call from Sravanti's friend, we asked for the number of the mobile she'd texted her on. We then were able to ring Sravanti back and get her exact location. Just over two hours later we'd obtained permission from the authorities here to pick her up. We set off for the hotel with a police car in support.

'As I think you know, Khaldoon Khan was tipped off we were on our way up to the room. He'd tried to drag his sister out – presumably to a new location – but she'd fought back and he was forced to flee without her.'

'Is she OK?' Iona had asked without thinking. 'Sorry, Detective Khan here. Is Sravanti OK?'

'Yes. A few lumps and bumps, but she's fine.'

'Did it appear anyone else was part of the operation?' asked O'Dowd. 'Or was it just the brother?'

'It appears to be just the brother, why?'

'If Khaldoon was in Pakistan for terror-related activities, would there not have been –'

'Oh, she's convinced the trip was in order to marry her against her will. She has not mentioned anything else. It was to be to a son from a family in the village where her parents grew up.'

'DCI Sullivan speaking: that village is located in the tribal areas of Waziristan?'

'Correct. She'd even been given a photo of him by the brother, Khaldoon.'

'Why then,' asked Sullivan, 'did the brother flee? Is an arranged marriage attempt – if that's the correct terminology – such a serious offence?'

'That's a fair point,' Wilson replied. 'She'd been tricked into the trip in the first place. It was, she'd been told, their last chance to visit an ailing grandmother, who, as it happens, isn't so ill after all. Sravanti had told her brother she would get him locked up for his part in the deception.'

O'Dowd placed his elbows on the table. 'Do you think that's why she was there?'

'It all seems to fit, why?'

'We're looking at it from this angle: Sravanti was really going to be carrying a bomb. That's what she had come to Pakistan for.'

Wilson said nothing for a second. 'You think she is some kind of jihadist? A suicide bomber?' He sounded incredulous.

'Whether she knew that was why she was there is another question.' O'Dowd's jaw was tight.

'Erm, that's . . . frankly, that seems unlikely to me. I've just spent over an hour with the girl. She's thoroughly Westernised. The fact she was tricked into coming out here – she's angry, upset, confused . . .'

'A change of heart, maybe?' O'Dowd said. 'A loss of nerve? What about if the arranged marriage story was a cover the brother was using to lure her into Waziristan?'

Iona could hear it in O'Dowd's voice; he was trying to make the facts fit the theory. The pressure of making progress with the case was skewing his judgement.

'So,' Wilson replied cautiously. 'The brother first gets Sravanti out here with a sick grandmother story. He then changes it to an arranged marriage one. But really, he's lining her up – and this is his own sister, remember – as a suicide bomber.'

'Why run when he knew the police were coming?' Sullivan demanded, shooting a supportive look at O'Dowd.

'He was keeping someone against her will, for a start,' Wilson replied calmly. 'He just assaulted her while trying to get her out of there. Have you seen the *lathis* – the sticks – the police carry out here? They really like to swing those things, believe me. Khaldoon will have known that.'

O'Dowd placed a clenched fist on the table. 'Mr Wilson, you're not party to a lot of the information we have at this end. We have evidence to strongly indicate Khaldoon was involved in terror-related activities. So would you mind going back and questioning this girl from the angle we're talking about? Either as a knowing or unknowing accomplice of the brother.'

They all heard the sigh come from the speaker. 'OK, I'll try. She's with the embassy doctor now. Emotionally, she's all over the place. She knows she's shamed her family – she's terrified now that she's on her own. And she's probably right.'

The door opened and Fairfield stepped into the room, a laptop in his hand. He looked at the super with raised eyebrows. O'Dowd held up a finger. There was a hectoring note in his voice as he spoke again. 'We need to know if she has ever met an individual

called Nirpal Haziq. He worked in the same office as Khaldoon.
We are currently seeking Haziq in relation to several recent
murders here in Manchester.'

'Right, I've got that.'

'We are also trying to locate two girls who've gone missing
from care homes in this region. Khaldoon had only booked seats
for himself and his sister on that flight, but we need to know if
the sister is aware of him arranging transit for any other females
recently.'

'You think she'll be able to answer that? I'm pretty sure she
was duped into all this.'

'Would you just ask her?' O'Dowd's face was going red.

'Fine. Have you any names?'

'We have profiles, not actual names. I'll have the details
emailed over.'

'OK, I'll look out for it. Anything else? I need to—'

'That's all, thanks.' O'Dowd cut the call and immediately
turned to Sullivan. 'I want two officers on the next flight over to
Islamabad. No way I'm leaving this with that clown. You can
decide who goes. Now, DS Fairfield, what is it?'

He moved round the table. 'CCTV from the lobby of the
sheltered housing place where Libby Williams lived.'

O'Dowd looked hopeful. 'Does it show Haziq?'

'Not Haziq. Someone, but not Haziq.'

Officers shuffled to the side so Fairfield could sit next to
O'Dowd. Immediately, people were out of their seats and
crowding round behind him. The acuteness of the angle Iona
found herself at meant the screen was little more than shifting
patterns of light.

Fairfield clicked the pad. 'Here he is, entering the lobby at
seven thirty-six, that's eight minutes ahead of us.'

Iona's teeth clenched. Eight minutes.

'Now watch, see that? The bastard walks in and gives the
camera his middle finger; he knew this footage would be viewed.'

O'Dowd's elbows came down on the table with a bang. 'Play
it again.'

'Sir?' A detective spoke up on the far side of Fairfield. 'Can
you freeze it as he's approaching the doors? Before he keeps his
head down. I might know who that is.'

Fairfield fiddled with the keyboard and moved his hand away. The officer moved closer, regarding the screen intently. 'I think . . . I don't know. I worked for Stockport Division before here. We had a serial burglar – and that really, really looks like him. Bloke called Liam Collins. A total shitbag.'

TWENTY-EIGHT

Iona was shutting down her computer. The two officers chosen from Sullivan's team had each gone home to hastily pack a bag. At least they can get some sleep on the flight, she thought as waves of emotion washed through her. Strongest among them was a nagging sense of doubt. The investigation just didn't feel right. O'Dowd seemed to her more and more like a man blundering about in the dark, hands hopefully scrabbling for a light switch.

Now the theory was Haziq was working with Collins. Between them, the two men were murdering people like it was a competition between them. Iona could see Collins as a killer – a miserable childhood spent between Manchester and Blackpool, spells with foster parents and in care homes, school drop-out, long record for burglary, assault, racial abuse, ABH, GBH. He'd then kept out of trouble for almost five years, only to reappear in the old people's home lobby, all his old defiance back.

What Iona had a problem with was someone like Haziq working with someone like Collins.

A disconsolate sigh from across the table broke her thoughts. Martin. Did he feel it, too? This impression of having taken a wrong turn, of going off track. She looked across to see his head was bowed. His green biro was balanced between his finger and thumb, waggling back and forth as he struggled over something. She was still surprised he'd chosen to move to the desk opposite her while they were working together: as the more junior officer, she'd assumed that inconvenience was coming her way.

She cocked her head. He was looking down at a copy of that day's paper. He was on the puzzles page.

'You any good with these things?' he asked, glancing up once the question was out.

'What is it?' she replied noncommittally.

'Su-bloody-doku. I keep having a crack at them. Always end up giving up.'

'Which paper?'

He flipped it over to check. *'Manchester Evening Chronicle.'*

She sat up. It wasn't like Martin to ask for help. Even if it was just a newspaper puzzle. 'They can set quite nasty ones. Regional papers don't, normally.'

'You sound like an expert.' He gave her a quick grin. 'It's the top row. My mum always says if you can crack one row, it all falls into place.'

She wanted to say that depended on a few other factors. 'You realize it's not far off three in the morning? It'd probably be quicker to wait outside the all-night garage and get today's edition – it'll have the answers for that one inside.'

He laughed. 'Lateral thinking. I like it. But seriously, this'll just bug me.'

'Let's have a look, then.'

He folded it over and spun it across. She stopped it with one palm, scrutinizing the numbers before her. As she suspected, it wasn't hard. But telling Martin that would probably only dent his ego. He'd mucked it up straightaway by putting a three in at the corner. No way was that right. 'Whoever sets these things is so sneaky.' She pretended to agonize over it for a few seconds longer. 'How about if you swap the three in the corner for a five? Will that help?' She quickly completed that corner for him and passed it back. 'Does that work?'

He looked at it for a while and eventually smiled. 'Eight goes in on the other side. I think we're winning. Nice one.'

'My pleasure.' She could feel his eyes lingering on her.

'So, we're checking out this care home first thing tomorrow?' She met his eyes. 'Yup.'

He checked around: only a few other detectives were at their desks. None was in earshot. 'Do you think we're wasting our time? I can't help feeling we are.'

Now he's confiding in me. Was it for real? 'Why do you say that?' she asked quietly.

He moved the paper to one side. 'Nirpal Haziq.'

'What about him?'

He hunched forward, voice low. 'He doesn't feel right to me.'

She raised her eyebrows. Then why the hell, she thought, did you cut me down back there when I raised the question of how he got to Poynton?

'I'm sorry.' He briefly fluttered a hand. 'That comment in the progress meeting just popped out.'

'Even though you also doubt he's the person we should be looking for?' She recalled his condescending tone when he'd spoken up. 'You just wanted me to look clueless in front of everyone?'

'No, I didn't.' His face altered slightly. 'Well, I did a bit. But you were only too happy to make me look a twat in the offices of CityPads.'

She frowned. What was he on about?

'When I made that joke? The woman asked where our uniforms were and I said it was a dress-down day. At which point you said not to listen to me. You were all a regular team, I was an oddball. Full of it, according to you. Remember?'

She couldn't dredge up exactly what she'd said. Wasn't it just banter to set the women at ease? 'You took that to heart? Really?'

Now he looked cross. 'Iona, this isn't my team. I'm with Palmer, normally. The others don't know me. You left me looking like a right prat.'

Guilt took hold. So this was what it was about. My God. Part of her wanted to laugh at how ridiculously sensitive he was being. But at least he could be sensitive, unlike so many of the blokes in the unit. She found herself looking at him in a new way. 'Well . . . I'm sorry. I didn't mean to do that. I thought it was just mucking about, trying to release a bit of the tense atmosphere when we all came trooping in.'

'It was – but you didn't need to start making me the butt of your jokes. You of all people: you know what it's like being the new kid. Not easy, is it?'

She felt her throat tighten. That was a reference to when she'd joined the unit under DCI Wallace. Her boss who, it transpired, had done his best from the very start to make sure her career in the CTU never got the chance to even start. And all because he was racist. Probably a misogynist, too. 'I think that was a bit different.'

'Was it? I don't know . . . I mean, the odd whisper goes round, but I've never really heard what actually happened between him and you.'

She started gathering her things as quickly as she could. 'Yeah, well. It was different, OK?' Her voice was raw and she could feel a prickling in her eyes as it all started coming back. Damn it!

'So what did happen? Tell me.'

The tricks he'd played to turn opinion against her. She could see once again the little Blu Tack figure he'd fashioned of her. Its oversized head and tiny, pointy breasts. All her colleagues laughing as – afraid to appear like she couldn't take a joke – she placed it on top of her own monitor. She stood, bag in hand. 'It's not something I want to talk about.'

'Where are you going?'

'Home.'

'Iona?'

The softness in his voice drew her eyes back to his.

'I'm not accusing you of anything. Really I'm not. You under-stand that, don't you?'

With a single nod, she turned and made for the doors. She wanted him to know the truth. She wanted to describe how Wallace had dug out a newspaper clipping that mentioned the nickname from her school hockey team: The Baby-Faced Assassin. Only Wallace had pared it down to just Baby. The runt of the team. The token female, half-Pakistani, at that. Their little mascot, never to be taken seriously. Certainly never to be one of the team. Never confided in, relied on, accepted.

She was halfway across the car park when her phone started to ring. Martin's mobile. She toyed with ignoring it. But his parting comment had – what? Showed a little empathy? Perhaps she had misjudged him. Maybe he wasn't such a backstabber. 'Iona here.'

'Hey, listen, sorry if I upset you.'

'You didn't.'

'You seemed pretty pissed off when you shot out the door.'

She came to a stop. 'It wasn't you, all right? It's what you were talking about. It's still hard for me, you know, to deal with it.'

'OK, that's fair enough. I just wanted you to know that, from what I can gather, the bloke was an utter bastard to you.'

His words brought fresh tears to her eyes. Blinking them back, she sucked in a lungful of air. It was still night, but a bird was singing somewhere. A starling or something. Fooled by the perpetual dawn of the streetlights, the thing was warbling with all its might.

'Iona?'

'Yes.'

'You're still there?'

'Still here.' She closed her eyes. *And you don't know how much you saying that means.* 'See you bright and early.'

'You know, Iona, us two working together? I reckon we could make quite a team.'

The pair of binoculars trained on Iona from the darkened office building on the other side of the main road were lowered. 'I think that's Detective Constable Iona Khan.' The man traced his finger along the row of photo identities. 'She's in DCI Roebuck's team, reporting to Superintendent O'Dowd.'

The man in the Redskins baseball cap kept the lens of the camera on her. 'She's cutting the call. Did you get it?'

The matchbox-sized device concealed at the base of the perimeter fence of Orion House's main car park was no more than thirty feet from where Iona stood. While she'd been speaking, her mobile phone signal was being relayed to the TETRA scanner on a table in the back of the unlit office. Numbers flickered on the glowing panel on its side.

'We had long enough,' the man sitting beside it murmured. The apparatus he was gazing at had been made in America and was authorized for use only by its intelligence services and certain other countries it chose to equip.

A moment later, the encrypted signal had been cracked. 'We're in,' he announced. 'Her number and the one she was just connected to.'

After capturing the registration of the car the female detective unlocked, the man in the baseball cap turned round. 'Then let's hear what was being discussed.'

TWENTY-NINE

The headlights of Liam's car shone briefly through the kitchen windows as he swung on to Nina's drive. She immediately stubbed out her half-smoked Sobranie in an ashtray already crowded with filters. He'd rung ahead to say the visit had been a success – but only just. Her Dell had been in the old woman's flat which, fortunately, was on the ground floor; he'd been forced to escape through a window when someone had started knocking on the door.

Back in his car, he'd passed a police vehicle racing in the direction of the home. So he'd turned round and driven back past the house. His suspicions were correct: blue lights were flashing on the driveway and, even before the care home was out of sight, two more, unmarked, vehicles had raced up the short drive. It meant the police were closing in. They needed to get out of the country as fast as possible. He opened the kitchen door and walked towards her.

'Where've you been?' she hissed, snatching the laptop from his hands and placing it on the breakfast bar. It was hers. Absolutely no doubt about it. Her eyes lifted to the ceiling with relief.

He watched her as she breathed out, arms dangling limply at her sides, fingertips twitching minutely. Like she was tapped into another world, communicating with the gods. Finally her head turned to him and she smiled.

'You've done well, Liam. We're safe.'

'You wanted to know where I've been?' He shook his head. 'Driving through country lanes shitting myself. I nearly didn't come back, Nina. Nearly just did one. We're not safe. They've almost worked this out. I didn't know if they might already be here when I drove up the drive.' He felt a muscle in the corner of his mouth spasm and tried to turn it into a bleak smile. 'I did her as well, Nina.' He regarded the laptop as if some element of her lived on within the machine. The organ music. 'They can't catch me for this. I'll not die in prison.' His cheek muscle fluttered again and he pressed his thumb against it, crushing the flesh against his molars. 'I fucking won't.'

She stepped up to him, brushed his hand away from his face and gently cupped his cheek. Her thumb moved back and forth across the spot of skin that had taken on a life of its own. 'Do not worry. Everything is arranged.'

'What's happening with the flights?'

She lowered her hand to gesture at a stack of bags by the dining table, the holdall full of hair extensions balanced on the top. 'You need to pack some things. Not much; you won't need much. A plane is coming for us tomorrow at four, the private airfield out near Woodford.'

He looked out of the window. 'A private flight. You arranged that?'

She nodded. 'All the paperwork from the office I've put in the firepit by the patio. There are boxes of files there, too.' She opened the laptop and turned it on. The wallpaper image was different. She tried her password but it didn't work. How silly to think she could check the hard drive for the information that meant so much. She closed it. 'Burn this, too. Take a hammer to it, then burn it. Along with all the files. Everything.'

'What about the two in the cellar?'

She checked her watch. 'Madison needs to be at the airport in an hour. Her flight goes at seven fifteen. The ticket is for Beirut, but she'll be met at Istanbul. Chloe needs to come with us; she has no passport.'

Liam's top lip peeled back. 'Why bring her? Let's leave her. Lock the fucking cellar and leave her. She's baggage we don't need.'

Nina crossed her arms. 'We don't travel without that girl. The payment for her is our ticket out. No girl, no flight.'

He rubbed at his head. 'This isn't good. Me and you? It won't look strange. You're the VIP, I'm your minder. What's she? The maid?'

Nina looked at her watch then took keys from her pocket. 'She's coming. Now, I'll get Madison up here. You make sure she's on that flight then come straight back.'

She walked through to the utility room, unlocked the top door, went down the narrow steps, selected another key and opened up the second door into the basement. A suitcase was leaning against the wall. 'Madison, are you ready? Liam's here to take you to the airport!'

The two of them appeared in the lounge doorway. Madison, hair now in a short bob, looked self-conscious and apprehensive.

'Come, Madison. It's time to go.'

She turned and hugged her friend, arms grasping her tightly. 'I don't want to go on my own.'

'You'll be fine,' Chloe replied. 'Don't take the best room, you hear? I want the one with the biggest balcony and largest bed and—'

'Come on, we have no time!' Nina barked.

They broke their embrace and Madison wiped a tear from her eye. 'It won't be the same without you.'

Nina took in the girl's long, slender legs and high breasts. She would be popular, wherever she ended up. At least for the first few months. And Chloe? Nina suspected her journey would come to an end far, far more quickly. 'You'll be seeing each other in a few days. It's hardly worth saying goodbye. Now, Madison, we must go.'

At the bottom of the stairs, Madison reached back and gave Chloe's hand a last squeeze. With a tight-lipped smile, Nina closed the door and relocked it. Then she made a scooping movement with both hands. 'Up! Come on, we haven't got long.'

As soon as Liam's car was off the drive, she got her phone out. A male voice ordered her to wait. A couple of clicks later, he spoke.

'Tell me what's happening.'

'The laptop is here, in front of me.'

'It is the one?'

'Yes.'

'You are certain?'

'Yes. There's a scratch in the corner of the screen. It's mine.'

'Good. Now destroy it.'

'I will. And the first one? She's on her way.'

'Excellent. The second?'

'She's ready, too. We're both ready.'

'What about Khan, the policewoman?'

'I have an idea for her. The plane will need to be ready. It must happen fast.'

'You will need to move fast, Nina. The plane will wait for fifteen minutes only. Arranging this has cost me a lot of money. It leaves after those fifteen minutes whether you're there, or not.'

'Will . . .' She realized her voice had lifted. Nerves were making her sound shrill. She started again more slowly. 'Will you be there? Are you coming to get us? To get me?'

'You mean, will I be on the plane?'

'Yes.'

He laughed. 'Swooping in to your rescue, carrying you up and away into the clouds?'

She didn't know what to say. He used jokes like snake oil, to wriggle out of an answer.

'Nina, I'm coming to get you. Are you happy now?'

'Yes. Thank you. I . . . I'll need Liam.'

'Why?'

'To help carry them. Chloe is a large girl. The female detective is very small, but I cannot handle two people. Not on my own. Even getting them into the car.'

'Very well. But Liam does not come to the airfield. Arrangements are for one car to go airside and three females to go on board. You, the negress and that detective. I will have people ready to help get them on board. Liam must not still be with you by then.'

'OK.'

'And Nina? It's vital we have both of those girls. A very important client has been assured of Khan. Do you understand?'

Probably the Russian, she thought. The one with the enormous yacht. She wondered once again who was taking delivery of Chloe. 'Yes.'

THIRTY

Iona's legs felt like they were on remote control as she plodded back across the car park of Orion House. Watching one foot follow the other revived memories of doing her Duke of Edinburgh's Gold award. Her group had completed the fourth day of the expedition after a night when storms had lashed their tent from sunset to sunrise. Damp, cold and exhausted, she remembered urging her friends to keep going as they squelched along a sodden sheep trail that led to the final checkpoint.

As the side entrance of Orion House drew closer, she wondered where her life was going. Will I still be making my way into a building like this in five, ten, fifteen years' time? Dog-tired from the demands of an investigation that just doesn't let up? I'm twenty-six years old. Could I even do this stuff in my forties? Do I want to still be doing it in my forties? No. In my thirties? Not sure. She thought about her older sister, Fenella. At home with her kind husband and gorgeous twins. Preparing the little pair their mushy food. Shaking soft toys that played little tunes.

What about me? Her hand paused, door card ready. I want a baby at some point. Two. Even three. She knew the smile on her lips was twisted; it had come from self-pity. I don't even have a boyfriend. Not even close to one. Martin's face appeared in her head. She didn't want it to, it just did. He was smiling. Oh my God, she groaned to herself, swiping her card in the reader and yanking the door open. Get a bloody grip, you desperate cow.

Her phone went off. She fished it from her pocket, extending one foot behind her to stop the door from banging into her. Jim's name on the screen. That's all I need right now. For a moment she hesitated. Her conscience prodded her and she pressed green. 'Morning, Jim! You're up bright and early.'

'Yeah, and you. I'm on earlies. I went past your house and saw the car wasn't there.'

She wished he wouldn't do that. It wasn't exactly a detour on his part, but it still felt like he was checking up. 'Right.'

'Everything OK?'

'Knackered. But apart from that, yeah, I'm good, thanks.'

'Good.'

There was a pause. Iona felt herself wondering if this was a personal or professional call. She knew which she'd prefer it to be. 'So, what's up?'

'Oh, sorry. It's about the girl who died.'

Which one? she almost asked. The one you were investigating until we came along and snatched it from you? Or one of the others? 'Emily Dickinson?'

'Yeah. I've been going over the reports. Well,' his voice altered as an accusatory tone crept in, 'the parts people like me are allowed to view.'

She stepped back out of the door and it swung shut with a loud click. 'Jim, you know the score. It's not me going over things with the black pen.' She hoped he wasn't going to ask anything awkward; this was a work phone. All calls were recorded.

'Yeah, sorry. Only jealous.'

She blinked with surprise: the fact Jim had also applied to the CTU – and failed to get in – was a sensitive point, to say the least. Sometimes she wondered if it hadn't been the start of the end of their relationship. To hear him joking about it was a real turn up. 'Don't be. I can't remember the last time I had a proper night's sleep.'

He laughed. 'Listen, prime suspect in this is the Haziq character, right?'

She was still working out a response when he spoke again.

'Don't worry, we've been given his description, told he's pretty much the main priority. Him and the colleague, Khaldoon.'

She wondered whether to mention Liam Collins, but decided against it. 'Yeah, that's correct.'

'And you're also looking at him for the two other students, Philip Young and the Irish girl, Donaghue, wasn't it?'

'Yes – anyone who bought one of a batch of laptops that went missing from the office where him and Khaldoon worked.'

'CityPads?'

From the way he asked the question, Iona wondered if he was now pumping her for information. Fishing for details that didn't appear on the version of the report that had been circulated round the various divisions. She wished she had a copy of it to hand. 'Where are you going with this, Jim?'

'I don't know – just looking for threads, like we're supposed to do.'

Please don't, she thought. You haven't got enough information to do that. And besides, it's no longer your job. 'OK.'

'Emily Dickinson's laptop, the Dell. She had it in a carry case when it was taken from her. Same thing happened to Philip Young – is that correct? He was attacked and the Dell along with its carry case was—'

'Jim, I'll have to stop you there.' Her eyes wandered to the bland office block across the road. Half the units in it seemed permanently empty, judging by the lack of life in the place. 'You're asking me for details outside the Emily Dickinson murder.'

'Except they're not, are they? Outside her murder – not really.'

Now he sounded peevish. She hesitated. 'The murders appear to be the work of one person, yes.'

'Wow. Really? I'd have never thought that.'

'Come on, Jim. You know my hands are tied on this.'

'Oh, cheers. That's appreciated. Thanks, Iona.'

Great, she thought. Now he's moved on to sarcasm. Next it'll be straightforward bitterness. 'I'll check, OK? Find out what I'm permitted to tell you. I'll call you back.'

'Don't put yourself out on my part, please. I'd hate to think I'm inconveniencing you lot, trying to help get this guy caught. That would be inexcusable, wouldn't it?'

Bloody hell, now he's ranting. 'Give me a bit of time. I'll call you.'

'That's very good of you.' The line cut.

She held the phone away from her face to look at it. That, she thought, is why I couldn't live with you any longer. You can be such a complete arse.

Martin was still at the desk. As she weaved her way across the office she studied him for as long as she dared. He was slumped sideways, chin on one hand, gazing down at something. The posture gave him a boyish air, a kid yearning for the school bell so he could get outside and collect conkers. Or whatever boys liked to do. She wanted to ruffle his hair.

'How do you girls do it?'

She looked to her left. Sergeant Fairfield was in his seat grinning up at her. There was a cup of black coffee before him. 'Bugger all sleep, and do you look like shit? Nope.'

'Don't I? The bags under my eyes feel pretty bad.'

'Bags?' He scoffed. 'You haven't got bags. Want to see bags?' He pointed across his desk. 'Check out Taylor. His are more full than Victoria Beckham's on the way back from the Champs Élysées – or wherever the hell she does her shopping nowadays.'

'They don't live in Paris, you imbecile,' Taylor shot back. 'He doesn't even play for PSG anymore.'

'I imagine they keep an apartment there. It is, after all, so very la-dee-dah.' With both hands, he raised an imaginary handbag, shooting Iona a mischievous glance at the same time.

'Bitter blue,' Taylor retorted in a sing-song voice. 'Can't stand the fact Beckham played for United, can you? All the goals he scored for England – you should worship our David like the deity he is.'

'Rather eat soot,' Fairfield muttered, attention going back to the bacon roll next to his coffee.

Iona had taken three steps before Taylor spoke again.

'Rather take millions from some dodgy sheikh, try to buy success and still fail, you mean.'

'Children, children,' Iona called back. 'Not this early in the morning, please.'

As she took her seat, Martin looked up. 'Hey, I forgot to get a bloody paper on the way in.'

'Do you want one? I don't mind nipping back out . . .'

'Nah.' He shook his head. 'I don't think I'm ever going to make it as a professional Sudoku player. Time to accept it and move on.'

She smiled, wondering where the one from the previous day had gone. It didn't appear to be on his desk. 'Nothing back from the embassy in Islamabad, I suppose?'

He wrinkled his nose. 'The doctor said she had to sleep. Yeah, I thought. That would be nice, a bit of sleep. Who knows when we'll get anything out of her. Not until Hamilton and Baguley get there, I suppose.'

'And Collins?'

'The whole city is looking for him and Haziq.'

'So, what are you working on?'

'Oh, just the notes from the old people's home.'

A needle got her, right in the chest. 'Who . . .?' She felt her competitive side kicking in and checked herself. 'You're doing those?'

'Yeah, Roebuck asked me.'

She glanced across to the DCI's office. He was in there, reading through print-outs. A voice was going off in her head. Why wasn't I asked? Why didn't Roebuck give it to me? Martin's not even a proper member of the team. 'Let me know if you want any help.'

'Would you mind?'

'Course not.' She was about to add that it was always a good idea to have someone else check your work when he lifted his hands, forefingers extended.

'My two-fingered typing technique is shocking.'

She wondered if the twitch she felt was a mental one or if her head had actually moved. He's asking me to do his typing. Is he taking the mickey? Nothing in his eyes suggested he was. 'Really? I hadn't noticed.'

He picked up on the sarcasm in her voice and lifted an eyebrow. 'When did you learn to touch-type so well, anyway?'

'Lunchtime option at school.'

He shook his head. 'Swot.'

She pecked clumsily at the air, eyes crossed for added effect. When she refocused, he was looking at her with more than an amused expression. She looked down. She could feel the heat in her cheeks. Something just sparked, she thought. Or did I just imagine that? A nearby printer was whirring away. Someone was humming a tune. Noises seemed sharper. A phone was replaced too forcefully. It sounded like the plastic might have cracked. She was wondering if her blush had subsided enough for her to look up when a door opened and Sullivan's voice rang out.

'They just lifted Haziq! We got him, we fucking got him!'

People were rising out of their seats. Someone roared, 'You beauty!'

She looked at Martin but his back was turned to her as he applauded in the direction of the DCI. She should be standing, too. She got up and started to clap. But the movement felt jerky, unnatural. It's not him, a part of her said. He's not who we should be looking for.

THIRTY-ONE

The man in the baseball cap studied the back room wall. Stuck to the bare plaster was a cluster of photos. All had been shot from the window of the main office overlooking the car park of Orion House.

Iona was the latest addition. A Post-it note next to her listed her name, number of her mobile phone and car registration. Various other members of the investigating team had been similarly profiled, including DCIs Roebuck and Sullivan.

Further along the wall was another grouping of photos and scraps of paper, this one far more sparse. Next to a copy of Jade Cummings' photo was a newspaper photo of Teah Rice. Alongside that were two index cards marked Girl X and Girl Y. Another newspaper clipping, this one a report of Eamon Heslin's death, sat below them.

'Soup?' a voice whispered.

He turned to the doorway. There was a cup in the outstretched hand of the man who stood there. 'Thanks, Eli,' he replied softly.

The office that had been provided for them had a bathroom with a toilet and a small kitchen area equipped with a microwave and kettle. They were living on non-perishable foodstuffs, mainly tins, cans and packets. UHT milk for their muesli. Still, it was far better than scooping rations direct from foil wrappers, contents half-cooked by the relentless desert sun.

There was a rustling sound in the corner as the man whose turn it was to sleep moved in his sleeping bag. The man in the baseball cap took his soup then stepped from the room, carefully closing the door behind him.

'The female detective is leaving the main building, accompanied by a male,' announced a voice from beyond a sheet of dark netting which had been pinned to the ceiling a couple of metres back from the windows. A whirr and click as more photos were taken.

'Who is he?'

'Mid-to-late twenties, not sure of his name. They're heading towards her Micra . . . no, they've passed it. Continuing along – she's got a call on her mobile.'

The man in the baseball cap set his cup down and reached for the panel of the scanner on the table. 'She's number seven, right?'

The colleague who'd brought the soup checked a listing by the piece of equipment. 'Correct.'

Iona's number, pre-programmed in, appeared on the backlit screen and the speaker made a couple of muted ticking sounds as the machine patched in.

'. . . I didn't get back to you, Jim. It all just kicked off in there.'

'Yeah, how come?'

'We lifted Nirpal Haziq. Trying to access his own flat, can you believe?'

'Stroke of luck. Where's he being held?'

'On his way here, apparently. Though I'm not sure for how long.'

'Is he talking, yet?'

'No commenting it, so far.'

'Did he have any of the laptops with him?'

'Unfortunately, not.'

'So you still only have the one?'

'Possibly two. The remains of a Dell were recovered from Heslin's premises. But it's too damaged to say where it came from.'

'What are you up to now?'

'Heading out.'

'I can tell that. Where? Aren't you sticking around for the Haziq interview?'

'I should be so lucky. Us foot soldiers? They give us our orders and we follow them.'

'So where are they sending you?'

'There's plenty of other stuff needs wrapping up. The two missing girls, for a start. Who, where, when, how. We still need plenty of answers.'

'So they've got you doing that?'

'Yes. We're heading to a care home over in Heaton Chapel.'

'The laptop you've got – the one you think is probably Haziq's. I wanted to ask you—'

'Jim, I didn't have time to check what I could and couldn't share. Sorry. Let me speak to Roebuck when the opportunity comes up. I'll call you as soon as.'

'Iona, all I wanted to ask was—'

'Jim, I'm with a colleague. I'll call you back, OK?'

As soon as the call cut, the man in the baseball cap pointed to the backroom door. 'Move her details to Roebuck's, she's in his team.' He pressed a few buttons and the number Jim had been calling from came up. He noted it down on a fresh index card.

'They're stopping at a silver Audi, ending in CYP,' the voice by the window stated. 'He's unlocking it. Getting the full registration now.' The camera clicked again.

The man in the baseball cap took it off and tossed it to Eli. 'Follow them. Haim, you as well. See where they go!'

'Who was that?' Martin asked, reaching for his seatbelt.

'A sergeant with the City Centre division. He was on the Emily Dickinson case until . . .'

'We took over.'

'You guessed it.'

'But he's still sniffing about?'

Iona could anticipate the next question; why's he ringing you? 'I used to work with him when I was based in Bootle Street.' She shrugged. 'He wants to know what's going on. Can't blame him, either.'

'Suppose so.'

As the barrier lifted and they emerged on to the A635, she kept her head still, pretending to look at the road ahead while actually having a good nosey round his car. It was clean and smelled nice; an air freshener was tucked away somewhere. Not one of those cheap dangly ones with their cloying, floral reek. This was more like an essential oil. Something musky, sandalwood maybe. She liked it.

When Martin had offered to drive, Iona felt relieved. Doing his typing was one thing, and then driving him round – that would have raised all sorts of questions in her head – about his levels of arrogance, his willingness to use people. But he'd offered to drive.

A few CDs were lined up in a rack near the handbrake. Adele, of course. Amy Winehouse. Ella Fitzgerald. Janis Joplin. Nina Simone, even. He liked his female vocalists, then. And not the cheesy ones, either. Singers with a bit of oomph.

'Wonder how long before he rats out Khaldoon,' Martin said with a sideways glance.

On their way out of the office, all the talk had been about whether Nirpal would take the get-out that would be offered by whoever got to question him: Khaldoon was the leader, he'd organized the trafficking stuff; Collins was the violent one; Nirpal

had just been dragged in. It was obvious he was, at heart, a
decent guy. That was easy to see. He'd been led astray. Possibly
coerced by that nasty Khaldoon and Collins. He didn't deserve
to spend the rest of his life in a maximum security prison. The
chance of extradition to face detention in a far less savoury
country. Give us the full details about the other two and we'll
make sure the judge knows how you helped us, how you bitterly
regret getting mixed up in all this.

Iona hunched a shoulder. The bloke was being held under the
Terrorism Act. That meant there was no need to even charge him
with anything, not for twenty-eight days. It was a long time to
spend alone in a windowless cell.

'My money's on Wednesday morning. Three days and he'll
crack.'

'You went in on the sweepstake? I thought you had doubts
about him.' She tried to seek out his eyes, but he kept them on
the road.

'Well, once it went over two hundred quid, I thought it was
worth a punt.'

'What are the rules if you're all wrong? Do you get your
money back?'

Martin sniffed. 'You still think this guy's nothing to do
with it?'

'I certainly wasn't going to put any money on it being him.'
Within twenty minutes of Nirpal Haziq going into custody, the
investigation had been scaled down. Officers who'd been drafted
in from other units were swiftly sent back. Support workers were
being allocated other roles on different cases. It was touch and
go whether the two of them were staying together. But the pair
of missing girls needed to be traced. It was assumed Nirpal – or
Khaldoon or Collins once found – would supply that information;
but, in the meantime, officers would continue to visit the care
homes girls had absconded from.

It just wasn't being pursued with quite as much urgency. The
difference in O'Dowd's tone had left Iona seething. There'd been
a gloating look on his face as he'd announced the new arrangements. He thought the thing was all but cracked. Now it was just
a matter of tying up loose ends. Roebuck had even said that,
after they'd visited the care home, they were free to go home

for a few hours. Grab some sleep and be back in for a briefing at five that afternoon.

With a weak dawn trying to light the sky, they drove in silence round an almost empty M60. Sunday mornings, Iona thought. The near total lack of cars was a touch surreal. Slightly unsettling. Like everyone but them had been told of a killer virus.

As their turn off came up, Martin said casually, 'That Forced Marriage Unit. Nearly one thousand five hundred cases it dealt with in 2012. Didn't think it was so big, did you?'

An image of her father appeared in her mind. 'No.'

'It's a shocker. Imagine turning up for school. Just an empty desk where the kid sat. What's happened to so-and-so? Where is she? No one quite knowing. I wonder what the teachers tell the kids.'

Iona fiddled with the glove compartment catch, her father's face clearer in her mind. 'I'm sure an approach has been worked out in those cases.'

'Probably. I feel sorry for the poor girls. Shoved into a new life. Meet your new family. This is your husband. This is where you—'

'It's not just girls.' The words came out too fast. She felt his stare. 'My dad . . .' She took a breath in. I've never told this to anyone before, she thought, staring straight ahead.

'Your dad . . .?'

'He . . . the reason he came to Britain. I'm pretty sure it was to escape an arranged marriage back in Pakistan. It's never talked about, not openly. But . . . I think it was.'

'Really? Shit.'

He sounded genuinely taken aback. No stress on the words, not treating her sudden admission like a juicy morsel. Scandal fodder. She glanced right. His eyebrows were half-lifted. 'This isn't for the office, right?'

'Of course not,' he immediately responded. 'Christ, of course not. When did he move here, then?'

'Years ago. When he was about thirty. He's from quite a wealthy family, back in Pakistan. There's no contact now. Nothing. He arrived in Britain on his own. I think he fled – whether he was married, or about to be, I'm not sure.'

'And then he met your mum here.'

'Not in Manchester. Scotland. He ended up lecturing at

Glasgow University. She was working in the admin office. We moved down here when I was six.'

Martin tapped a finger against the steering wheel. 'Wasn't he something to do with hockey? Your nickname – that's what you were called in your hockey team.'

The Baby-Faced Assassin, Iona thought. 'It's how I got into Manchester High School – a sports scholarship.' Fond memories of the hours she spent mucking about with her dad came back. He used to take her along to the university's pitches after the students had finished training. Speed dribbling, controlled dribbling, Indian dribbling. They'd spend hours weaving through cones, spinning round them, shooting on the run, reverse passing. It was their time together. Dad and daughter. Fenella never showed any interest.

'Who did he play for?'

'Pakistan.' Saying the word used to make her feel uncomfortable. It had connotations among certain people in Britain, especially outside Glasgow in the late eighties. Her and Fenella had been the only non-white kids at their school. She'd heard all the paki jokes there were.

'The national team? Seriously?'

Saying Pakistan when it was about who her dad had played for felt completely different. She relished saying the word. It was so strong, it demanded to be said with pride. 'Yeah, he played in the 'eighty-four Olympic games. I used to wear his gold medal.'

Martin laughed. 'Until you won a few of your own, I'm guessing.'

She smiled. Her school team had cleared up in quite a few competitions. And she was top scorer: from the moment she was selected for the First Eleven. Small, slight and usually dismissed by other teams – until she started ghosting through their defence and slotting the ball into the net. 'What about you?'

She'd seen the notices in the kitchen about the five-a-side football team that played over at the Pits, a load of AstroTurf pitches near Ardwick. She'd spotted him a few times heading off with the others from the office, kit bags over their shoulders.

'I play a bit of football, but it's not serious. Though I was scouted once.' He puffed his chest before dramatically letting it fall. 'When I was nine. Reddish Rovers. Didn't pick me, though.'

She grinned in response. 'This is it – left here and it's at the end.'

They turned into a street lined on each side by large, detached houses that had all seen better days.

THIRTY-TWO

'Detectives Everington and Khan to see Diane Finnigan.'

'It's open, come in.'

The short hallway beyond ended at a second door, this one with a wire mesh window making most of its upper half. A woman, mid-thirties, dull brown hair tied back, was stepping out of a door further along the corridor. She was wearing jeans and a baggy cardigan that didn't quite hide her paunch.

Iona pulled the second door open. 'Diane?'

'Yes, come through, we can talk in my office.' She stepped back, out of sight.

'Big old place,' Martin murmured.

Iona glanced about. It was typical Victorian; high ceilings, wide stairway, ornate ceiling roses and huge skirting boards. The green fire exit sign and strip lighting were incongruous. 'Built for a wealthy cotton merchant, I should think,' she replied. 'Back in Manchester's heyday.'

They proceeded down the corridor, the clear plastic runner feeling sticky underfoot.

Diane was in her office, already sitting back at her desk. She had a weary look about her. Clearly, police visits were nothing new. 'You're here about the absconders,' she stated, pointing at two empty chairs. 'Madison Fisher and Chloe Shilling?'

'That's right,' Iona replied. 'Thanks for seeing us.'

'No, it's fine. I submitted a report to the police.'

'Yes.' Iona glanced at the whiteboard on the wall behind the woman. Staff rota, women's names except for one – Patrick Spencer. He had the green shifts, Mary had blue, Diane yellow, Justine red and Anna orange. 'And they've been missing now almost a week?'

Diane nodded. 'I rather think they're together, since they went missing at exactly the same time.'

'Have they ever gone off together before?' Martin asked, crossing his legs, sounding half-interested.

'Not to stay out all night. Chloe has a few times on her own. As a pair, they'd arrive back late, but they'd always turn up, eventually.'

'Where would Chloe say she'd been when she stayed out all night?' Iona asked.

'At a boyfriend's. Don't ask me who.'

'Chloe is seventeen?'

'Yes, that's right.'

Iona slid out the profile for Rihanna. Everything but the photo had been blanked out. 'Do you think this is her?'

'Oh my God,' Diane's hand was over her mouth. 'That's Chloe.'

Iona looked at Martin who was rapidly uncrossing his legs. 'You're certain?'

'Absolutely. That is Chloe Shilling.'

'Iona? Have you . . . ?'

She slid out Shandy's profile. 'And her?'

'Madison Fisher. Why are their photos on that . . . what is it? A form of some sort?'

Martin had his phone out. As he made the call, Iona returned the sheets to the folder. 'Stuart? Martin Everington. Can you get word to Roebuck or an equivalent rank; we have an ID for the two missing girls.'

Iona knew a team would soon arrive to take over. She sat forward. 'Would you describe the two of them as close friends?'

Diane's eyes didn't budge from the folder holding the two profiles. 'I suppose I would. They both go to the local school – walking to and from it together. But they'd go shopping together, too. Or looking round shops, at least. Saturdays in town.'

Iona pictured the girl gangs who'd hang around on Market Street or hover outside Burger King in Piccadilly Gardens. If there were ten girls, at least five would be speaking at any one time. Loud, breathless comments. Sometimes directed at one another, sometimes at nearby lads, sometimes into mobile phones. Voices always full of delight or disgust. Life one big drama.

'Chloe is more problematic,' Diane said, lowering her voice. 'She's been here the longest of any. We've had issues with her arriving back under the influence of alcohol on several occasions. Madison actually does quite well, academically, when she bothers to apply herself.'

'How many girls live here?'

'We can accommodate sixteen. We rarely dip below that number for long.'

'And these girls are sent to you by social services in the north-west?'

'Some are. We have contracts with several other boroughs, too. One in Birmingham, Islington, one in Leeds; those are our main ones.'

'Where are Chloe and Madison originally from?'

'Chloe's a local girl. Cheetham Hill, originally. Madison is from Derby.'

As Linda Bakowitz described, Iona thought. Stockport: preferred destination for the country's care home overspill.

'Where is everyone?' Martin piped up. 'Seems very quiet.'

'This early on a Sunday? Most will be in their rooms asleep. A few will be up, maybe doing their hair, make-up, perhaps even homework. You never know.'

'They all go to school, do they? I thought, you know, there'd be a few who are . . .'

Iona looked down, embarrassed by what Martin was implying.

'Excluded?' Diane said, a brittle edge to her words.

'Did either girl ever mention anything that gave you cause for concern?' Iona asked. 'Anything about a change of scene, here or abroad?'

'Certainly not to me.' Diane thought for a second. 'Actually, Jas is in the telly room. She's quite friendly with Chloe. Let me fetch her.' She scooted out of the office and down the corridor.

'They all go to school, do they?' Iona muttered. 'Nice one, Martin.'

He flicked a finger. 'Well, you know,' he whispered. 'I thought care home kids spent all day playing truant and going shoplifting. For glue.'

She shot him a look to check he wasn't being serious. To her relief, there was a sarcastic grin on his face.

'This is Jasmine.'

Iona looked round to see Diane ushering in a girl of about sixteen. She had thick hair that had been teased out to form a black cloud about her head. Her dark skin was dotted with small pimples. 'Hello, Jasmine.'

She nodded cautiously as Diane pulled a chair over from the wall. 'Jas, did Chloe or Madison mention anything to you about going abroad?'

'Like a holiday?' She had upper and lower braces. Purple blobs dotting her white teeth.

'Possibly. Or just to leave the country,' Iona said, keeping things as general as she could. 'Maybe a holiday with a couple of blokes they'd met. Or to earn money. Or to meet someone who'd contacted them. Anything, really.'

Jasmine picked at a thumbnail that held the remains of some red polish. 'Chloe was always going on about some scam. That was her thing, getting rich.'

'What kind of scams?'

'Rubbish stuff.'

Iona spotted the wary glance in Diane's direction.

'Jasmine, no one's interested in if she was breaking the law,' Iona stated. 'Isn't that right, Diane?'

'No,' Diane blustered, catching Iona's loaded look. 'We're more concerned about making sure she's safe.'

Jasmine picked at her nail again.

'She's been missing for a while,' Iona prompted. 'We're getting really worried about the complete lack of contact.'

'She said about getting cash one time. Like she was going to get loads.'

'Doing what?' Diane asked.

'It might have been a nightclub. The name was like a cocktail.'

Iona tilted her head encouragingly. 'How do you mean?'

'You know, Club Libra, like that.'

'Cuba Libra?' Martin corrected. 'That's a cocktail.'

'Not that. It was a name. Club something, I'm sure. Soda? That might have been it.'

'Club Soda,' repeated Iona. 'And this was in Manchester?'

'Don't know.'

'Had they both been offered a job there?'

'Don't know.'

'How did they hear about it?'

'Some woman they met in town, I think. She told them.'

'And she said it involved earning cash – they were going to earn cash?'

'Yeah, but Chloe always went on about finding ways to do that.'

'As opposed to trying hard and passing her exams,' Diane said pointedly, eyes on Jasmine.

The girl ignored the comment.

'And she didn't give you any hint where this place was?' Iona asked.

'Nope.'

'Ever hear Madison mention it?'

'We didn't talk.'

'OK. Club Soda. Thanks. We'll look into it.'

'By the way,' Diane announced. 'You should know Chloe has no passport. She's never been abroad.'

I know, Iona thought. Her profile mentioned it. Not wanting to reveal the fact, she looked back. 'And Madison?'

'She has. The last care home she was in took them to Holland, I think. A camping trip. Anyway, she has a passport.'

'Do you have it?'

'No – it would have been with her personal possessions. They have lockers.'

'But it's not now?'

'No. I checked to see if she'd cleared all her stuff. I couldn't see a passport.'

'OK,' Iona replied, making a mental note to get the team who took over to check with the Border Agency if a Madison Fisher had recently left the country.

THIRTY-THREE

The indicators on Martin's Audi flashed. He yawned. 'I am cream-crackered. You want a lift home? We don't need to be back in until five.'

She looked back at the care home. The team had arrived half an hour before, including a couple of officers from the Child Protection Unit. After briefing them on everything relevant, Iona and Martin had headed for the exit.

'And even then,' Martin added, 'there won't be much to type up – not with this lot now on it. You'll have it done in no time.'

Comments like that: even though he said them with a smile, she still couldn't make out if they indicated arrogance on his part. 'Suppose not.'

As they pulled out of the car park, Martin spoke again, face averted as he checked for oncoming traffic. 'Can I drop you off, then?'

Her mind fast-forwarded. Jo would have stayed over at her boyfriend's. Alice usually headed to her fiancé's place in Rochdale at the weekend. The house would be empty. She saw Martin's car pulling to a stop outside. Would he expect to come in for a coffee? She remembered the way he'd looked at her across their desks. Has he planned to be asked in for a coffee? 'Er, my car's at Orion House. I'll need it to get in later.'

'I could swing by and collect you. You're West Didsbury, aren't you?'

How did he know that? She didn't remember mentioning it. 'Yes.'

'Which road?'

'Fog Lane.'

'Well, I'm only East Didsbury. Going back to Ashton now will cost us a good hour, there and back.'

She sensed a set-up and hesitated. He'd already turned right. That was away from the M60 ring road that led them back to Ashton. 'OK, yeah.'

'Cool.'

They drove for a while in silence. The city was now stirring – dog-walkers or joggers the main signs of life.

'Club Soda,' she announced. 'Does that sound right to you?'

Martin shrugged. 'Sounds a bit cheesy, somehow. What's that old Wham! Song? The summer one – Club Tropicana, isn't it? Fun and sunshine for everyone?'

Iona smiled. 'And the drinks are free.'

'Maybe that's what makes the name seem cheesy to me.'

'No, you're right. Soda's an odd word, too, don't you reckon? American. They call fizzy drinks soda. Lemonade, Coke. What we call pop.'

'Doctor Pepper,' Martin drawled. 'Rank, that stuff is.'

'Strikes me as a bit young and girly. Club Soda: sparkling bubbles, froth, good times. Could be some sort of escort place.' She lifted her phone and went to the web browser. 'Club Soda, here you go. A type of fizzy water made by Canada Dry.' She scanned the entries further down. 'Bloody hell, it's the name of a nightclub.' She clicked on the site. Images of the club's interior glistened with reflected gold. 'Gross.' She turned the screen to Martin who took a quick glance.

He grimaced. 'More bling than Saddam Hussein's bathrooms. What does it say?'

Iona read out the text. 'Club Soda. An exclusive club for those with discerning tastes. Chartres Street, Beirut, Lebanon.'

'Lebanon? It's in Lebanon? Jesus, Iona. That girl blew up on the border of Lebanon, didn't she?'

Iona was nodding, a tingle racing up and down her arms.

'This has dodgy stamped all over it. What else does it say?'

She had already started working her way through the other sections. 'Membership costs on request. Isn't that polite-speak for saying, if you're bothered about prices, this isn't the right place for you?' She looked up and felt her lower abdomen tighten. They were on Fog Lane. Her house was just ahead. 'I'd better ring this in, in case they don't follow up on it straight away.'

'Definitely. Which number are you?'

'Fifty-four – it's a bit further along.' Her call was picked up by Stuart. She barely had time to relay the information to him before Martin slowed to a stop.

'What did he say?'

'Was taking it straight to an indexer.'

'Good. Well, here you go. Door to door.'

'Thanks.' The silence suddenly engulfed her. He seemed to be sitting there with an air of expectation. She stuffed the phone into her handbag then scrabbled to undo her seat belt. There was a click and the strap across his chest suddenly went slack. She'd hit the wrong button. Oh, no, that looks like I was – 'Wrong one. Shit. Sorry.'

The clip edged its way across his thigh then caught in the folds of material at his crotch. She threw her own seat belt off and grabbed at her door handle. 'Thanks, then. Shall we say four o'clock?'

'Four o'clock it is.' He was reinserting the clip, smiling as he did so. 'Sweet dreams.'

It sounded inappropriate, saying it to a colleague. 'See you later.'

She shut the door and scuttled up the front path, knowing her face had turned bright red. Nightmare! Total nightmare. And I swore. Oh God, I never swear. I was like a flustered schoolgirl and he just sat there, cool as anything. I made a total fool out of myself. Oh God. Oh God. She heard his car pulling away but couldn't bear to turn round.

The alarm gave its robotic protest as the front door opened. It sounded like something off a game show. Neee. Neee. Iona just failed. Neee. Neee.

'You can shut it,' she murmured, keying in the code to cut it dead. Silence. Emptiness. The chill of a house with no one in. The moment when his seat belt lost its tension was trying to nudge its way back into her mind. Would he have thought . . . A car revved outside and she hurried into the front room to peer through the net curtains on to the street. What if it was him coming back? What if he climbed out and knocked on the door? Would I let him in? I'd have to. But it was only a red saloon accelerating away. She glimpsed the rim of a baseball cap on the driver's head. Martin wouldn't have thought I deliberately undid his seat belt, would he? But scrabbling around and swearing; that was even more obvious. And he was smiling. Smiling!

There was a note on the kitchen table from Jo, a junior architect who worked for a big outfit in town.

Hi Iona, not seen much of you lately! Any chance you can leave a tenner? We stocked up on essentials the other day, receipt's in the jar. See you soon, doll. Me and you are way overdue a good catch-up over a cold bottle of SB. Love you.
XXXXX

Iona slid a ten-pound note from her purse, trying to work out the last time she'd had more than a quick cup of tea or slice of toast from the house supplies. It seemed like weeks.

Her bedroom felt cold as she kicked off her shoes. Flicking the fan heater on, she stood before it and let warm air wash across her feet. Once some feeling had returned, she drew the curtains and climbed into bed. Almost eight thirty. Seven and a half hours before he's back to pick me up. She set her mobile's alarm for half-three then lay down.

Club Soda. Was there a chance the place was involved? A tacky-looking club thousands of miles away? Jim's last call popped into her head. Christ, he'll be expecting me to have rung back by now. Khaldoon's sister. Awake by now? If not, they must have sedated her. Will Nirpal talk soon? Assuming he's anything to do with it. And I'm not sure he . . .

Opening her eyes, she immediately looked at the bedside clock. Great. One hour eighteen minutes of sleep. She stared at the ceiling. Something popped into my head, just now. It woke me up. What the hell was it? Jasmine. Something related to Jasmine. She said it was a woman who'd mentioned Club Soda to Chloe and Madison. Gangs sometimes used women to lure girls in for them. A trust thing. You just didn't think a fellow female would set you up like that. To be raped.

Iona clamped her eyelids together. That wasn't it. Think! It was something else . . . something to do with it not being a man. A woman. Her eyes snapped open. The CCTV. The woman in the footage when Teah Rice went off the motorway bridge. Why didn't she stay at the scene? She'd been speaking to the girl. Could she be the same woman who'd approached Chloe and Madison? The lure. Another thought hit home. One that made Iona sit up in the bed. What if Teah Rice was trying to get away from her? She had realized it was a trap . . . the promise of work in a foreign club . . . it was all lies. She was running away and the woman was actually trying to get her back.

Iona scrabbled out of bed and pulled the laptop out of her bag. Moments later, she was clicking on the CCTV footage once more. The woman in the Parka coat with its fur-lined hood was speaking to Teah. You could tell that from her hand movements. The occasional tilt of the hood. As if she was reasoning with her. Imploring her. But Teah just stared straight ahead. The woman took a step closer, her right hand stretching out. Teah's head moved. An almost imperceptible shake. A rebuttal, or refusal of some kind. The woman edged closer once more and Teah stepped out into space and was gone.

Iona continued to watch, all her focus now on the woman. You could tell she was shocked; she seemed to grow an inch as her back straightened and her shoulders stiffened. But then the hand went back into the pocket and she turned round. Her concern ended, like a switch had been flicked. She didn't check to see if Teah had survived the fall. She didn't ring the emergency services. She just strode out of shot, head bowed. She'd lost Teah. Too bad: it was time to move on. That's what her body language seemed to say.

The clip finished and Iona watched it all again. The narrative seemed to fit. It really did. She picked her mobile up and called the station, unsure of whom she should be speaking to.

Her call was transferred through to the incident room. This time, Euan picked up. 'Hey, I thought you were getting some zeds in?'

'I was, but something . . . I had a thought about the case.'

'A dog with a bloody bone, you are, Iona. One of them little fluffy terrier things. They might be cute to look at, but . . .'

'It's about the Teah Rice footage. Who's in?'

'I can put you through to Martin. He's at his desk.'

'Who? Martin Everington?'

'Yeah.'

Iona glanced at the curtains. She heard his car pulling away once more. The echo of his parting words. Sweet dreams. Was this his plan? 'When did he show up?'

'About an hour ago.'

Which meant he must have gone immediately to the office

after dropping me off. No way could he have gone home. And I can't get in because he persuaded me to leave my car and rely on him for a lift. She felt like she was in a chess game. One where she'd walked into a trap. Suddenly, the alignment of her opponent's pieces wasn't quite so innocuous. 'What's he doing?'

'Not being able to talk too loudly, for obvious reasons; he's working on something. When he first got here, he went into Sullivan's for a bit. Then he came back out . . . I thought it was a bit odd you weren't with him. I heard him saying to someone about you being at home getting your beauty sleep.'

Iona was closing her laptop and looking for her shoes. 'What's he doing right this second?'

'He's on the phone. Someone at the Forced Marriage Unit, I think.'

A stone hit the bottom of her stomach. And I trusted him. Worse, I confided in him about my dad and why he left Pakistan. 'Has word come from Islamabad, then? Has the younger sister talked?'

'Not that I know. But they got Khaldoon at a police checkpoint. He was on a bus on its way to a place called Wana, in Waziristan.'

Martin, in Iona's mind, had turned into a cartoon character. Fat wheels spinning as his souped-up buggy raced away. Eat my dust, you stupid woman. 'Where was this checkpoint? Islamabad?'

'A few hours outside. But that's where they're taking him, now.'

'I'm coming in. Thirty minutes, tops.'

'You want me to give Martin a shout?'

'No.'

'Shall I tell him you're on your way?'

'Euan? Don't tell him a bloody thing.'

'OK.'

'Cheers, Euan. See you in a bit.' She pressed red and darted off down the stairs. The local taxi number was on the fridge.

THIRTY-FOUR

Martin's eyes lifted for a moment then dropped. She hadn't completed her next stride before he looked back up. 'Iona.'

Confusion was now all over his face as she sat down at her desk and turned her computer on. He glanced at his watch. 'What are you doing here?'

'Working. You?'

He sat back. 'Yeah, working. Wasn't I coming to get you at four? How come . . .'

She kept her eyes on him as her screen flickered into life. 'I thought you were heading home after dropping me off?'

'I was.' A hand was directed at Sullivan's empty office. 'I was on the way when he called me. The FMU wanted a full report on the Khan family for when they interview Khaldoon. Muggins here got the job.' He held up a sheet partly covered by text. 'This is draft number three.'

Iona stared at the piece of paper. 'The FMU asked for that?'

'Something about next steps – gauging whether it's feasible for Sravanti to return to her family, once she's been repatriated. I've been trying to collate the parents' and siblings' interviews.' He cocked his head. 'How did you get in?'

Suddenly, the thirty quid she'd just blown on a taxi seemed foolish. 'Jumped in a cab.'

'A cab? Why did you get a cab?'

'How else was I going to get here? My car's here, remember?'

'You could have rung me. I'd have come and got you.'

'I thought you were in bed. Asleep.'

'Yeah, but I wouldn't have minded you calling me. If you had something worth rushing in for . . .' He looked at her again.

She could almost hear the thought striking the inside of his head. You'd decided to come in without me. And you were happy to pay for a cab to leave me out. She broke eye contact to adjust her mouse. Brilliant. Now I look like the sneaky one.

'Why have you come in so early?' He was staring at her now. His voice was guarded.

'It was . . . I'd nodded off. You know when something pings into your head – I had one of them. It woke me up.' She shrugged. 'Probably nothing.'

He was still staring. 'You want to tell me?'

She glanced at Sullivan's office. You idiot, Iona. You got this completely wrong. And now it looks like you're holding back on him. 'Of course. You know the CCTV footage of Teah Rice as she goes off that bridge?'

He nodded.

'The girl we spoke to in the Appleton House care home mentioned that Chloe Shilling had been approached by a woman in town. Do you recall?'

'Vaguely.'

'It was to do with the Club Soda place. This woman tipped them off about it.'

'Are you sure? I thought Chloe Shilling had loads of schemes for money-making.'

'She did, but Club Soda was the one the woman mentioned.'

He frowned, obviously not quite so convinced.

'So,' Iona pressed on. 'It occurred to me: what if the woman Chloe mentioned is the same one talking to Teah Rice in the CCTV footage? Some of these gangs – sex traffickers – they use a woman to lure the girls in. She convinces them there's nothing to worry about, that it's all good fun, the blokes are fine . . . she lays the trap.'

Martin sat up. 'This woman is approaching vulnerable girls, you mean? Selling them a story about making easy money in a nightclub? Something harmless – cocktail mixer, cloakroom attendant or whatever?'

'Exactly.'

His head turned and he sent an appraising look in the direction of his boss's empty office. 'Could be . . .'

Iona craned her head. The only DCI in his office appeared to be Roebuck. 'Where's Sullivan?'

'Up with O'Dowd. Helping him get his report ready. Apparently the Home Secretary contacted the chief directly. The Israelis want to know exactly what's going on and we've been told to give them what we have.'

'What? Everything?'

Martin nodded glumly. 'Seems so.'

'I thought we had until Monday morning before that happened,' Iona murmured.

'They moved the goalposts. The power of diplomatic pressure.'

Iona looked further to her left. Roebuck was in his office putting the phone down. We'll have to take it to my boss, not yours. Her flicker of triumph was instantly swamped by a wavelet of disgust. Why, she asked herself, must you always keep scores? The bit of her that would never shut up immediately fired back a reply: because everyone else is. 'What do you reckon, then? I thought we could try the children's unit, see if they have anything on known female groomers.'

Martin tapped a finger. 'I don't know. It depends on if the woman is the link to this Club Soda thing . . . and from that, you're making another connection to it being her in the Teah Rice footage. I thought that woman was a Good Samaritan.'

'Check the footage. The way she walks off without even calling for an ambulance is really odd. I think the body language indicates that Teah knew her. The conversation wasn't just, please don't do it. Life can't be that bad. It's deeper. She talks to Teah for maybe half a minute, reasoning with her. Honestly—'

'Did you two put a request in for an airport check? On Madison Fisher?'

Iona turned. Stuart Edwards was a couple of desks away, a sheet of paper in his hand.

'We briefed the team who took over,' she replied. 'They would have done.'

'Word from the Border Agency just came back.'

'Only just? When did the request go in?'

'After nine.'

She glanced at Martin; they sat on it for over an hour? That should have been one of the first things they did. Martin nodded back as he turned in his seat. 'And?'

'Departed Manchester this morning at seven fifteen.'

Iona felt the pulse in her neck quicken. 'Where to?'

'Turkish airways. A stop-over in Istanbul and then on to Beirut. Plane took off from Istanbul about half an hour ago.'

Iona shot a look at Martin. 'Club Soda, it's in Beirut.' She leaned forward and keyed the words in to Google. 'Here you go, Club Soda. An exclusive club for those with discerning tastes. Chartres Street, Beirut, Lebanon. We need to get word to Beirut airport – get her lifted the instant she comes off that plane.'

Martin came round the desks to look at the club's homepage once more. 'I don't get this.'

She couldn't understand his lack of urgency. 'Come on – the place is tacky beyond belief. It's a front.'

'Oh, I agree the decor is hideous. But a couple of the boys have been doing background checks.' He nodded to a pair of detectives working at the far end of the room. 'It's owned by an organisation with a string of places to their name. Casinos and hotels throughout the Middle East. A couple of holiday resorts. It all looks very above board.'

'Maybe on the surface. Roebuck needs to know about this.' As she started to stand, Stuart spoke again.

'Hang on.' He was still studying his print-out. 'She isn't en route to the Lebanon.'

Iona's head jerked in his direction. 'What's that?'

'She's not on the flight. Says here that her onward ticket wasn't processed.'

'Was the flight delayed, or something?'

He shook his head. 'She went through passport control in Istanbul over an hour ago.'

Iona sat down, her theory wobbling before her. 'But she left the UK.'

Martin sighed. 'Not with Chloe, though. Wasn't it Chloe who mentioned Club Soda?'

Iona nodded slowly, the buzz of adrenalin fading. 'Well . . . maybe they had to drive her there for some reason.'

'You know, Iona – this Club Soda place seems pretty legit to me.' He leaned past her to take control of the mouse. The arrow moved to a tab entitled Gallery and a new screen opened up. The row of thumbnails all had a label. 'Launch of the Emerald Palm Holiday Resort. Fashion show for a label I've never heard of. The birthday of Sheikh Kazan-something's daughter.'

Iona's legs suddenly felt tired. She sat back down.

Martin continued. 'It doesn't fit with a sex ring dealing in troubled girls from British care homes. I mean, why? It looks like one of the country's top venues.'

Iona pushed her hair back. 'Unless the club is being used as a story and, really, it has absolutely no connection to all this. Maybe the girls think it's where they're going – but end up somewhere completely different.' She searched Martin's face for any kind of agreement.

He gave a sad kind of grimace. 'Sorry, Iona. I'm struggling with this one. It would be good to know where the hell Madison Fisher is in Turkey, but Club Soda . . .'

I'm trying to make the facts fit my theory, Iona thought. Idiot! She'd been so sure she was on to something. A trail that would lead to the two missing girls. That's what comes of not enough sleep – your judgement starts to go.

'Everyone!'

She turned to see Roebuck standing in his office doorway. 'Nirpal Haziq has just commenced talking.'

The few officers who were in all started turning to the whiteboard in one corner.

'Two to half-two on Sunday afternoon,' someone said. 'Which lucky git picked that slot?'

THIRTY-FIVE

S moke rose into the pale November sky. Nina watched through the window as Liam threw on more files and sheaves of paper. He waited until the flames had engulfed them, too, then dropped the laptop into the middle of the pyre.

The weight of it caused fragments of ash and paper to swarm up, the larger ones soon abandoned by the updraft. They floated down to gently settle on the lawn. The similarity to falling snow took her back to the mining town from all those years ago.

As she turned away, her phone went. Unknown number. Him. 'Hello?'

'Is everything ready?'

'Almost.'

'The laptop – its contents . . .'

She glanced back at the window. 'Being burned right now. I can see the flames.' Liam was burying the machine beneath another layer of office records.

'And the female detective?'

'She's next. I'm making the call.' Her eyes lowered to the floor, to where Chloe waited. She'd told the girl to pack. 'As soon as the girl I have here's safely in the car, I'll ring the policewoman.'

'You must be at the airfield at four o'clock. Not arriving at four o'clock: you must be there at four o'clock, ready to go. Is that clear?'

She'd never heard him sound like this before. He was nervous. She suddenly felt afraid. 'I understand. We will be—'

'You must be there. It's . . . this is something . . .'

Now he was fumbling with his words. As if he was a schoolboy. She could hardly believe her ears.

'I will explain to you . . .' The reception faded, his words fragmenting into a disjointed buzz.

'I cannot hear.'

'Hello?' His voice was clear once more. 'I have made certain decisions. Ones that I now regret – but am unable to escape from. Zara. I am talking about Zara.'

Nina sagged against the worktop, felt the edge of it dig into her midriff. Zara: the name I gave to Jade Cummings. The girl who exploded at the checkpoint on the Israeli border. She closed her eyes.

'They want . . . the people who I am doing business with, they want this other British girl. I agreed it would be possible. Do you understand me?'

Chloe, Nina thought. Chloe is to carry a bomb for them. 'Yes.'

'We must get the one you have out of Britain and to these people. Then my obligations are fulfilled. I can – we can – start again somewhere new. As we were before, my jewel. Supplying the clients we know.'

'And the police detective? Where will she go?'

'To someone who uses girls only for pleasure.'

'The yacht?'

There was a pause. 'You are too perceptive. Yes, the yacht. Both women, Nina: we need both of them. The people I have

made arrangements with, they have other information. They told
me the Israelis are there – in Britain. Mossad. There is a team
of them there.'

She said nothing. They should never be in such danger. Why
had he placed them in such a position? He had always been so
good at business decisions. Now she was having to risk everything,
sacrifice everything she'd worked so hard for. Her eyes alighted
on the holdall stuffed with boxes of human hair. Madison's was
in there. A shade of yellow that delicate would get an excellent
price. One day, she thought, I will build up my business again.

'I will see you at four o'clock.'

She lifted her chin. He was coming! In person. She knew he
would. 'You will be there? You are on the plane?'

'Of course.'

His voice had that faint, metallic buzz once more. He's in the
air, she realized. A satellite phone.

'I will see you soon, OK?'

'OK.' She placed her mobile down as the back door opened
and Liam stepped through. Dark specks were stuck in his short
hair. His fingers were black. She was back again in the mining
town of Vorkuta. The line of men she had to service. They didn't
even wash their hands before grabbing at her flesh. Filthy fingered
animals.

'What?' He was looking at her with an uncomfortable
expression.

She smiled. 'Nothing. A memory, that's all.'

'It's done. The fire.'

'Yes, I saw. Thank you, Liam.'

'So we get Chloe into your car. Then what's next?'

'There is one more thing before we can go.'

'What's that?'

'I will ask for someone to come and see me.'

He looked nonplussed. 'Who?'

'Just a woman. Someone we're taking with us. When she
arrives, we need to subdue her. She must be with us on that
plane.' She reached into her pocket and took out the business
card Iona Khan had handed over to Martin Everington.

Liam stepped over and peered down at it. His eyes widened.
'Why are you ringing the fucking police?'

'Because the woman we need works for them.'

He laughed shrilly. 'That was a joke, yeah?'

'No.'

'We're kidnapping a policewoman? Is that what you're saying? Is it?'

She lowered the phone and stared at him contemptuously. 'How else do we start another life? Tell me. Do we earn our money picking fruit, maybe? Apricots and plums? Is that how we pay for a place by the beach? Will that buy us through the border so we just disappear?'

He raised both hands and pressed all his fingers into his temples. 'This is so, so fucked.'

'This is the last thing we do in this country, Liam. The money I know I can get for this particular woman – and it must be this woman – buys us a new start. Do you understand?'

He threw his hands at her. 'Fine. Let's fucking do it. Ring her. What's kidnapping a pig?' His voice was now wobbling with laughter. 'Add it to the queue of other stuff, do I give a shit?'

THIRTY-SIX

The tech room couldn't hold more than six people, so Alan Goss had set up his equipment on the table in a ground-floor meeting room.

Iona tried to get a clear view of what was going on, but every time the officers before her shifted, her sliver-thin view was lost. She considered asking to stand in front of them but decided that would be the sort of thing a child would ask. Worse, they'd probably stand aside for her with some comment that included the word baby.

'Right,' Alan resumed. 'We had this RAW file on the hard drive, if you recall. Completely unreadable – and no way of getting at it: not until Nirpal decided to tell us what would run it.'

Which he was happy to do, Iona thought, as soon as he got an inkling of exactly what he was being accused of. He'd gone very pale according to the officers observing the interview. He hadn't killed anyone. He knew nothing about what Khaldoon Khan was up to. He'd never heard of a Liam Collins. He certainly didn't know anything about a British national exploding at a checkpoint on the Israeli border.

'So,' Alan stated. 'I take the hard drive out of the laptop, insert it in the hard drive dock.'

Nirpal was claiming he had fled from CityPads because he thought they were there about his credit card fraud. That's all he'd done and the RAW file on the laptop would prove it.

Iona caught a fleeting glimpse of a black device with the letters, AKASA.

The IT guy had one hand lying on it as he spoke again. 'Then it's just a case of bringing in my old PlayStation from home and plugging that into the dock. Bingo, our RAW file reveals itself to be for a PlayStation. This tab?' He pointed at a little monitor. 'Nirpal's mystery file. The names, addresses and log-in details of several thousand PlayStation customers he'd managed to hack.'

A gruff voice spoke up from the other side of the room. 'Sneaky bastard.'

The shoulder blocking Iona's view shook as the officer laughed.

'Nothing else in there, as you can see,' Alan added.

'No profiles of girls?' Iona asked, fighting the urge to stand on her tiptoes.

'No.'

Assuming Goss was scrolling through the spreadsheet, she looked at Martin. 'Then he's just a scammer?'

He shrugged. 'Khaldoon Khan needed funds for whatever he's up to. They reckon Nirpal was providing them.'

Iona almost shook her head. It didn't make sense. 'Why would Khan steal – and then flog – his own money-man's laptop?' she whispered. 'Leaving Nirpal the focus of a huge manhunt, as a result?'

Martin shrugged again.

Iona knew the loft space of Nirpal's parents' house had been searched. There were several boxed smart phones and tablet devices up there which the parents could not explain. They did admit, however, that Nirpal regularly went up there to retrieve items he had no room to store at his flat.

'We need more on him than just a charge of credit card fraud,'

Roebuck said with a clap of his hands. 'The guy is neck-deep in this. He'll have a lock-up somewhere, a rented flat, a garage. We keep going at him. Khaldoon's due at a high security police station in Islamabad within the hour. I have a strong suspicion things will get a lot clearer then. Back to work, everyone.'

Iona moved away from the press of bodies heading for the door. Martin hung back beside her.

'You're not happy,' he murmured.

She watched her colleagues filing out. 'Haziq has never felt right for the murders.'

Martin sighed. 'Which is where Collins comes in.'

'Maybe. But not as part of a team with Haziq.'

'That's the theory they're running with. And we're in the wrong room.'

She thought about the Gold Command they were setting up along the corridor. People from MI5 and MI6 working alongside most of Sullivan's team, all focusing on Khaldoon Khan, Nirpal Haziq and Liam Collins as a terror cell.

They made their way out into the corridor. 'There's still Club Soda,' Iona stated.

'What about it?' Martin replied despondently.

'I still reckon there's something in it. The woman on that bridge. I don't know . . . it just seems odd, the whole encounter before Teah Rice jumped.'

'And you think the woman is also the person who approached Chloe Shilling with the promise of a well-paid job at Club Soda?'

She shrugged. 'Or am I just clutching at straws?'

He put his hands into his pockets and peered down at his feet. 'We haven't got much else to go at. Who do you want to take it to? Roebuck?'

She glanced at him. 'I don't mind. Whoever's free, I suppose. But it's us, Martin. We're a team on this.'

'Of course. But it should be Roebuck. You made the link, he's your boss.'

She stole another quick glance. 'It probably makes more sense. Roebuck's still got responsibility for the girls' disappearance.'

'Yeah, it makes sense.' He pushed open the door to the main office and ushered her through.

More desks of civilian support workers were empty. They've

scaled it back too soon in here, Iona thought. There's more to run with this. A lot more, I feel certain. And now we lack the resources to keep up. Roebuck was in his office, already talking on the phone. 'I'll catch him when he comes off.'

She sat down, spotted the call slip on her desk and groaned.

'What's up?' Martin asked, eyes hungrily sweeping Sullivan's office. Iona had already checked; he wasn't back down from the fourth floor, yet. She lifted the piece of paper. 'The Ice Maiden has rung. Wants me to nip out and see her.'

'Who?'

'Nina Dubianko.'

Martin's head turned. 'She rang? What about?'

He'd tried to sound casual, but Iona caught the interest in his voice.

'She's got some stuff about another client of Eamon Heslin. Needs to go through it in person.'

'And she asked specifically for you?'

There was no mistaking it: he sounded disappointed. It was showing, too, at the corners of his mouth. Nina hadn't asked to see him.

'That's what it says.'

'Oh.'

Such a simple word, but so loaded with feeling. It triggered a hollowness at the base of her throat. If he fancied me, she thought, he wouldn't look so gutted about her not asking to see him.

'And it has to be right now?' His head was bowed over his desk.

'Says it's urgent, yeah.' She keyed in the number and listened to it ring. The call was soon answered. 'Nina Dubianko? It's Detective Khan. You rang—'

The woman cut across her, speaking too fast. Her voice was more squeaky than she remembered. It had a whine of something that sounded close to alarm.

Iona listened to what she had to say.

'All right, madam, I understand. It's fine; if you only feel comfortable sharing this at your home, that's not a problem.'

Dubianko spoke again.

'I could be there within thirty minutes. OK. See you soon.' She cut the call and frowned.

'That sounded interesting,' Martin said, moving his keyboard closer to his monitor and starting to type laboriously with each forefinger.

She examined the slip of paper again as the slow click of his keyboard continued. 'Interesting and a bit strange,' she replied, thinking about how the woman's foreign accent had been showing through. She'd sounded tense and, at the same time, insistent. Maybe where her parents came from the police had time to make home visits whenever they were summonsed.

'Go on,' Martin said, busily stabbing at the keys.

He'll damage the micromesh, she thought, typing with that much force. She studied the top of his head. His shoulders were hunched as he hit the delete key several times in quick succession. Is he sulking? I think he is. One way to find out. She took a breath in. 'Why don't you go?'

He looked up. 'Mmm?'

She folded the piece of paper over and tossed it across the narrow crack dividing their desks. 'She probably only asked for me because it was my name on that card we left.'

She saw the look on his face: a kid on Christmas Day. She squashed down her own feelings of sadness. What were you thinking? A tall, statuesque blonde with pearly white teeth and sapphire eyes, or you? Who did you think he'd go for, given the choice?

'Seriously? What did she say?'

'It was about a client Heslin introduced her to once. A man who really creeped her out. She wouldn't say why.'

'And you want me to follow it up?' The typing was forgotten.

'I could sort out the FMU report miles quicker. And if Roebuck becomes free, I can collar him with the CCTV theory.'

He sat back. 'If you're sure . . .'

'It doesn't need two of us – and I think you'll enjoy feasting your eyes on the East European Goddess more than me.'

He gave her a rakish grin. 'Well, in terms of effective time management, it would be a more suitable arrangement.'

She nodded sagely, trying to look happy as she played along. 'Yes. I fully understand the professional nature of your decision.' Watching him eagerly grab his coat, her smile felt like it was painted on.

'I owe you, Iona.' He stood up and gave her a big wink.

She wanted to die. He winked! He actually winked at me. She waved a hand. 'Go on. Just try not to drool all over her nice carpet.'

He was now moving round the desk, one thumb directed at his computer. 'The document's on the screen . . . notes are all next to it . . .'

'That's fine. I'll see you in a bit.'

Once he'd gone, she stood up. That, she said to herself, is one to erase from the memory bank. Just count yourself lucky you didn't invite him in for a coffee. He would have looked at you like the lonely saddo you are. Her mind went to his wink and she shuddered. It had been dirty, lascivious. Like he fully expected the visit would lead to . . . she sat down in his seat. It was still warm. His buttocks. She saw Nina's long nails digging into them. Stop! She blinked the image away, focusing on the partial report displayed on the screen.

As Martin had said, it summarized the interviews conducted with Sravanti's parents and siblings. She skimmed over his notes; they were good. Succinct, to the point, no waffle. It seemed likely the daughter's fears were well-founded – the parents had been unwilling even to speak about the fact their son and daughter were over in Pakistan. But the interviewing team had managed to see the younger sister during school. According to her, the father had always been frank about his wish to see Sravanti married into a respectable family. The sister was afraid; she saw the same pressure beginning to bear on her. Iona thought about how her own father let her choose who she went out with.

The report was typed up within twenty minutes. Standing by the printer waiting for it to come out, Iona looked round the room. A group from DCI Palmer's team looked busy on something. The last civilian worker was clearing her place on the overspill desks. She carried a tray of print-outs over to Euan, who pointed to the stack on his side table. Iona wondered how many people were still working full-time on the missing girls. She was fairly sure no one from Sullivan's lot was still at the burned-out remains of Heslin's shop. There was the team assigned to the interviews over at the care home. Hamilton and Baguley would be asking questions out in Islamabad. Apart from that, she concluded, it's probably only me, Martin and Euan.

She wandered into Sullivan's empty office with Martin's report.

She had never set foot in it before. He had a picture frame by his phone. Not the usual wife or kids; it was Sullivan himself. He'd been snapped in a ski resort's mountain-top café. Aviator mirror shades and a big grin. It all spoke of ego to Iona. She glanced at the printed sheets in her hand. Should I just leave them on his desk? Presumably, the FMU people in Islamabad are waiting for the report. Best take it to Roebuck; he can sign if off and send it on. She was turning round when Sullivan's wastepaper basket caught her eye. A copy of the *Chronicle* was sticking out. She paused. It was open on the page with the Sudoku puzzle. Is that the one I helped Martin with? It looked like his green pen. He'd added a comment in the margin.

She checked the main office. No one was paying any attention. Bending forward, she lifted it out just enough to read the words: *10/10! She went for it BIG TIME.*

The paper dropped back. She straightened up and quickly walked out. The implications were sending ripples of nausea through her. It had been a ruse. He'd used the Sudoku puzzle to play her. She ran over the sequence of events. He bloody had! It was that simple thing – that request for help – that made me open up. The bastard. We agreed to make a fresh start after that, begin working together. And what has that led to? She looked at what was in her hand. Me doing his typing. Me being conveniently dropped off at my house. Me being edged to the side. Me being a complete and utter idiot.

She came to halt mid-step. Where had the whole Sudoku idea come from? Was it that initial interview with Philip Young? She continued towards her desk, remembering how she'd used the puzzle to get the student to relax. Did that mean O'Dowd was part of this? She imagined the man slipping a comment to Sullivan in one of their private meetings. Try Sudoku on her. She thinks she's an expert. That's the angle Martin needs to take with her. Trust me, it'll work a treat.

She sat down and took a couple of deep breaths. I could actually throw up right here. She considered her own waste-paper bin. I could. Right in there.

'You all right, sweetie?' Euan was looking over from his desk. 'Someone walked over your grave?'

She managed a tight smile. 'Just realized something, that's

all.' She checked her boss's office. He'd gone. 'Euan, do you know where Roebuck is?'

'Upstairs. With Sullivan, holding O'Dowd's hand as he updates the CC.'

Of course, she thought. Reporting all our latest findings so the Israelis are kept happy. Prove that we're making progress. 'I've just got this report – it's for the FMU guy over in Islamabad.'

'Oh – that's to go straight away. Are you OK sending it? Contact details are on Martin's desk. I am snowed under here.'

'Of course.' She walked round to Martin's side and looked at his empty chair. It still held the imprint of his arse. She didn't sit down.

THIRTY-SEVEN

'That's right, activity levels have dropped.' He plucked a stray thread hanging from the rim of his baseball cap. 'I'd say by, perhaps, thirty per cent. Purely from traffic coming and going.'

'That would fit.'

The voice at the other end of the line had sounded confident. 'Why do you say that?'

'We're just receiving an update. This has all come from up there, where you are.'

'And?'

'They've got Nirpal Haziq in custody. He's being held in Orion House.'

The man with the baseball cap looked at the anonymous building across the road. 'OK.'

'The sister of Khaldoon Khan was picked up in a hotel in Islamabad by people from the Forced Marriage Unit some twelve hours ago.'

The man lifted his head. 'And Khaldoon?'

'Yes. The Pakistani police got him at a road check. He was heading into Waziristan.'

'Is he alive?'

'As we understand, yes. He's being transferred to the Federal Investigation Agency and is due at their headquarters any minute. A team from the CTU and officials from the British Embassy are waiting to question him; we're pressing for an immediate update.'

'But he's in the custody of the Federal Investigation Agency?'

'Yes.'

He leaned back. 'So that's it. They will learn everything very quickly. He will talk.'

'We think it's all bullshit. They are not part of this.'

'Who isn't?'

'Khaldoon Khan. Certainly Nirpal Haziq. They aren't connected to the girl who took out the checkpoint.'

'I don't understand. Khaldoon was trying to get into Wazir—'

'Where he has relatives. We have a source in there now, on the ground. The story is good. It was a marriage, so forget Khaldoon. Teah Rice came from a care home. We believe how she was recruited links—'

The man with the pair of binoculars trained on Orion House announced, 'Car preparing to leave the compound now.'

'One second,' the man in the baseball cap said into the phone. He looked out of the window. 'Registration?'

'It's the Audi ending in CYP. He's just unlocking it.'

Another voice spoke out from the back of the office. 'The one that visited the care home earlier. Detective Sergeant Everington and Detective Constable Khan.'

The voice at the other end of the phone cut in. 'Stick with those two detectives! Did you copy?'

The man with the baseball cap waved his free hand. 'Eli, Haim, go. The Audi, keep with it.'

The man with the binoculars spoke again. 'It's only Everington. He's alone.'

'It doesn't matter,' the voice on the phone buzzed. 'You follow that vehicle and, if the female detective leaves, you follow her. They are your priority.'

By the time he'd got Chloe to the front door, Liam's breath was jagged. The girl's unconscious body pressed down on his shoulder. He kept his left arm clamped round her thighs as he manoeuvred her through the doorway.

'Are you OK, can I take her legs?' Nina hovered anxiously on the top step. 'She is heavy, isn't she?'

'Put it this way,' Liam replied through gritted teeth. 'I wish you hadn't slipped her the special pill down in the cellar.' He shuffled forward, a limp forearm gently banging against his waist with each step.

Nina's white Range Rover had been reversed back as far as it would go. The rear hatch was open and the tailboard lowered. He walked sideways down the set of steps and roughly deposited her slack form on to the edge of the boot. A layer of blankets had been arranged behind her.

'Fuck me,' he gasped, shrugging her off his shoulders. Nina held the girl's head as she fell back into the vehicle. Liam then grabbed both ankles, folded her legs in and stepped back. 'Like shifting a sack of wet cement, that was.'

Nina's lips were curled. 'She has been living like a pig, eating and eating . . . all she was interested in was eating.'

'Lots to hold on to there.' He extended a hand and slapped the girl's curving thigh a couple of times. 'Solid, that.'

'Push the legs further across, can you? We need room for the little detective.'

Liam did as asked, raised the tailgate, then reached up for the hatch and lowered it. 'When's this copper coming?'

'Soon. Move the car out of the way and I'll get the kitchen ready.' She hurried inside and paused just out of sight. Once the Range Rover's engine started, she checked her coat hanging by the door. The fur lining its hood was real fox, its padded panels filled with goose down. The thickness of it meant that nothing in the inner pockets showed up. She slid a hand inside and made sure the snub-nosed pistol was still hidden there. Many years ago, he had taught her how to use it. She had kept it safely wrapped in an oiled cloth ever since. Earlier that day, she had slid a full clip of bullets up into the stock.

THIRTY-EIGHT

Iona's mobile went and she answered it without checking the screen. 'Detective Khan.'

'Yeah, it's me.'

Her heart sank. Jim. Why didn't I look to see who was calling, first? 'Jim – hi.' He'll want answers about Teresa Donaghue. 'I'm really sorry, Jim – things have only just calmed down. I'm sitting outside Roebuck's now, waiting for him to come out of a meeting. Then I was going to call you.' She winced at her lie.

'Right. Thought you'd forgotten.'

'No. Not at all. It's just . . . you know how it gets sometimes.'

'The bag that Donaghue had for her laptop. It was nylon, says here. Made by a company called Binto.'

'That's on the notes you've been given?' She instantly regretted the comment.

'It is.' His petulant tone was back. 'Approved for general consumption, including us mere plodders.'

'Sorry, Jim. I didn't mean—'

'Looking through the reports, all the laptops taken from CityPads appear to have been in nylon bags made by Binto.'

'No – not all. Nirpal Haziq used a leather carry case for his. He's admitted the laptop is his, Jim. There's no question of that.'

'I know, I just saw the update. But he has only admitted the laptop was his. My question is: why would he be the only one from that company using a leather carry case, made by Dell?'

'I don't know. He wanted something flashier. One that would go with his suit?'

'What about this: that carry case wasn't with his laptop. Not when Khaldoon Khan sold it to Eamon Heslin. When it was sold to Heslin, it was in a Binto carry case, same as all the other ones from CityPads. The leather carry case was only put with Haziq's laptop when Heslin sold it on to Philip Young.'

Iona had the sudden urge to swallow. Her throat had gone

completely dry. 'The profiles in the carry case. You're saying they have nothing to do with Khaldoon Khan or Nirpal Haziq.'

'Why would they, if the carry case came from somewhere completely different? It's just a theory; it's the bag that's the key to who's killing the girls. They're after the carry case because they know it contains the profiles.'

'Oh my God, Jim.'

'What?'

'Nirpal's laptop. It had a locked-out bit of memory. IT just got into it; there's nothing there apart from stolen credit card details. No girl's profiles. None.' She checked Roebuck's office again. Empty, still. How long did it take to deliver their update on the latest findings? Or maybe he was in the new incident room. 'Jim, if what you're saying is right – and, believe me, it feels right – the entire investigation so far is screwed.'

'Hey, hey, hey, one for the thickoids in uniform. Do mention me when you hand this in, won't you?'

'Jim, I feel awful. I'm going to make damn sure, don't you worry.'

'I was only joking. You take it, Iona. It'll do your career far more good than mine. I'm going nowhere.'

'Don't be ridiculous, Jim. Listen, I'm going to check this with Nirpal Haziq. We've got him downstairs. I'll ring you right back, I promise.'

Nirpal's head came up as Iona stepped into the room. He'd been left to stew, just a plastic cup of water for company. He looked her up and down, clearly surprised by her appearance.

'DC Khan.' She took a chair on the other side of the table and looked him in the face.

His eyes cut to the CCTV camera mounted in the ceiling. Then he looked at the two-way mirror in the wall to his side. 'So you've checked out the laptop, yeah? You found the credit card numbers?'

'Nirpal. What type of carry case did you have for that laptop?'

'You what?'

'The carry case. What type did you have?'

He looked at the mirror, more concerned at who might be behind that. 'Listen, I didn't have anything to do with the murders! I never met Liam Collins. I'm a thief, all right? You got that on your tape? I'm a thief, I admit it.'

'Nirpal, answer my question, please.'

He flicked a hand in her direction, shaking the chain that ran from the table through the handcuffs attached to his wrists. 'I'm not talking to you, little lady.'

She stared at him, counting to ten in her head. It was a technique Jim had taught her: the power of silence.

By seven, he glanced back at her, face sullen. 'Fucking what?'

'You're not talking to me.'

He jutted his chin. ''S'right. You can hear properly. Well done. Now send in the other guys; I told them the truth about—'

'Would you talk to Mossad?' That got his attention. She kept her voice very low. 'You know who Mossad are, right? Good. They're here, in the building. They want you. They believe you are a terrorist. Not just the killer of a few students. You're a recruiter for al-Qaeda. A money man. They want you extradited. Will you refuse to talk to them over in Israel? When you're down in the basement of some detention facility that doesn't officially exist?'

She sat back and started counting to ten once more. She got to three.

'A red nylon carry case. Made by Binto. This is all . . .' He sat forward and tried to wrap his arms round his stomach. The chain clinked as it tightened. 'Jesus, I'm scared.'

'Was that laptop ever transported by you in any other type of carry case?'

'No.'

'Did you ever see any other type of carry case in the office at CityPads?'

'No.'

'Did you ever see Khaldoon Khan using any other type of carry case?'

His head shook.

'Any employee at CityPads?'

'No. We all had the same ones, all right?'

Martin parked in front of Nina Dubianko's house. The white Range Rover was tucked away by the side of the garage. As he started to climb the front steps, the door opened and she stepped out.

She was wearing a pencil line skirt and a silky blouse. The material rippled at chest height and he had to make a conscious effort not to look down. Her blonde hair was tied back tight. She looked businesslike. Powerful.

'Where's Detective Khan?'

Martin's step slowed. His hand was half-outstretched. She didn't seem to even be aware of it. 'Busy, I'm afraid. I came with Detective Khan on the previous visit.'

'I remember you.' Her eyes were searching his car. 'I asked for her.'

He let his hand drop. 'Miss Dubianko, we work as a team.'

Her higher position made it feel like she was looking down her nose at him. It was plainly obvious she didn't want him here. Maybe the information was of an embarrassing or humiliating nature. Something she only wanted to share with a fellow female. He tried to sound sympathetic and warm. Like a doctor. 'Whatever information you have, it can be delivered to me.'

She thought for a second or two then looked at her watch.

As she did so, he glanced at her breasts. Both nipples were pressing against the thin material. 'Miss Dubianko, shall we go into the house?' He stepped closer. 'It's cold out here.'

Abruptly, she turned on her heel, stepped inside and set off down a corridor towards the kitchen. 'I have an appointment; this must be brief.'

'That's absolutely fine.' He took out a notebook and pen. A line of bags were in the hallway. 'You have information on another client of Eamon Heslin?'

'Yes.' She gestured to a chair that had been placed away from the dining table, near to a side door. 'Sit.'

He obeyed her. 'Off on holiday?'

She glanced across, cigarette already in her fingers. 'Sorry?'

'The luggage in the hallway. Holiday?'

'Oh. That. Yes – a short break.'

Martin sat back, crossed his legs and gave her his friendliest grin. 'Where are you going? A bit of winter sun, maybe?' He could picture her in a swimsuit. One of those high-cut, plunging ones to show off her breasts and legs. Oh, yes. He could see her in one of those. Dripping with water from the pool. She lit her cigarette and he saw that her fingers were shaking ever so slightly.

'This person who came to see Eamon.' She took a long drag.

Martin scrabbled for his pen, not ready to take notes.

'He has some business in the city. Restaurants.'

'What kind?'

'They are Turkish. That is where he is from. He, I felt, was not an honest—'

Martin caught a tiny shift of her eyes to just beyond his shoulder. They'd widened fractionally: a warning look. He twisted round. The door directly behind him was closing. A man was closing the door. Martin saw his face. Recognition sparked. Who the hell? He started to stand. 'Sir, if you'd like to step out . . .'

The door suddenly swung back and the man burst through. The gap between them closed in an instant and Martin felt the dining table slam into his back. Liam Collins. It's Liam fucking Collins. A fist came down and Martin's vision ballooned into red. Another impact. Martin could feel his ears were being gripped. Another impact. He's smashing my head against— Another impact. He could feel the man's breath blasting his face. He gripped his pen in a fist and jabbed it up as hard as he could, directly at where the breath was coming from.

The pressure on his ears released. He shoved at the weight pinning him down with his arms and knees. He was beginning to see again. Liam Collins was half on the table. He was pulling the biro out from under his chin. A lot of blood followed it. Nina Dubianko was a shadowy form running for the door.

'Call the police,' Martin gasped, regaining his feet and trying to blink his vision clear. He groped for a chair and had begun to lift it when Liam launched himself again. They both crashed to the floor. Martin felt the chair splintering beneath him. A sharp, white pain lanced his kidneys.

He tried to get a hand up under Liam's chin so he could force the man's head back. Drops of blood were landing in his face and across his chest. He dug his middle finger into the man's throat wound. Liam was snarling. Blood caused Martin's grip to suddenly slip and Liam was able to duck his face down. He opened his mouth, clamped his teeth on Martin's ear and started wrestling his head from side-to-side.

Martin grabbed again at Liam's face, fingers searching for his eyes. They were scrunched too tight. He tried to find the throat wound again but the man's head was moving about too much.

Martin felt the tip of his ear starting to rip. He heard it. He got fingers into Liam's nostrils and pulled with all his might.

Nina walked briskly back into the kitchen. The two men were locked together, faces pressed tight. Martin's hips were bucking up and down. It looked sexual. She put the barrel of the gun against the base of Liam's skull and fired. He was grunting and rigid one moment, floppy the next. A lot of stuff flew out the front of his face and into Martin's. Fleshy lumps that glistened wetly.

Martin's eyes were closed. He was gasping out the corner of his mouth as he tried to shift the slack body off him. She altered the aim of the gun and fired three times into his face.

Iona's hand was on the door handle of Roebuck's office when she realized it was still empty. She looked around. A smattering of officers on the far side of the room. No sign of the office manager. Highest rank appeared to be a sergeant who used to serve in Wallace's team; he only ever glared at her or ignored her completely. At least Euan was in his corner, looking badly in need of sleep.

'Is Roebuck still upstairs?'

'He is,' he yawned. 'He did come down about five minutes ago, then his phone went and he shot up there again.'

'Shit.'

'Iona! Not like you to swear. What's up?'

She gestured weakly at the floor. 'Something about the stolen laptops. Any word from Islamabad?'

'Not sure; maybe that's why Roebuck shot back upstairs.'

'Sullivan also there?'

'I believe so.'

She surveyed the room again, unsure who to approach. Euan had turned back to the landslide of paperwork covering his desk. She returned to her own. The only people she could think of to ring were Jim and Martin. Jim could wait for his good news until later. Right now, she needed to alert her colleagues about what Jim had figured out. Martin was her logical first call. He was, after all, the senior rank in their supposed partnership. She hesitated. Would he try and fob her off? Maybe stall things long enough for him to get back and double check what she was asserting? Probably; that would allow him to be alongside her as they reported the discovery. She scolded herself; this was no time for petty point-scoring. The entire investigation had been fatally flawed. She needed all the back-up she could muster if she wanted to be taken seriously.

His phone rang through to his recorded message. She couldn't believe it.

'Martin, it's Iona. Call me the second you get this. I mean the second. It's vital you do, OK? Bye.'

She placed her handset on the table and looked once more at Roebuck's deserted office. This was ridiculous. Do I just head up there and knock on O'Dowd's door? No. They could be on the phone to the chief. It could be a conference call, the Home Secretary patched through from London. She checked the time. Ten past three. What the hell should I do?'

'Gunshot. I just heard a gunsh— another one, two, three.'

'From where?'

'Inside the house.'

'Visual contact?'

'Negative. This bush extends round to the rear of the property. I'm moving to my left. There's a barbecue on the back patio. Smoke's coming from that. I can see a female! She's in the kitchen. One body on the floor – no, two. I repeat, two. Lying on the kitchen floor. She has a gun in her right hand.'

'What's she doing?'

'Smoking.'

'Smoking?'

'Standing there, smoking and looking down at them. One might be the detective, I can see an arm. He's wearing a dark blue jacket. I think it's him.'

'She's taken out a detective?'

'Her or the other person did. No one is moving – wait. She is, now. She's left the room. What shall I do?'

'Can you confirm identity of the detective?'

'Negative. Not from this position.'

'Can you get closer?'

'Not without breaking cover. There's twenty metres of lawn between me and the house.'

'Understood. But we need to know what's—'

'I can see daylight. She's at the other side of the house. The front door is open. She's got . . . bags. She's moving bags outside. On to the front steps, the car is parked out there.'

'You mean luggage?'

'Yes.'

'Identify the bodies while she's doing that. Go.'

The Mossad agent emerged from the rhododendron bush and sprinted across the swathe of grass, phone in one hand, a gun in the other, barrel directed at the ground. He sank into a crouch against the back wall of the house. 'A lot of ash in that barbecue thing. Possibly the casing of a laptop, too.' He peeped in at the base of the patio window. 'It's him. The male detective.'

'Martin Everington?'

'Yes. Unknown male lying partially across him. I'd say she did them both while they were struggling. Head shots.'

'Follow the female, Eli. She's key to this.'

'Follow the female?'

'Correct.'

'These two in the kitchen?'

'Nothing to do with us.'

THIRTY-NINE

Iona's call was answered on the phone's third ring. 'Nina Dubianko? It's Detective Khan. You rang and left me a message a bit earlier. Hello? Are you there?'

'Yes.'

Iona heard the other woman making a small panting noise. She looked at Martin's empty seat. 'Sorry, is this a good time?'

'No. I mean, yes. Well, I am in kind of a hurry.'

'I understand, Miss Dubianko. I won't keep you. Has the other detective called by? The one I was with when we visited you before?'

'Who?'

'Detective Everington.'

'Everington?'

'Has he been to see you?'

'No. I thought you were coming to see me. You said you'd be here by now.'

The woman sounded flustered. Slightly out of breath. Iona had a sudden vision of her straddling Martin, looking down at him as he mouthed up at her, I'm not here, I'm not here . . . 'I . . . it wasn't possible. He hasn't been?'

'No.'

The single word answer sounded strained. Something was going on at the other end of the line. Iona closed her eyes. Please, Martin, do not be . . . coupling with this woman. Not now. Not at this very moment. 'It sounds like I'm disturbing you.'

'No. It's OK.' She let out a little breath. 'I am moving some stock to my car, that is all. I have a business appointment I must get to. There.' Her voice relaxed a notch. 'It's done.'

'OK,' Iona continued uncertainly. 'Would you mind asking Detective Everington to call me if he arrives before you set off.'

'I am leaving now. In the next few minutes.'

'Oh, right . . .'

'Detective Khan. I know something. I think it's important.'

'Yes, you said.' She used the pen in her hand to sweep back a strand of her fringe. 'Would you like to tell me?'

'Yes.'

'OK. I'm listening.'

'Not over the phone.'

'Sorry?'

'This client of Eamon Heslin. I am not comfortable saying more about him over the phone.'

Iona frowned. Was the woman trying to suggest her phone – or house – had been bugged? Surely not. Unless the client was some kind of IT type. 'You believe this individual could represent some kind of threat to you?'

'Yes.'

'A physical threat?'

'He . . . I have heard rumours. About him and women. Can we meet? Please?'

There was something about how she was speaking. You don't sound that on edge for no reason. You know something vital to this investigation, Iona thought, whether you realize it or not. 'Of course, Miss Dubianko. If that's what you'd prefer.'

'Yes, it is. Can you come and meet me now?'

'Now?' She looked across at Roebuck's office. How long before he reappeared? Probably long enough to nip out and see this Nina woman. 'Where? At your house? Because my colleague is due there any minute.'

'No – I have to go to this appointment now. But you could meet me there. It's not far.'

Iona delayed her reply. A part of her was screaming: if the black leather carry case is connected to this client that Nina knows about, you could be walking back in here with all the answers. 'Where would that be?'

'Woodford. Near Bramhall. There's a Holiday Inn, by the side of the Manchester Airport Eastern Link Road.'

'I know it,' Iona replied, calculating travel times. 'I could be there in about twenty minutes.'

'That would be perfect. Shall we say the car park of the Holiday Inn at twenty to four? I'll be in a white Range Rover.'

Don't I know it, thought Iona. 'See you there.'

She swivelled round and reached for her jacket. 'Euan? If Roebuck reappears can you get him to call me? Or Martin Everington, for that matter. I'm just heading out. Should be back in an hour.'

Halfway to the door, she came to a stop. Car. It's at my house. She wanted to stamp her foot. Keys to the pool cars were kept in a little wall cabinet behind the office manager's desk. She reached in and unhooked the nearest ones.

The moment Iona's call ended, the man in the baseball cap stood. 'Tal, let's go.'

The voice came back at him through the black netting. 'We're terminating observations?'

'This is it, Tal. It's happening right now. Target is the woman Khan just spoke to. Come on!'

His colleague hurriedly placed the camera on the floor and slipped under the sheet of dark material. 'We're following Khan?'

'Yes. She's going to meet the woman calling herself Dubianko. Eli and Haim are following her.'

The other man was checking the wall display in the rear office. 'Red Micra.'

The man in the baseball cap was already making for the door.
'I know. Registration starts MY09.'

FORTY

Iona tried Martin's phone twice more on the way round the
M60. Answerphone. What was he playing at? Ignoring work
calls like that: if Sullivan had been unable to get hold of him,
he would find himself in serious trouble. Then again, he'd probably answer a call from his boss in a flash.

The Renault felt quite good once she got it into fifth. It was one
of those people carriers. Pale green exterior, grey interior. As it
sped along in the fast lane, she mulled over the situation. Could
Nina and Martin really have been . . . Would Martin be so unpro-
fessional? Would Nina? She was hurrying to a business appointment,
after all. She wouldn't even have had time to shower. Iona grimaced.

Nina had been doing something; the strain in her voice gave
it away. Samples of hair didn't weigh much – so, when she said
she was packing stock for a business meeting that was highly
unlikely. Martin would probably ring at any moment, claiming
he'd got a flat tyre or something. He'd been changing the wheel
and so hadn't heard his mobile in the car. He'd say he'd just got
to Nina's house, but there was no one in. How convenient.

'The Renault. She must have been in that green Renault. Fuck!'
He punched the dashboard. It was twenty-eight minutes to four.
They'd been sitting in the lay-by along from Orion House for
six minutes. He lifted his mobile and hit a speed dial number.
'Where are you?'

'Behind her. I think we're somewhere near an airport.'

'Is it called Woodford?'

'That was on a sign we just passed.'

The man in the baseball cap clicked his fingers at his colleague.
'We need the M60, westbound, now!'

The car pulled out. Immediately in front of them were blue
motorway signs.

'We're on our way. Rendezvous is a Holiday Inn somewhere near Woodford.' He scanned the map across his knees. 'OK, I see it. Just stay with her, we'll be there soon.' By the small white square marked hotel was a large expanse. Dissecting it were two dotted channels in the shape of a cross. The words by it read, Woodford Aerodrome. Private airfield. He immediately hit another speed dial number. 'We have a target. It's happening.'

'Where is the target?'

'By a private airfield. I think she's about to flee. What I can't work out is why she's trying to meet a female police detective first.'

'How certain are you she's connected?'

'Very. She's just taken out a member of the CTU who went to question her. I need a decision.'

'Secure the target. Take her alive.'

'And then?'

'Be in contact. There is a safe house within thirty minutes of Manchester.'

'The observation post by Orion House is unmanned. We left everything in there.'

'That will be taken care of.'

'What about sideliners?'

'What sideliners?'

'This female detective the target is meeting. She may obstruct us.'

'Remove her.'

Iona reached the roundabout where the turning for the Eastern Link Road branched off. Manchester Airport was probably a mile away; a Virgin plane was hanging in the sky above. Its wheels were down and the thing was low enough for her to see into the housing of its landing gear. Stowaways sometimes hide in there, she thought. Clinging to a ledge, suffocated or frozen within minutes of leaving Nigeria or Liberia or wherever it was they were trying to escape from. Tiny, illegal cargos. How many dropped from the planes to fall, unnoticed, into the desert or sea?

The Holiday Inn came into view. The roof of the low building was almost level with the raised link road. Iona peered down into the car park as she took the slip road. There were only about a dozen cars there. She didn't spot Nina's Range Rover until she was at the very end of the slip road. There it was, parked right at the back, as far from the motel as it could possibly be. The woman really was nervous. Iona spotted her then. Smoking, as usual, her gaze fixed on the traffic up on the road above.

Of course, Iona realized. She's expecting me to be in something small and red. Iona went to signal left. Her fingers recoiled from the indicator as if the lever carried an electric charge. Nina Dubianko was wearing a cream-coloured parka. It had a fur-lined hood. The exact same coat from the CCTV of Teah Rice's suicide.

She let the Renault roll past the entrance and her hand clamped back on the wheel. Another forty metres of road then a sign. Deliveries only. A single lane led behind the main building. Iona risked another glance over her shoulder. It was the same coat. The one worn by the mystery woman on the motorway flyover. The corner of the building cut off her view.

'Eli, what's happening?'

'Nothing. She's by her car chain-smoking. Watching the traffic passing by. She keeps checking her watch.'

'Any sign of the female detective, Khan? I think she's in an olive-green Renault Scenic. She's certainly not in a red Micra.'

'Negative.'

'Where exactly are you?'

'To the left of the main entrance. We're facing towards the building, parked alongside a black Mercedes. I'm watching in the rear-view mirror.'

'Very well. Stay where you are. We're ten minutes away. Be ready to acquire the target as soon as we arrive.'

'No problem. She's parked at the far end. There's no one here to see.'

Iona drew to a stop in the loading bay and tried the rear entrance. Locked. She jogged to the corner and looked round it. A swathe of gravel ran along the side of the building to the next corner. A border of grass beside it, sloping up to a row of conifers at the top. She crawled up the shallow incline, head turned in the direction of the car park. As she got higher, the sound of traffic from the road grew louder. She made it to the small trees just before the end of the car park came into view. Perfect. She crawled between two of the narrow trunks. A chalky cluster of dry dog faeces lay next to the right-hand one. Once she'd squeezed through, the trees formed a barrier between her and the expanse of asphalt. She started forward. Nina was there, a phone held to her ear. Iona's mobile went off. Shit! She lay flat, the phone digging into her stomach, its sound muffled. Five rings and then the answer-phone kicked in. As soon as it did, she lifted her chest and took it out. Unknown number. She watched Nina as she spoke for a few more moments, then hang up and light a new cigarette.

Iona went to her messages. New one, received today at three forty-three p.m.

'Detective Khan? It is me, Nina Dubianko. Can you please pick up?' A pause. 'I am here, at the Holiday Inn. You are late. I am parked at the end of the car park. It is easy to see me. I will wait for seven more minutes.'

The woman sounded more than stressed. She was freaking out. Iona called the office. Surprise, surprise, on asking for Roebuck, she was put through to Euan. 'It's me, Iona.'

'Iona? The signal is atrocious, you're hardly—'

'I'm whispering. Listen, Euan; send a unit to the address of a Nina Dubianko. She was on the list of Heslin's clients recovered from his offices. I think Detective Everington may be at her address. He could be injured.'

'Martin's at the address of—'

'Listen! I am watching the Holiday Inn car park on the Manchester Airport Eastern Links Road. I need back-up. Nina Dubianko is here. She is the woman from the Teah Rice footage. I believe she knows the whereabouts of Madison Fisher and Chloe Shilling. She could well have recruited Jade Cummings. Got that?'

'Jesus Christ, Iona.'

'You must get this message to Roebuck.'

'OK.'

'I'll keep visual contact with Dubianko. Hurry!'

At exactly three fifty-five, Nina Dubianko slung her half-smoked cigarette to the ground. After studying the surrounding car park with great care, she opened the door to her Range Rover and got in.

As the man sitting in the passenger seat of a blue Volvo parked to the side of the Holiday Inn's main entrance lifted his phone, Iona was crawling backwards to the gap in the trees. She raised herself to a crouch, shouldered her way through and raced down the grassy slope. When she reached the bottom her phone began to ring. She ignored the call, concentrating on retrieving her car keys instead.

Seconds later, as she turned right back on to the Links Road, her phone rang again. 'Euan, she's on the move!'

'Roebuck just called you, why didn't you pick up?'

'I couldn't. I was returning to my vehicle.'

'Stay on the line.' He spoke away from the phone. 'Sir? She's here.'

A second later, her boss's voice filled the car. 'Iona? What's happening?'

'She's on the move, sir.'

'State your position.'

'Heading away from Manchester Airport. We're almost back at the roundabout at the end of the East Links Road. Sir, has anyone got hold of Martin Everington?'

'Iona, you sure she's the one from that CCTV footage?'

'Yes. Fisher and Shilling absconded from their care home because a female fed them the story of a well-paid job overseas.'

'Don't worry about details. I need to know, is she alone?'

'Yes.'

'How close are you?'

'One car behind. We are now at that roundabout. She's indicating right.'

'Back-up is minutes away. Just stay with her, Iona. Gavin, progress?' A faint voice responded, too indistinct for Iona to make out actual words. 'Iona? An armed unit is only a few minutes off. What's happening now?'

'We've reached another mini-roundabout. It's now all fields, sir. We're heading east on the A5149. She's accelerating – no, she's slowing, now. She's indicating. Sir, it's some kind of airfield, I think. I can see one of those windsocks behind the hedge. There's a control tower. Is it a private airfield? I can see several small planes lined up by a runway. She's driving towards the only building. The terminal, it must be. She's stopped. I think she's making a call.'

'Keep your distance; they're almost with you.'

'Sir.'

'That is an order, Iona. Support just got to Nina Dubianko's property.'

'Is Martin there?'

'Iona, he's dead.'

She felt cool air on the roof of her mouth. Her lips were open.

'Iona? It's likely the woman shot him. Do not approach her. Is that understood?'

The man with the baseball cap was hunched over the map, speaking calmly into his phone. 'There's a roundabout. The turn-off for the Eastern Links Road is off that. Do you mean that one?'

'No, do not take that turn. Go straight over. I repeat, straight over. You get to another roundabout. Take the first left off that one.'

'On to the A5149?'

'Yes. Two hundred metres is a right turn. It's for a private airfield.'

'Woodford Aerodrome?'

'Yes.'

'She's in the main car park. A green Renault Scenic followed her in. It's now parked on the far side.'

'That's the detective. Where are you?'

'Out on the road.'

'What's the target doing?'

'She's in her car. Possibly talking on the – no, she's moving. She's approaching the security building. She is now going to the side of it. There's an entry point for getting airside in the fence there: a barrier with metal panelling below it. The security guy has gone round to her window. They're talking. Discussing something. He's now walking away from the vehicle, going back to his hut. He's raising the barrier! The barrier is – the detective. She's out of her car.'

'Repeat.'

'She's out of her car. She's running. She's running in the direction of the Range Rover!'

*   *   *

Iona's vision bumped and jarred each time a foot struck the hard tarmac. She was aware of her keys bouncing about in her pocket. It set up a weird rhythm in her head, the thud of her trainers and the metallic chinking. When she'd seen the barrier starting to go up, she'd known she couldn't stay in the Renault.

She'd run almost fifty metres and had yet to breathe. When her words came, they exploded out of her. 'Lower that barrier! Lower the barrier!'

The man in the security booth looked through the window, the whites of his eyes clearly visible. Iona was holding her badge in front as she closed the remaining distance. 'Police! Lower it!'

The far end of the barrier had lifted by about five feet. Now the hum of the motor cut and the thick metal pole stopped moving. The end of it quivered briefly. Iona also came to a halt. She was about twenty metres to the right of the Range Rover and about four metres away from the perimeter fence. Coils of razor wire looped along its top. At the base of the fence was a yellow container. Black letters on the lid said, rock salt.

For a second, no one moved. Then the door of the Range Rover swung open and Nina climbed out. She had a gun in one hand, a mobile phone in the other. 'Get here!' she shrieked at Iona.

Raising her hands, Iona stepped back. 'Nina, just stop. Please, just—'

'Here!' She beckoned jerkily with the barrel. The security guard peeped from the doorway of his booth. The gun swung in his direction. 'Back!'

Iona was judging distances. She could take cover behind the plastic container at the base of the fence. What would that buy her? Twenty seconds before Nina walked over and forced her back to her feet. Where was the back-up? Roebuck had said a few minutes. They must be close. The airfield seemed eerily deserted.

'Now! You come here!'

Nina's face was frightening. Her eyes had darkened to black and her lips were stretched tight against her teeth. Iona suddenly knew they were false. Too perfect. The woman took a few quick steps closer. 'Now!'

Hands still raised, Iona edged forward.

'Quick, quick!' Nina was now walking backwards, retreating to the rear of the vehicle. 'Quick!' She put her phone in her pocket and released the catch of the Range Rover's boot. 'In! Get in!'

Iona shuffled closer. What was the woman doing? She wants me to get in there? Is she taking me hostage? Nina's eyes slid to the airfield. Iona risked a quick glance, too. Not all the planes were parked up. One stood slightly apart.

Nina was gesturing once more with the gun. 'You get in.'

Iona skirted round the vehicle, keeping as far back from it as she could. With each little step, her view into the boot increased. A trainer. Two trainers. Legs. Someone is under the blankets. Now she could see the person's head. Iona stopped. It was Chloe Shilling. She's got Chloe Shilling in there. Iona turned to Nina. 'Where's her friend, you bitch?'

'Get in!' Nina's words cut the air like a car alarm.

'There is no way—'

The gun clicked as the safety came off. Nina stepped closer. Iona's vision was taken over by the small black circle pointing at her face.

A phone warbled. Gun still on Iona, Nina scrabbled for her handset. 'I'm here.' She nodded eagerly. 'At the barrier! Can you not see me?' She looked towards the runway. 'I am just fifty metres away.'

Iona stole another glance at the airfield. The plane – some kind of small jet – had now moved to the end of the runway. A light at the tip of its wing winked. It was parked in a loading area. Everything suddenly clicked and Iona felt her stomach writhe, like a snake had pushed into it from her intestines.

'Yes, she's with me! They both are. The black girl, too. You cannot see me? Why can you not . . .?' Nina's face suddenly crumpled. Her eyes went to the plane once more. She whispered, 'You said you would be. You said . . . you said . . . but . . .' She coughed and her voice was hard once more. 'OK, I am coming now.' The phone was lowered. 'Get in the car.'

As Iona moved forward, the motor controlling the barrier started again. Iona looked fearfully to her side. But the heavy metal pole was sinking down, not rising up. The rim of the metal skirt slotted into a runner in the tarmac. Nina let out an animal snarl.

Cars. Iona could now hear car engines. Two vehicles shot into view, undersides rasping as they took the speed bump at the car park entrance without slowing. Iona could see two figures in each vehicle but it wasn't the armed response unit.

The vehicles skidded to a halt ten metres away. Front corners almost touching, they formed a V shape. Doors opened. The people slid out behind them. Iona could see each held a gun. But they weren't wearing anything with the word police on and neither were they identifying themselves. They watched in silence.

Iona looked at Nina. Her lips were twisted tight, lower jaw moving rapidly up and down.

'Put the weapon at your feet.' The words had come from the one wearing a baseball cap. He had the trace of an accent. North American? Nina's mouth was still working.

Out on the airfield a slow whine started up, rapidly gaining in strength.

'No.' Nina's voice was small, desolate. 'No.'

The two men at the outer edge of the V suddenly broke left and right. They ran at a half-crouch, weapons directed at Nina. She loosed off a shot. Neither man slowed. Hand shaking, she fired again. The other two were now out, racing straight at the Range Rover with their weapons raised. 'Put it down! Put it down!'

Instead, Nina whirled about and ran for the barrier. From the edge of her vision, Iona could see the security guy. He was lumbering towards the main building, cheeks puffing out. The two outer men had altered direction and were now closing in. A pincer movement. Beyond them all the tone of the plane's engines lifted. It started moving away with surprising speed.

'Wait!' Nina wailed, now within metres of the chest-high barrier. Her phone was flung aside as she jumped at it. Her chest connected with the upper edge and she scrabbled for a second with one arm. For a second, Iona thought she might haul herself over. But her grip slipped and she fell back.

The other two men were about to pass Iona. She stepped out into the path of the one wearing a baseball cap. The leader. 'Who the hell are—'

He hardly checked his step. The hand holding the gun went down. The other came up. Iona just had time to see something in his grip. Olive-green, same as the Renault. Two stubby arms at the top. Almost like a catapault with no rubber band. He thrust it at her shoulder. She felt herself fly backwards into the side of the vehicle. Then she bounced off and crashed to the floor. Mini tornadoes of agony bounced up and down her limbs, crashing into each other and ricocheting off in other directions. She could feel her back arching, teeth clamped together. Breath hissed from between her molars. *I've been tasered.*

When she opened her eyes seconds later, she could see Nina. Her back was pressed against the barrier, gun switching from side-to-side. Her eyes were mad. A strand of hair had come loose and it swung across her face like a pendulum. All four men were closing rapidly. The threat of her weapon seemed to make no difference. They were relentless. In the background, the jet's engines were roaring. Iona could feel tiny vibrations in the ground.

The men were within four metres of Nina when she let out another animal moan and stuck the barrel in her mouth. The weapon cracked and her blonde hair parted as the top part of her skull jumped up into the air. As she slid down the expanse of metal, the plane rose up behind it, now birdlike in size and getting smaller.

The men descended on her like hyenas. The quilted parka was yanked open and searched. The mobile phone went into the jacket of the leader. Then they were marching back, weapons vanishing from sight. They stopped at the Range Rover and pulled open the doors. She heard the sounds of them rooting about inside the vehicle. One of them spoke.

'Female in the back. Unconscious.'

Iona could only move her eyes. She looked at her hand beside her face. Each finger was curled in, nails buried deep into the skin of her palms.

Then they were moving on. A second later, car doors shut, engines revved and they were gone.

Iona lay on the tarmac. Muscle control was returning to her fingers and toes. Her jaw loosened. Noises. The sound of her breathing, quick and shallow. People speaking from over near the main building. The cars' engines, merging with the plane's fading rumble. And behind that, weak but getting stronger, the sound of a siren.

EPILOGUE

Iona let the drone of the vicar's voice wash over her. Manchester Southern Cemetery was immense. While at school, she used to pass it all the time. With Dad as he dropped her off on the way to his job at the university. Or on a coach, taking the school's hockey team to away matches.

Then, it was just a space running along on one side of the road; she'd barely given a thought to what lay behind the thick iron fence. Her eyes wandered across row upon row of endless graves. There were two other burials going on as far as she could see.

A production line.

The thought was unfeeling and she forced her attention back to the people around her. Martin's mum and dad, eyes downcast, faces drained of life. The sight of them made her want to cry. About a dozen from the CTU were alongside her, Sullivan and O'Dowd included. She was the only member from Roebuck's team. Towards the edges were a few uniforms; colleagues from Martin's early career in the regular police. Nearest the family were a few members of the very top brass, including the ACC. A young female civilian on the far side of the grave sniffed loudly. A girlfriend, Iona guessed. A plane was banking up into the layer of blue. As it tilted, sunlight winked through its line of windows.

Iona's mind went back to the private airfield at Woodford. The jet had logged a course for Barcelona, southern Spain. But it had never cut in from above the Atlantic. Morocco or Algeria seemed the likely destination, but no one was sure.

Whoever had organized that jet was, surely, the person behind the entire operation. He might have had his UK business ruined, but, apart from that inconvenience, he seemed to have got away completely. Iona wasn't so sure. It was commonly acknowledged within the CTU that the team who'd tried to snatch Nina were with Mossad. The Israelis had lost four soldiers in that checkpoint explosion: the search for Nina's controller would never end.

Although diplomacy dictated that accusations of a secret Mossad cell being in Britain were never aired in public, Iona had heard that the Israeli ambassador had been quietly called in to see the Home Secretary. But he'd known nothing of any covert operation running alongside that of the CTU. Nothing at all.

Nina's firearm had been used to murder Martin and Liam Collins. Efforts to map her life story were quickly derailed when it turned out that Nina Dubianko had died in 1963, aged six years old. The entire identity of the woman had been artificially constructed on a copy of a dead child's birth certificate.

Of Nina's victims, Chloe Shilling was back in care. The Club Soda story had all been false; the establishment did employ foreign females, but mainly recruited via dance schools or modelling agencies. All workers were legitimately – and willingly – in the country. Madison Fisher was gone and Iona tried not to think about where she might be or what she was doing. Her details were with Europol and British embassies throughout the Middle East.

Khaldoon Khan's younger sister was due to be repatriated to Britain. Her family didn't want her back. Social services were working with Karma Nirvana, a charity that helped girls who'd escaped from forced marriage arrangements. It was hoped she could be placed with a family rather than going into care. Khaldoon Khan was due to be released from custody in Pakistan. He had stated his intention to stay in the country.

Iona glanced down at the mound of earth to her side. A small beetle had emerged from beneath a half-buried pebble. Its legs were moving with frantic speed as it scrambled for purchase on the layer of fine, dry soil. Centimetre by centimetre, it climbed higher. Iona wondered how long it could continue before tiring. The thing showed no sign of giving up and she liked it for that.

Roebuck had seen her a few days before. She'd gone to him about the message Martin had written by the Sudoku puzzle, tormented by what it meant. Was O'Dowd in on it? Were they all manipulating her? Roebuck had looked embarrassed. Yes, O'Dowd had passed the snippet to Palmer, Everington's boss. He, in turn, had passed it on to Sullivan. Roebuck had known about it, too. They'd decided to see how she and Martin worked together; whether it was worth looking at them long term as a team.

Soon after, Martin had reported to Palmer that she was hard to work with. She had trouble, according to him, about opening up, about working as a pair. Sheepishly, Roebuck had pointed out it wasn't the first time people in the CTU had said it. She was – undeniably – very competitive. You only had to look at her record, from school onward, to find plenty of evidence of that. Not that it was a problem, he'd added hastily. Unless it impinged on her ability to operate within a team. The Sudoku thing was a ploy thought up by them, that was all. A way for Martin to try and find some common ground, to build a connection with her. She'd remembered the words he'd written and had recoiled.

10/10! She went for it BIG TIME.

People were beginning to move. The service had ended. The questions were in her head again. Am I overly ambitious? Do I see everything as an exercise in winning? Me versus the rest of the unit? But I reported that it was Jim who'd worked out the mix-up with the carry cases. He told me to take the credit for it and I didn't.

She was aware of how thinking about Jim made her feel. I miss him so much. I need to see him, in person. We have to have the conversation. The booze. If I can help him to stop, if he managed to properly—

'Iona?'

She looked round. Martin's family were getting into a black saloon parked nearby. Everyone was hanging back, waiting for them to be driven off. It was a sergeant in Sullivan's team who'd spoken. He'd never been anything less than nice to her.

'We're heading to the Abercrombie on Bootle Street for a few drinks.' He gestured at the uniformed officers. 'Where Martin used to go before the CTU. You coming?'

She thought about the city centre pub, a regular haunt of the officers who worked in the police station next door. Jim, she knew, had a day off. He'd be at home, doing nothing. Probably as good a time as any to see him. Sit down, discuss where they both stood, see if there was any chance the two of them could give it another go. She looked at her colleagues hovering in the vicinity of the vehicle. Sullivan was among them. It would be a chance to have a quiet word. Explain how sorry she was about Martin. The doors of the saloon were being gently closed.

She looked at the sergeant. 'Is everyone going?'

'Yeah, for a tipple, at least. Most of us aren't due back on duty, are we?'

No, thought Iona. We're not. She could see Jim, sitting in his house, all alone.

'So,' the sergeant was walking towards the waiting group. 'Is that a yes?'

Iona wasn't sure.